Face Me
When You Walk Away

Face Me When

by the same author

GOODBYE TO AN OLD FRIEND

Brian Freemantle

You Walk Away

G. P. Putnam's Sons, New York

For my parents, in small repayment

As the Russian saying goes, 'Trust not your brother: trust your own eye, even if it's crooked.' This is the soundest basis for understanding one's environment and for determining one's behaviour within that environment.

ALEXANDER SOLZHENITSYN
NOBEL PRIZE SPEECH

Prologue

Josef Bultova prepared his death with the utmost care. For the camp authorities to find out would mean hardship even greater than that which he was committing suicide to avoid.

It had taken him a long time to reach his decision, because he was a survivor. Certainly he had begun his imprisonment as such. On the train of prison cages taking him to the labour-camp complex at Potma, 230 miles from Moscow, he had sold his expensive, Zurich-purchased wrist-watch for just two roubles. And then he had blackmailed the incriminated soldier into buying fifty-kopek bags of tea for prisoners to boil, complete, in miniscule amounts of water, to make a near-narcotic mixture of tannin with which they washed out their surroundings in just thirty minutes of blissful intoxication. Each bag sold for one rouble, so within six months he was rich by the standards of the camp.

But gradually the realization had enveloped him, insidiously, like the consumptive mist which always clung to the camp.

No limit had been imposed upon his sentence. Or on the exile to follow. And slowly Josef accepted he would spend the rest of his life on a starvation diet of cabbage soup and sour fish, horse-whipped to drag a brick truck from loading point to delivery bay in a perpetual, mind-numbing circle.

So he decided to die.

The camp commandant was harsh on suicides. As an example to others, anyone interrupted was punished to the point of the death they sought before being carefully coaxed

9

back not to life, but to bare existence. From the moment of discovery, the would-be suicide was marked by a specially striped uniform, as in the Nazi concentration camps at Dachau or Bergen Belsen. And they were subjected to the grossest humiliations, cleaning quarters where prisoners lived like animals, eating food that even the prisoners had rejected as inedible, becoming pathetic male prostitutes in a camp that had forgotten women.

So Josef was cautious, planning his act meticulously, telling no one.

His tame guard, to whom he paid twelve roubles for the thin rope, may have guessed, but his knowledge involved him. And Josef never let the man forget he could become a prisoner in his own camp if the authorities discovered their association.

It was a Sunday night, exactly seven years after his sentence, when he made the attempt. He stood on the lavatory stall, the rope looped around a rafter, and stayed for several minutes trying to inhale courage with each breath. Finally, he fitted the noose around his neck and lowered himself gently until his legs swung just above the floor.

As soon as the rope tightened and he began to choke, he panicked. He groped out for support and twisted wildly until his feet regained the stall.

Back on the bare shelf upon which he slept, Josef twitched with fear, weeping at his own cowardice. Tomorrow. He would definitely do it the following day.

Early in the morning, the guards came, shouting for him by name. Josef stood mute. An informer had witnessed the attempt and exposed him, he decided. Or perhaps the guard *had* talked.

'Josef Ivanovitch Bultova?'

Josef nodded. Why his name? Usually it was just the number.

'Seems you're a lucky man.'

'Lucky?'

Just one word was difficult. He kept his head down in case the twine had burned his throat.

'Someone has decided it's not a crime after all to have so many friends in the West. They're setting you free. With a pardon.'

Josef Bultova bequeathed the rope to the man next to him in the barrack block, the only friend he had made in the camp. His name was Asher Medev. He was a Jew who had tried to hijack a plane to get out of the country, consumed with the thought of getting to Israel.

Often Josef wondered what had happened to Medev.

Chapter One

One of the Czar's favourite Archdukes, a man of confused tastes but great wealth, had built the dacha for his mistress. And around it the opulent atmosphere of a whore's boudoir still clung, like perfume gone just slightly stale. The villa was surmounted by four bonnet-shaped towers, ornately carved and castellated, each containing observation rooms from which the plump hills around Moscow could be surveyed. It was fussy and vulgar and reminded Josef of the cardboard castles that sprang up upon opening those illustrated fairy-tale books in the West.

The building represented an era most despised and vilified in modern Russia, which was why Josef had insisted upon it when he had been rehabilitated. Having to accede to his demands had been humiliating for those who had jailed him, and it remained a wedding-cake monument to a mistake they had publicly made and of which they were constantly, publicly, reminded.

He well knew it was a dangerous, even stupid gesture. And made for such a small circle of people that it was largely meaningless. But Josef was an overwhelmingly vindictive man, which made him so successful in the vocation he pursued.

Josef enjoyed the privileges he exacted, yet was cautious of them, like a starving man who hesitates to accept bread from his rescuers because he fears a trick and can't believe it won't be snatched away at the last minute. He was, in fact, plump with good food, yet fit from the saunas and the gymnasium equipment installed both here and in the Moscow apartment, for fitness was important to a man who flew 200,000 miles a year for discussions in any of five languages on subjects too delicate for direct government involvement, yet important enough for him to be accorded treatment at ambassadorial level at home and abroad.

He stretched, a short man with a weight problem badly concealed by shorts and singlet, the rimless spectacles giving his chubby, round face the look of an owl that has discovered where the mice live. He felt blown up with contentment, tight and about to burst, like a balloon at a child's birthday party.

She came up alone from the lake, the sunhat he had insisted she wear trailing from her hand, so that the early summer sun faded the blondeness of her hair almost white, her scrubbed face shining with perspiration. She was walking too fast for the heat, with head-down determination, as if to slow and admire the odd attraction of the villa would betray the revolutionaries she admired. He knew she was embarrassed by the house and his privileges, and smiled, indulgently, wondering how long it would take for her idealism to become bruised. Perhaps it never would, he conceded. Being his wife, with the dacha and the Moscow apartment shared by no one, with cars always available and foreign travel rarely denied, would mean she was cosseted against the harshness of a life she had chosen to adopt.

'Hello, wife,' he said.

'Hello, husband.'

It was becoming their secret intimacy, the way they used the new titles like foreigners encountering a strange word.

'You promised to speak Russian,' she complained. 'I'll never become fluent if we keep using English.'

She had still been reading modern languages when they had first met, when she visited Moscow two years before with the Oxford University party, and she retained the anxiety of a student who must learn every word of the lesson to please her tutor.

'My apologies,' he said, mock serious. Josef was ten years older than his wife. He supposed she had transferred the tutorial respect.

She came lightly up the steps and sat down in the creaking wicker chair. She was wearing Western-style jeans and a shirt knotted around her waist, so that her flat, hard stomach was bare. Her modest breasts did not need the support of a bra.

She stared out over the spectacular view towards the lake and the rolling meadows of the estate. Nudged by a bossy wind, formal gatherings of polite daffodils bowed and curtsied to each other. Soon it would be night, and a muslin of flying things swirled over the lake, unsure whether to absorb the last of the heat or seek shelter in the eaves of the boathouse. It was growing cold at night now.

'It's lovely,' she conceded, begrudgingly.

'Then try to enjoy it more.'

He bit off the sentence, aware of the ambiguity. She looked down at her bare feet, nipping her lower lip between her teeth, and he knew she had felt it.

'I'm sorry,' she said, hesitantly.

'Pamela, darling. Don't. It was a clumsy expression. I am sorry.'

He knelt beside her but she refused to look at him.

'It's so bloody stupid,' she protested. 'I mean, there's no reason. I love you. I really do.'

Now she turned to him, as if the reassurance needed the emphasis of a direct look.

'I know,' he placated, softly. 'Look, we've been married exactly five days. You're two and a half thousand miles from home, trying to adjust to a whole new way of life. And being treated in that ridiculous way by your parents was bound to upset you.'

'The fact that my idiot father called me a traitor is no reason why I can't make love to my husband,' she argued, weakly.

15

'I didn't say it was. It's a contributory factor.'

He kissed her, very lightly, aware of an almost imperceptible tensing.

'See,' she pleaded, knowing he had noticed it. 'I'm like a schoolgirl on her first date.'

He straightened. His knees had begun to hurt. He pulled up another lounging-chair and sat alongside, putting himself where they would not have to look directly at one another.

'You're making it into a bigger problem than it is,' he warned. 'If you think constantly about it, the psychological barrier will get bigger.'

'I can't stop thinking about it,' she said.

He took her hand again, which stayed listless in his fingers.

'Darling,' he said. '*Making* love isn't love. It's a part of it. An important part, certainly. But not all. If I'd wanted sex, I could have got it without marriage. You know that.'

'But you're ... ' she stopped, unable to find the expression.

'What?' he prompted, curiously.

'Oh, I don't know. So worldly, I suppose. You could have had your pick of some of the most attractive women in the world. I feel you expect so much. And all you get is a frightened virgin who can't stop shaking.'

He squeezed her hand, anxious to stop the conversation.

'And he doesn't actually help, being here,' she protested, lifting the book in her other hand. He detected the lightening of her depression and was grateful. He hadn't noticed the book.

'Where is he?'

'Down by the lake,' she said. 'Near the boathouse, watching the birds feed off the insects. He says he likes it there ... because he doesn't have to be with people.'

'How much have you read?'

Pamela considered the book and then tossed it on to a glass-topped table.

'Nearly all,' she said.

'And?'

'It's wonderful,' she said, shrugging again, annoyed at her inability to express herself better. 'Oh, that sounds so trite. It's more than wonderful. It's like seeing colours for the first time ... '

She was seized by her simile, but embarrassed by it.

'That's what I thought when I was reading,' she said, glancing at him to see if he would sneer at her difficulty in finding the proper admiration. 'It's like painting with words.'

Josef nodded, accepting the approval without a smile of criticism. She relaxed.

'Are the other books as good?' she asked.

Josef nodded. 'I don't pretend to have any literary criticism, but I found them magnificent.'

'If only he'd bathe. Or even wash occasionally,' complained Pamela. 'He smells like an old man, all musty and discarded.'

'I told him about it the second time we met,' said Josef. 'He stared at me in complete astonishment and then didn't speak for an hour. You know he can't stand criticism.'

'I don't understand it,' said Pamela.

'Until perhaps six years ago, he had never seen a bath,' defended Josef. 'The roof of his family home is still covered with sods of earth. There's no lavatory. If they want one, they use the backyard. Or in the winter, a small shed. There's no closet. The shed merely protects them against the cold ... '

'You mean ... ?' interrupted Pamela.

'Yes. For everything.'

'Christ.'

'In the winter, for warmth, the peasants from whom Nikolai comes rub their bodies with grease. It permeates their underclothes and forms a sort of skin.'

'Ugh,' grimaced the woman. 'Does Nikolai still do it?'

'Of course not. And he does bathe, occasionally. But getting him used to personal hygiene isn't going to be easy.'

17

'Is that why he upsets you, because he smells?'

Josef stared at her, unsettled. 'Upsets me?'

Pamela nodded. 'I've never seen you behave with anyone like you do with Nikolai. You're withdrawn, apprehensive almost. You're rarely like that with other people, even men with high ranks who are much more important than Nikolai. I've thought sometimes your arrogance must upset a lot of people. But with Nikolai it's different.'

Josef hesitated, unaware it was so obvious.

'I do something that no one else in Russia can do,' he began, slowly. 'There are only about twenty men like me in the world. We're like diplomats without the open support of the countries we represent. We negotiate ... open channels of discussion. Nearly always it's involved with trade, huge deals on governmental level. The last project I was involved with, bringing a French motor plant under licence to Russia, was worth nearly thirty million pounds. That's the sort of thing I'm used to. I know how to do it, perhaps better than anyone else, even among the other nineteen or twenty ... '

'Then why?'

'Exactly. Why? This isn't something I've done before. Or am likely to do again. I'm nervous because I don't know the rules.'

'So you might make a mess of it,' judged Pamela, lightly.

For several minutes, Josef looked at her, tenderly. In many ways she was as innocent as the author.

'That's the problem,' he said, finally. 'I mustn't make a mess of it.'

Pamela missed the importance of the remark. She grass-hoppered away.

'Why does Nikolai drink so much?' she asked.

Josef gestured, uncertainly. 'Nerves, I suppose. From an earth-roofed hut to being a public figure in the largest country in the world in little more than six years is pretty awe-inspiring.'

'It isn't just nervousness,' argued Pamela. 'People take a few drinks for courage, but Nikolai's drinking is ridiculous.'

'I know,' said Josef, thoughtfully. 'I'm worried about that, as well.'

They were quiet for several moments, happy with the beauty of the grounds surrounding the dacha. Josef tugged at Pamela's hand and she looked at him. 'I'm sorry he had to be brought here,' he said. 'But it's important I get to know him completely. There was no other way.'

She smiled. 'Darling, I don't mind.'

She glanced behind her, towards the Archduke's idea of a love-nest.

'You could accommodate an army here.'

They saw him coming from far away, initially little more than a movement that formed itself into a figure walking quite aimlessly and uncaring of any observation. Once, quite obliviously, he relieved himself against a tree, steam rising in the cooling summer evening.

'Just like home,' muttered Pamela. It was a bad attempt to cloak her embarrassment.

Mist came like that in the evenings at Potma, thought Josef, not isolated little pockets to be picked up and jostled by the wind, but huge, rolling blankets that locked and clung to that which refused to dissipate during the day, covering everything like a shroud. It had been odd, he thought, caught by the word, how everyone had died with what appeared to be a smile on their faces. Happy to escape, he supposed.

Nikolai Balshev saw them and waved, his hand going straight to the gesture from buttoning his flies. His utter innocence destroyed any offence. He was very slim and pale and although his hair was long, almost to his shoulders, it was so blond and fine he appeared to be balding. He wore rough serge trousers and a peasant's smock. The dress, thought Josef, was an affectation, an attempt to impress them. Nikolai stopped, looking up to the low veranda, completely still and unmoving. It was an attitude of which Josef had become aware almost immediately they had met. It reminded him of a nervous animal, a gazelle or a chamois maybe, head tensed to one side, constantly alert for flight. Nikolai saw his novel lying on the table.

'Well?' he demanded of the woman.

'It's very good,' said Pamela, disconcerted, words jammed by the directness.

'Very good!'

Nikolai's baby smooth face creased at the inadequate praise. He needs constant reassurance, like an unsure child, decided Josef. So the invitation to criticism was false, like the clothes.

'No, not just good,' groped the girl. 'It's wonderful ... I don't think I've ever read anything like it.'

Nikolai nodded, better satisfied.

'Sure?'

'Really.'

'That's what others say ... ' he paused, turning slightly, and with the young man's full attention upon him Josef felt for the second time that afternoon like a tutor being respect-fully addressed by a student.

'Josef likes it, don't you Josef?'

'I've already told you,' said the older man. 'It'll be recognized as one of the best examples of Russian literature.'

Nikolai smiled, happily. Josef had made the remark several times in the last five days, but the author never appeared tired of hearing it.

'You really think so?'

'You know I do.'

The performance over, Nikolai came on to the veranda, edged a chair alongside them and sat down, staring out towards the lake. Silence settled as heavily as the mist in Josef's recurring dreams. Nikolai knew they were on honeymoon, but it never occurred to him they might wish to be alone and that his presence was an intrusion. Josef studied the younger man sitting alongside Pamela, reminded again of their similarity in colouring. They could be brother and sister, he thought. Nikolai did not notice the attention, but Pamela turned, raising her eyebrows in helplessness.

'Have you discussed supper?' she asked, seeking neutral discussion.

Josef sniggered, unable to suppress his reaction to the situation.

'Caviar, borsch and some wild boar. With wild strawberries to follow.'

Now it was Pamela's turn to laugh. 'My pompous M.P. of a father maintains a town house in Eaton Square and a country seat in Buckinghamshire. And he doesn't dine on beluga and wild boar.'

Josef joined her amusement. He knew she was impressed and it pleased him. Pamela's lightness slipped away. 'Somehow,' she said, 'it seems wrong that we live so well.'

'Why?'

'Wasn't this what it was all about? If we could discover a seventy-year-old menu, we'd find the Archduke ate caviar and wild pig. And had fresh strawberries and champagne.'

'I hope he did,' said Josef. 'It would show more taste than his interior decorating.'

He saw she refused to be amused.

'It *is* different, you know,' he said. 'The peasants aren't animals any more. And there's no such thing as a classless society, no matter how perfect your socialism. There are always those who lead and those who follow. And the leaders provide themselves with a better life-style for taking the responsibility. That's not really unfair, surely?'

'But your life is so similar to what things must have been like before 1917 ... ' She glanced at Nikolai. 'And people still live in sod huts way out in the country.'

Josef sat looking at her, arrested by a doubt. Could he any longer afford to exact the punishment from those who had jailed him? Before he had only had the danger to himself to consider and he'd decided the challenge with great calculation, aware there was no safety net beneath the tightrope he was erecting for himself and that the applause would be louder if he fell rather than kept crossing. But now there was Pamela. Just as his life-style would protect her from the harder aspects of Soviet life as long as he remained indispensable, so his collapse from favour would impose upon her greater problems than those of the poorest peasant for whom she felt sorry.

'I love you,' he said. It sounded like an apology.

Embarrassed by the affection, she snatched a sideways look at Nikolai. A finger was exploring his left nostril and he seemed completely occupied by the view of the lake.

She looked back. 'I love you, too,' she said, breaking a moment then blurting on, in a whisper. 'And I'm so sorry.'

At that moment, the telephone sounded inside the dacha and Josef's balloon of happiness popped.

Chapter Two

It was a small room in the Ministry of Culture, away from the Kremlin complex, and only four members were present. Uli Devgeny, a member of the Central Committee of the Supreme Soviet and the man who had signed the imprisonment order against Josef, had been appointed Minister four years before. He sat, smiling, content that at last he had complete control over a project in which Josef was involved. Vasily Illinivitch, the deputy Minister, who sat on his right, was also on the Central Committee. Illinivitch puzzled Josef. The man acted as a liaison between the Praesidium and several committees for which Josef had worked, so there was no one else with whom the negotiator had closer contact. Yet the man was a perfect stranger to him, resisting all but official contact. Josef suspected intense ambition behind the reserve and acknowledged that Illinivitch's unique function gave him unrivalled opportunities to ferment purges. Did he, wondered the negotiator, covet Devgeny's Ministry? Or was there something else?

'I don't think you know our other comrades,' Devgeny introduced, formally. 'Alexandre Ballenin,' he said, gesturing towards a white-haired man squinting myopically through pebble-lens spectacles. 'And Dimitry Korshunov.'

Korshunov was sallow, greased hair like a tight-fitting hat. He stared expressionlessly across the intervening table, revolving a pen between his fingers. Ballenin, Josef knew, was the man who had first recognized Nikolai's ability, when his manuscripts had been sent from Kiev.

Devgeny was a huge, bull-like man, almost too big for his surroundings. Thick, black hair capped a florid face blotched with the bubbles of too much vodka, and the hands which lay flat before him were matted with wiry, black hair that protruded from beneath his shirt-cuffs. He wore a badly tailored, double-breasted suit, with all three buttons fastened, even though he was sitting, so that the material creased around his body, like sagging skin about to be shed by a snake. A dangerous reptile, thought Josef. An anaconda. Or a python, which would crush its victims to death, very slowly. Devgeny was over sixty and had taken part in the siege of Leningrad. In the end, the rumours said, when the German withdrawal had become a rout, he'd made commando raids among the weakened, frightened stragglers, strangling them with his bare hands. There were other stories, too. It was said that during the siege, at the worst part, Devgeny had survived by eating the flesh of people who had died around him.

Josef's father had never believed the stories, but then the old man had never believed anything involving Devgeny. And had died because of it. Josef's father had been one of those rare revolutionaries, born into the aristocracy but a man who embraced the overthrow of a system he recognized as corrupt. In Devgeny he had seen an opportunist as evil as any who existed in the Czarist court, and had openly opposed Devgeny before the Praesidium when they considered the ambassadorship the man so desperately wanted. The Praesidium had been persuaded, recognizing in Josef's father the man fitted to the role, despite his age. So Josef's father had become perhaps the best ambassador Russia had ever had in the immediate post-war period and Devgeny had stayed in Moscow, plotting the old man's downfall. And when he had succeeded, he had dragged Josef down, too. And then been made to look ridiculous before the Central Committee, who had to concede the need for someone like Josef to bridge a necessary gap between the countries of the

24

world. So the well-practised hatred had transferred from father to son.

'How do you like our young genius?' asked Devgeny.

Josef saw Ballenin frown at the disparagement.

'A little odd,' offered Josef.

'Men of genius don't have to confirm to normal standards,' defended Ballenin. 'They are extraordinary men.'

Devgeny ignored the statement. Josef felt pity for the old man's unawareness.

'Things are developing in Stockholm,' said Devgeny.

'I still don't like the idea of getting involved,' began Josef, guardedly.

Devgeny smiled. He looked capable of eating another human being, thought Josef. Or crushing him.

'It's a problem of your own creation,' said the Minister, happily. 'There's no one else we can possibly consider for the job.'

'But in a strange field, I could be unsuccessful,' warned Josef.

'Fail!' mocked Devgeny. 'But you never fail, Comrade Bultova. "Russia's unofficial ambassador," isn't that what they call you? "Mr Fixit." There's scarcely been a man since Stalin who has manufactured the personality cult like you.'

'There is common sense in manipulating the Western press,' sighed Josef. Almost lecturing, he continued, 'As I've explained many times before, a man with a reputation for negotiating astuteness has an in-built advantage over an unknown in any business dealings. That's basic psychology.'

Devgeny turned to the other three. 'You will come to learn,' he said, 'that psychology enters into Comrade Bultova's reasoning quite frequently. He even studied it at Harvard, the American university, in his youth.'

Josef refused to accept the bait.

'I thought I was to be allowed my honeymoon,' he said. Devgeny would expect protest and be suspicious if it were not made.

'You were,' said Devgeny, in a voice showing it had never been the intention. 'But as I said, things are happening a little faster than we anticipated.'

'Like what?' demanded Josef, emphasizing the truculence.

'Nikolai is on the Nobel prize short-list,' announced Devgeny.

'We knew that weeks ago,' said Josef. He allowed the exasperation to leak into his voice. Devgeny was achieving too much superiority. 'We're already engaged in negotiations with Western publishing houses.'

'But we didn't know the other possibilities. There is a black American, Aaron Jones, whom no one thinks has much of a chance. I gather he's been listed for political reasons.'

'Doesn't the whole thing degenerate into politics?' asked Josef. He had to interrupt, to prove he wasn't frightened. Devgeny ignored the question.

'Nikolai,' he listed, like a quizmaster announcing prizes. ' ... Aaron Jones ... '

He paused, theatrically. Fool, thought Josef.

' ... and Lin Tsai-Fu.' Devgeny was pleased at the effect upon Josef. 'From Peking,' he continued. 'His poetry and descriptive powers are said by those who've read him in the original to be magnificent.'

'So ... ' began Josef.

'So your task becomes incredibly important,' cut in Devgeny, uttering the thoughts that butterflied through Josef's mind. 'It would be very unfortunate for a member of the People's Republic of China to be selected and fêted as a better writer than a Russian ... '

Devgeny smiled, looking straight at him, like a cat that has finally exhausted an elusive mouse.

'The Nobel Foundation have intimated quite clearly that they wish to nominate Nikolai,' continued the Minister. 'But they're nervous of another Solzhenitsyn problem. Before his name leaks out, they want a positive assurance from us that there'll be no difficulties.'

Josef stared across the table at him, cautiously. 'The decision is irrevocable?'

'Such suspicion, Comrade Bultova!' mocked Devgeny, still smiling. His teeth were green and discoloured near the gums, where he never bothered to clean them. Josef remembered his own had been like that when he had left the camp.

'Just careful,' said Josef, preparing a defence. 'I want it clearly understood by everyone what I am required to do.'

There was an unintended tinge of desperation in the statement. His eyes remained on the man facing him across the table, assessing his chances later of being able to establish his caution before any examining body. Only Ballenin would be honest, he decided. But his account would be overwhelmed by the other three. The flicker of fear returned. Poor Pamela, he thought.

'So I will give them the assurance?' he queried.

'Of course you will,' said Devgeny, like a schoolteacher addressing a particularly dull student. 'But we expect much more of you ... '

'There is no way I can influence the actual selection, for God's sake,' erupted Josef.

Devgeny gazed at him, theatrically surprised. The tip of Josef's hysteria had just been visible.

'I wasn't for a moment suggesting you could,' said the Minister, enjoying his superiority. 'Please let me finish.'

Sweat pricked out on Josef's face. Devgeny would be able to see it and guess the fear, he thought.

'It's been decided that Nikolai is a good Russian,' continued Devgeny. 'He's someone of whom Russia feels proud.'

'What's the point you're making?' probed Josef. He was irritated at Devgeny's determination to manipulate him and pride was fuelling his anger.

'If Nikolai gets the award, he will become ... '

He paused. He had waited a long time, Josef thought. He wanted to prolong it as long as possible.

27

' ... What's the expression your Western friends would use, Josef? A hot property?'

Josef sat without replying.

' ... Yes, that's it. A hot property. So as well as negotiating with the publishers in England and America with whom you've already established contact, we want you to accompany him on publicity tours to those countries.'

Surprise robbed Josef of response for several moments. Desperately he tried to isolate the snares that Devgeny was laying.

'You're going to let Nikolai tour the West ... ?'

'But it'll be easy for him, Josef,' broke in Devgeny. 'He'll have you to guide him. And nothing can go wrong if you're looking after him, can it?'

For a long time, the five men sat in complete silence.

Then Josef said, 'Of course, there's no guarantee he'll get the award.'

The hope was too discernible and Devgeny smiled.

'Oh, but that would be too bad,' said the Minister. 'We've made our minds up. I can't stress strongly enough how distressed we would be if China got an award we regard as ours.'

The nightmare that night was one of the worst. When he awakened in the Moscow apartment, he was unable to breathe and almost lapsed into unconsciousness before forcing air, by sheer strength of will, into his lungs. In the bathroom he discovered there were no sleeping pills. The briefcase in which he kept a supply when he was travelling was empty, too, so he dragged the padded quilt from the bed and sat, cocooned in it, staring out over the capital until the first fingers of dawn appeared, squeezing life into the city.

He could have commanded a king's ransom for a quilt as warm as this in Potma, he thought. He wondered if Medev had been brave and succeeded in the attempt he had been too cowardly to accomplish. Probably, decided Josef. Medev had always been the braver of the two.

Chapter Three

The feeling between them was so real Pamela felt she could stretch out and touch it. Upon reflection, she supposed it had begun six nights before, immediately Josef had telephoned from Moscow saying he had to go the following day to Stockholm. But at first she hadn't noticed it. When it had begun to register, she had dismissed it as the gradual developing confidence of someone who had spent twenty-two years in a narrow, closed environment of a village two hundred miles from Kiev. Then the uncertainty had developed until she felt permanently uncomfortable with the man. She would go back to Moscow, she decided. Perhaps tomorrow. Or the day after. Certainly by the week-end.

'Why are you so quiet?'

The remains of their meal lay between them and Nikolai fingered the wine bottle, staring at her over the rim. His new confidence irritated her.

'No reason.'

'Of course there is. Missing Josef?'

'Naturally.' She tried to convey coldness.

'Why naturally?'

'My dear Nikolai,' she said, pompously, regretting the words as they came, 'I don't really think it proper for a guest in my husband's house to examine whether or not I miss him.'

He laughed at her, genuinely amused.

'My dear Pamela,' he mocked back. 'You are exactly five years older than I am. You'd have to be at least twenty years my senior to speak like that.'

Embarrassed, she laughed with him. 'I've still no intention of discussing Josef with you,' she said, primly.

'Why not?'

'Why should I?'

'Because you're unsure of your marriage.'

For a moment, she was unable to reply.

'What ... ?' she tried.

'Oh come on,' he said, impatiently. 'You're frightened of it. Of marriage. Of Russia. Of Josef ... of Josef, most of all ...'

'I'm not.'

The denial came a little too swiftly. 'Of course I'm slightly unsure ... any woman would be. But it's only the strangeness of the country ... getting used to it. It's nothing to do with my marriage.'

She didn't have to offer explanations, she thought.

Again he laughed. 'Then why were you apologizing so deeply the other day on the balcony?'

The blush came back. She felt it spread over her neck and chest and recalled the remark to Josef on the veranda the day he'd been summoned back to Moscow.

'I don't know ... '

'Yes you do. You said you loved him. But that you were sorry. I think I know ... '

'I don't want to know what you think.'

She should create a scene and storm from the room, refusing to carry the conversation further. She remained seated. He lounged in the high-backed, curved chair, twirling his glass. He added to it from the bottle and gestured towards her. She shook her head. Never once did he take his eyes from her and determinedly she gazed back, refusing to be stared down.

'If it embarrasses you, then I won't pursue it,' he said, dismissively.

'It doesn't embarrass me,' she blurted out, instinctively.

'What doesn't?'

She slapped her hands against the table. 'Stop insulting me,' she said, angrily.

'I'm very important to your husband,' he announced, incongruously.

'Not as important as he is to you.'

Nikolai nodded, accepting the rebuke. 'Why can't you make love to him?' he said, abruptly.

'I ... '

She had to go now. The only thing to do was to leave the room and tomorrow order him from the house. Was he important to Josef? He hadn't involved himself with writers before, she knew. And Nikolai seemed so sure of himself. He leaned across the table and added more wine to her glass. Slowly, she sipped it.

'I want to stop this conversation.'

'Why?'

'Because you're rude and impudent and because there's no reason for continuing it.'

'Why haven't you asked me to leave in the last six days, since Josef has been gone?'

Oh God, she thought, he imagines I'm attracted to him.

'Because ... ' Pamela paused, confused. His sudden change of attitude bewildered her.

'Because you didn't want me to go,' completed Nikolai, positively.

'You're playing with me.'

'What?'

'You're acting out some part,' she accused. 'Like an experiment.'

He smiled. 'Perhaps you're right.'

'Then I find it offensive. And I think you should go.'

'All right,' he said. He gulped his wine, spilling a little, then stood up.

'I didn't mean now,' she protested, lamely. She looked at

her watch. It was after eleven. 'There's no way you can get back to Moscow tonight.'

'You could drive me.'

'I don't choose to become a chauffeuse at half-past eleven at night after drinking nearly a bottle of wine.'

He sat down and emptied the second bottle of imported Volnay into her glass.

'Please stop it,' she pleaded.

'Stop what?'

'Oh don't. You know what I mean.'

She swallowed, trying to conceal the nervousness from Nikolai by dabbing her lips with her napkin.

'I didn't mean to upset you,' he said, appearing contrite. 'I was rude. Please forgive me.'

He smiled openly and again he was the guileless, shy young man she had met two weeks before.

'I'm so unsure of myself,' he blurted, suddenly.

She waited, her bewilderment growing. Was he a lonely, scared man, seeking friendship? Or was it part of the game she had earlier accused him of playing?

'Sometimes,' he went on, 'I almost wish it hadn't happened to me.'

He was stirring his wine with his finger. She'd seen someone do that in a film, years ago. She tried recalling the title and failed. It had been a bad film, she remembered, full of phoney mannerisms.

'Why?' she asked.

He smiled at her. 'Because I don't know if I can do it … '

He halted, ashamed that he was badly expressing himself. It seemed difficult for him to continue. 'People expect so much of me. And I know it's going to get worse. I want the prize, God how I want it. But I'm terrified. Anyone who wins the Nobel prize must be a special person. I don't feel special. Just frightened.'

'Josef can help you.'

32

'He can tell me what knife to use and what wine glass to pick up and how to address important people,' agreed the writer. 'But that's like putting on a cloak to hide a hole in your trousers.'

He sipped his drink.

'Do you know?' resumed Nikolai. 'At home they thought I was the village idiot.'

Pamela laughed, knowing he meant her to. It wasn't an act, she concluded. He did need a friend.

'Why?'

'Because I scribbled in books,' he said. 'The local party secretary, a man called Georgi Polenov, actually came to the house to complain. He said I was setting a bad example, refusing to work. If I were excluded from the co-operative, then others would want the same privileges.'

Nikolai stopped, staring at her. 'They wanted me to work in the fields,' he remembered, disbelievingly. 'I was supposed to drive a machine that packed wheat during the harvest. Every time I tried, I broke it.'

It was difficult not to laugh again. Thank God, thought Pamela, for the napkin.

'I was lucky, meeting Polenov,' said Nikolai. 'He was a refined man, mourning the old era.'

He poured brandy into her glass. It seemed pointless to object.

'The only way he could do it was through his pretension to literature,' said Nikolai. 'He would even, at times, refer to Dickens and Shakespeare as if he had read them, which I'm sure he hadn't. But he had read Amalrik and Solzhenitsyn in *samizdat* ... '

He stopped, like someone helping another across steppingstones in an eager river.

'Do you know of *samizdat*, the underground method of printing and circulating prohibited material?' he asked.

Again Pamela stifled a laugh. For the first time in his life, she thought, he was talking confidently to someone.

33

'I had heard of it,' she said. Then, allowing him the indulgence, she added, 'But I was never quite sure what it meant.'

He smiled, enjoying the role, like a child with the monologue in the school play.

'He sent my stuff to some friends he had cultivated among the Writers' Union in Kiev. They were impressed and sent it here, to Moscow. Luckily for me, Comrade Ballenin read it.'

Nikolai added more brandy to her glass, then to his.

'Oh God, how Kiev frightened me,' he reflected. He looked directly at her. 'Would you believe,' he said, 'my father had never been there. Never once in his whole life. It was like hell, something mothers frightened their children with. "If you are naughty, I'll send you to Kiev." We didn't call it by its real name. It was always the "big place", as if to mention its correct name would call down a curse.'

Nikolai was talking hurriedly, spurred by memories. Sometimes Pamela, whose Russian was still imperfect, had difficulty in immediately understanding him. Alcohol was blurring some of the words. Did peasants really feel that about Kiev or Moscow, she wondered? Or was he romanticizing the whole thing? He began to laugh and she thought he was lapsing into complete drunkenness.

'I was absolutely terrified the first time I went there,' he started again. 'I had the address of Polenov's friend in the Writers' Circle, but everything was so big and I couldn't find it. I went around and around all those concrete buildings. Everyone was far too busy to help me. And then I wanted a toilet. I didn't know how to find one. I was walking around, pigeon kneed. And finally I found a park; I was quite sure I would get arrested, but I couldn't wait any longer. So I peed against a tree.'

Pamela sniggered.

'It wasn't funny,' protested Nikolai. 'I was so frightened

34

of park-keepers or police that I still wet my trousers. I walked around for an hour until it dried. I chafed my legs red raw.'

Remembering a nephew to whom it had happened in London, Pamela said, 'Yes, it does.'

The child had been six years old, Pamela recalled.

'I tried a trolley bus,' went on Nikolai. 'And it went five kilometres the wrong way before I realized it. So from then on I walked everywhere. I get very tired. I nearly always got lost, so I would begin journeys hours before any appointment.'

Pamela felt a great sadness for the man. How could anyone so naïve create such beauty with words, she wondered.

'It was marvellous when I got back home, though,' he reminisced. 'I wasn't the village idiot any more. I was important now. People who a year before would have slammed the door in my face welcomed me for some vodka or to share their borsch.'

He stopped again. His finger was in his glass, stirring. He looked up, suddenly, staring directly into her eyes.

'I liked it,' he admitted. 'It will be the fame that I'll enjoy. I could manage it. It was enough, really. I'd been to the big place. They were not quite sure what I had done, but they knew it was something special. The fame wasn't mine, really. It was theirs.'

Pamela pretended the cheese she had been nibbling had caught in her throat and coughed, so that she was able to bring the napkin to her eyes. He stretched over the table, taking her hands.

'I am a selfish person,' he confessed. 'I don't mean to be. But I haven't the experience to behave otherwise. I know I've intruded upon you and Josef ... I've cluttered your honeymoon even ... '

'No, please ... ' protested Pamela, automatically.

35

'I have,' he said, ignoring her protest. 'And I know there are other things that must offend you ... '

He motioned with his hands, helplessly.

'Stop,' demanded Pamela. She felt numbed. It was like watching somebody inject themselves with a local anaesthetic and then perform their own autopsy.

Nikolai sat waiting. He looked very small, she thought, just like the nephew who'd wet his pants. The child had done it to draw attention to himself, she remembered, because his sister had a new dress and was earning all the praise. In England, she recalled, there had been a quiz programme where contestants had to rearrange words on magnified boards. She had never been able to understand their difficulty as they scrambled around, aware of the enormous clock which timed their progress. She was like one of the contestants, she thought. She knew the words, could see the sentences even, but she couldn't put them into the right order.

'I'm sorry ... ' she started. Why did every sentence begin with an apology?

' ... if I've hurt you,' she started again. 'Then I'm sorry. I didn't understand ... strangely, it seems we're very much alike — two very frightened people ... '

The silence grew brittle between them. There was no clock. No fawning compère with lacquered hair and plastic teeth was going to suddenly appear and apologize because she had run over time. Why couldn't she arrange the words in their proper order?

'Perhaps we could help one another,' she said. That uncertain feeling bubbled at his look.

'I just want to know everything,' he stated. He was looking away from her, tracing imagined patterns on the table.

'Everyone says I can write. They use stupid words, like brilliant and genius, which have no value. How can I write about things when I don't know about them?'

36

He looked at her pleadingly.

'But *Walk Softly on a Lonely Day* is a wonderful book,' she said.

For once the accustomed flattery didn't work. 'How can you write about love without knowing what it is?'

'But ... ?'

'I am a virgin,' he announced, flatly. He drank again, avoiding her eyes, ashamed by the admission.

Pamela strained for something to say.

'I tried once,' he wandered on. 'I really did.'

He was defensive, as if she would doubt him. 'It was in Kiev, the third time. I paid a woman, a prostitute ... '

He looked at her. 'It was thirty roubles. I wanted the best. I saved for nearly three months.'

To have laughed would have bruised him, she thought. Again she covered herself with a napkin.

'Do you know, they ask you for the money first?' he said, conversationally.

'No, I didn't,' said Pamela. 'But I suppose it's sensible.'

She began experiencing a feeling of unreality.

'Why?' he asked.

'Well, you could always leave afterwards, without paying ... once you'd ... once you'd done it ... '

They were like strangers in a foreign country, trying to follow an inadequate map.

'Yes, I suppose you could,' he said. 'That never occurred to me.'

He relapsed into silence. Pamela sat waiting.

'It wasn't any good,' he said, breaking the pause. 'It wasn't her fault,' he added quickly, as if the reputation of an unknown whore needed protection. 'She was very good. At least, I suppose she was. She did everything she could to help me. She was kind, too. I cried. But she didn't laugh. She said it often happened to men the first time. Especially on their wedding night ... '

He looked directly at her. 'That's why I asked about you and Josef.'

'Oh,' she said. The stupid response annoyed her, but there seemed little other contribution she could make. She felt her antipathy towards the man evaporating into pity. His increasing confidence towards her was a compliment, she thought, an indication that he felt at ease in her company. She felt guilty.

'I'm sorry,' she said, the familiar response.

'What for?'

She shrugged. 'Just sorry.'

Because of the cold evenings, she had asked for a fire to be lit in the massive hearth of the dining-room. Now it was dying. The last log cracked and collapsed upon the white ashes in a tiny explosion of sparks. She shivered.

'It isn't Josef's fault,' she confessed. Having held back for so long, her offer was over-generous. 'It's me.'

'Why?'

'I don't know,' she said. 'I wish I did.'

'Frightened?'

'I suppose so.'

'There's an excuse for you,' he said. 'It's supposed to hurt, the first time. But what can I hide behind? It doesn't hurt a man ... '

He hesitated, arrested by a doubt. 'Does it?' he asked.

'I don't know,' she said. She shivered again.

'Let's go by the fire.'

He stood up, carrying her glass over to one of the cavernous chairs that bordered the hearth. She hesitated, then followed. He had remained standing and when she reached him he pushed her gently into the chair, lowering himself on to one of the bear rugs that the Archduke had once shot. The skin had been badly treated and the bullet hole was still visible, high, behind the animal's ear.

'Poor bear,' said Nikolai, pushing his finger into the

wound. 'What a stupid thing to do, kill an animal just to cover the floor with the skin. And it wasn't even looking.'

He kissed her knee. She didn't realize it immediately and then she felt his lips on the soft part of her leg, on the inside of the knee.

'Don't.' She shifted.

'Why not?'

'Because I say not.'

'Offended?'

'No. I just don't like it.'

His arm was propped against the seat, supporting him, so that his hand was against her thigh. She could feel the pressure. He smiled at her. She smiled back.

'Why don't you like me?' he asked.

'I do ... don't be silly.'

'You've not been the same, without Josef.'

'Of course not.'

'Towards me, I mean. You've built a wall.'

'I haven't,' she said, feeling the emptiness of the denial.

'It's made me sad,' he went on, dismissing what she had said. He looked up at her from the floor. He seemed so small and vulnerable. 'Because I wanted us to be friends. I thought I could relax with you. But I offend you.'

He looked away. She stretched out, putting her hand on his arm.

'Oh don't, Nikolai. I'm sorry if I've been withdrawn. I didn't mean to reject you.'

He kissed her hand, snailing his tongue between her fingers. She tried to withdraw it, but he held it there with the hand with which he was supporting himself. For a long time they sat there, her hand in his. The fire went lower, spluttering to stay alive. She felt the wetness of his mouth on her leg again, but didn't bother to protest. She felt heavy with wine and tiredness. At last he shifted, rising to his knees and crouching before her. She knew what he was going to do, long before he moved, and could have avoided it by rising from the chair, because at the last moment he hesitated. Instead she sat there, unmoving, like an animal hypnotized by the glare of a poacher's torch. It was a clumsy kiss, lips dry. Then his tongue edged between her lips, against her teeth, which first clamped shut and then parted and he moved on to the chair, his body partially covering hers. He kept one hand against her leg, the other caressing her face. Her hands were on his shoulders, supporting him.

'My leg's gone to sleep,' he gasped. 'Kneeling like this, half on, half off the chair. It's gone to sleep.'

She sniggered.

He smiled, standing before her and putting his weight on his left leg to restore the circulation. Unspeaking he held out both hands to help her from the chair.

'No.'

'Yes.'

'Please, no.'

He stayed, hands reaching out.

'I'm frightened,' she said.

'So am I.'

He leaned, grasped her hand and gently pulled. She stood before him, their bodies touching. They came together naturally this time, without awkwardness, mouths searching. Not speaking now, he turned, arm around her, guiding her from the room. She moved with him, without protest. Near the room she and Josef occupied she stiffened, but he led her past, to his own bedroom further along the corridor. Again he was clumsy, fumbling with the zip at the back of her evening skirt, then the buttons of her blouse.

'You'll have to help me.'

She undressed, then hesitantly edged into the bed. The sheets were cold and her teeth began to vibrate. She felt him get in alongside. For a long time they lay without touching.

40

Then his fingers covered hers. And then he moved, his mouth fluttering over her body, his tongue hard and probing. She stayed stiff and unyielding, legs together. She excited him. He brushed against her hand, kneeling over her. Then he took her hand and placed it on him and she felt him grow. There was wetness on her stomach and she touched it with her other hand and realized he was crying. A great gush of pity engulfed her. With Nikolai she did not feel the desperation she knew with Josef, the anxiety to appear sophisticated. Nikolai was as innocent as she was, so he wouldn't recognize the mistakes and be offended or amused by them. She felt her legs parted, easily, and realized the tension had gone from her. Nikolai nuzzled below her, then moved over. She still held him, tightly, the last tiny attempt to prevent it happening. He was suspended over her, supported on his arms, waiting.

'Please,' he said. The cold wetness of his tears dropped against her chest. Gently, frightened for both of them, she guided him into her.

'It's too big.'

'No.'

'Yes,' she said. 'It'll hurt.'

'No it won't. I promise.'

She had kept her hand between them. He moved it away. He stayed just inside her, moving very gently. She was hardly aware of the increased pressure.

'Does it hurt?'

'Not really.'

'Is it good?'

'I don't know.'

She supposed she should match the rhythm, but she couldn't quite adjust to his movement. She began to feel sore. He quickened, suddenly, and she gasped, disappointed, aware it was going to end before she felt anything.

'No. Wait.'

'I can't.'

'Please.'

'I can't.'

He erupted inside her, shuddering movements shaking his body. Then he fell over her, head into her neck, panting. She stared upwards into the darkness, eyes opened wide. It had to be better than *that*. It hadn't been anything. She felt very wet. She shifted slightly and he moved off her, head still by her shoulder.

'We're not virgins any more,' he said. He sounded proud. 'Was it good for you?'

She felt his head move away at the question. He was looking at her in the darkness. Always the need for reassurance, she thought.

'Yes,' she lied. 'It was wonderful.'

He missed the sadness in her voice, leaning over and clicking on the light. She turned her head away from the glare.

'You're crying,' he said.

She didn't reply.

'Is it happiness? Was it that good for you?'

She nodded. 'Of course.'

When the effects of the wine subsided, she began crying openly, desperately, sobs jerking through her body. Once she turned to Nikolai, reaching out towards him. He was snoring, small, bubbly sounds. He shrugged her hand away.

Chapter Four

Count von Sydon was an undeniably imposing man, thought Josef. He wore his snow-white hair long, almost to his collar, but carefully trimmed. So, too, was the beard, contrasting with the mahogany-brown face. He dressed with matching attention, his suit bordering on the flamboyance befitting a man associated with the arts and sciences, but stopping short of a style that could be criticized or laughed at. Josef sat opposite the Nobel Academician in the discreet chamber off the main dining-room of an hotel in the old part of Stockholm and watched him dab his lips with a white silk handkerchief drawn from his jacket sleeve. Josef wondered from whom he had copied the mannerism. The Count had made himself into a composite picture, decided Josef, a jigsaw of mannerisms and behaviour copied from admired men whom he had encountered in twenty years of life devoted to the Nobel Foundation. Strip them away and there would only be a grey outline left, like a child's drawing ready for colouring.

Josef had known everything about the Count, long before they had hesitantly shaken hands fifteen minutes earlier. Successful negotiations depended on complete knowledge, so in advance of any discussion Josef had detailed dossiers prepared by the relevant Russian embassy upon the person with whom he was becoming involved. The Stockholm embassy had done particularly well, he thought, correctly identifying the Count as a poseur who had successfully cloaked his deficiencies to become the embodiment of the Nobel Foundation.

The Count ordered coffee for himself. Josef chose mineral water.

'It was good of you to come,' said the Swede. He was ill at ease, seeking safety in cliches, decided Josef.

The Russian shrugged. 'It was good of the committee to consider Balshev for the award,' he said, matching the banality.

'But it must be quite clear,' stressed the Count, 'that this is an unofficial meeting.'

'Quite,' agreed Josef.

'It has no standing whatsoever,' emphasized the old man.

It was sad, thought Josef. Aloud, he said, 'The fact that I, rather than anyone in an official capacity, have come from the Ministry of Culture must indicate our acceptance of that.'

'Good,' said the Count, smiling. 'But I feel you will appreciate my concern.'

'Concern?' asked Josef, innocently.

Count von Sydon appeared unsure.

'I can talk openly?'

'Of course.'

'Solzhenitsyn was an embarrassment, a great embarrassment. There was criticism ... unpleasant comment ... when he would not leave Russia for the presentation ... '

'It was unfortunate,' agreed Josef.

'Oh please,' said the Count, anxiously. 'Don't infer annoyance at your country on my part. But it's important that the Foundation is above politics.'

'Of course,' said Josef. He wondered if the man had ever expressed an opinion.

'*Walk Softly on a Lonely Day* is a wonderful book,' the Count said, abruptly. 'A work of art.'

'It is,' agreed Josef.

'I believe the committee think very highly of it.'

Josef sipped the mineral water, allowing the old man to wade deeper. The silence stretched out.

'... But I ... the Foundation ... well, it is important that we avoid a repetition ... should Balshev be nominated, it's necessary for us to know that he will accept the award.'

Although the words were splintered, the Count had spoken rapidly, avoiding the other man's eyes.

'I can assure you,' said Josef, formally, 'that my country regards it as a great honour that one of its writers is being considered for the nomination. If Balshev is chosen, then he will definitely be allowed to travel to Stockholm.'

Count von Sydon sat back, sighing, the tension leaking from him. Life, he thought, was very pleasant.

'Wonderful,' he said.

There seemed nothing else to say.

'It would give me great pleasure ... indeed I would be honoured ... to offer you lunch,' said the Swede, after several minutes' silence. 'But I'm afraid that might be difficult.'

Josef looked at him, not helping, his face blank.

'You see,' continued the other man, the unease returning, 'I am quite well known in the city ... '

He smiled, shyly. 'I've been connected with the Foundation for a long while. I've a certain amount of local notoriety ... '

Josef nodded.

' ... And you', continued the Count, 'are even more well known. I do not think there are any good restaurants in this city where we could go together without being recognized ... '

Count von Sydon paused, swallowing. He regretted embarking on the conversation, Josef knew.

'To be seen together, in advance of any announcement by the committee of any award, literary or otherwise, would be very damaging to the Foundation,' said the old man. 'The Foundation's reputation for impartiality could be jeopardized.'

'I understand perfectly,' said Josef. He inhaled deeply,

45

preparing himself. 'As I said, my country is deeply honoured at being considered for the award.'

Count von Sydon frowned at the repetition.

'The Praesidium of the Supreme Soviet itself sent me here to assure you of Balshev's attendance ... '

'But ... '

Curtly, Josef held up his hand. He had to be in command now, for the rest of the meeting.

'I must impress upon you', he went on, 'that having gone to so much trouble, my country would be deeply offended if the award went to another writer.'

Count von Sydon's face cleared, then clouded immediately.

'My dear sir, are you trying to tell me ... '

'I'm not trying to tell you anything,' cut off Josef, sharply. 'We started this meeting on the understanding of honesty. My country wants to do nothing that will embarrass the Foundation ... although we realize that any disclosure of this meeting would be embarrassing to both you personally and the organization you have worked with for so long. Especially after the Solzhenitsyn problem. We are completely aware of the difficult questions that would be posed ... of explanations that would be demanded ... it could do the Foundation irreparable harm ... '

Count von Sydon sat absolutely still, gazing at the Russian.

'But I have no power ... no way ... '

'That's not really true, is it? You are a man who has devoted his life selflessly to the Foundation. Your reputation and integrity are immense and your views are respected by the Literary Committee.'

'But you're asking me ... '

'I'm asking you to do nothing. I'm just making the position clear.'

Count von Sydon straightened in his chair. 'This is despicable,' he said.

46

Josef humped his shoulders. '*You* sought this meeting. You asked for guarantees. I see nothing despicable in requesting similar assurances.'

'I refuse to do it,' said the Count, stiffly. 'You are right. I *do* have influence. And I shall use it to ensure that someone other than Balshev is nominated.'

Josef sighed. 'Count,' he said, almost gently. 'The initial conversations you had with our embassy were recorded. So was my telephone call to you. You have been photographed entering this hotel, today. And your departure will be recorded, too, as mine will. We can prove connivance and produce evidence and pictures of your participation. Neither China nor America would accept the award under those circumstances. We are quite prepared to publish everything and permanently damage the Foundation.'

The Count stood, scraping the chair backwards, looking down contemptuously at the Russian.

'We look forward to hearing from you,' concluded Josef.

Back in the hotel, Josef made telephone reservations for the next part of the journey and considered trying to call Pamela. Telephone connections to the villa from outside the country were bad, he knew. Instead, he wrote her a letter, then ate an early dinner in his room, staring out over the darkened capital. Much later, as he was undressing, he found a scrap of bread from the dinner-tray in his jacket pocket. He frowned. It was only under great stress that he unconsciously reverted to the prison-camp routine, hoarding things, especially food. Medev had been very good at it, frequently stealing food unseen in the camp from the commandant's kitchen. Always, the Jew had shared it with him. It hadn't happened for a long time, reflected Josef. Before lapsing into what he regarded as sleep, he ate the bread.

Chapter Five

The choice of Vienna for his meetings with the British and American publishers was Josef's, decreed by no other consideration than that he liked Austria. The people remembered how to live, he felt. Like a sensible widow who survives happily after the death of her husband, remembering the good times and not distraught by the emptiness of the future, Austria had accepted its time of greatness was over and refused to mourn. He liked a country where women put on their favourite hats and dressed up to take afternoon tea and *Sachertorte* with other women with whom they had exchanged the same gossip the previous day, wearing the same hats.

Russia, he thought nostalgically, had forgotten how to wear pretty bonnets.

He stayed at the Hotel Sacher because it had character like the elderly, behatted ladies in its glass-fronted tea-room adjoining the lobby. There would be, he believed, many similarities between the Vienna of 1915 and St Petersburg or Moscow. Perhaps, Josef conceded, he was enamoured with nostalgia.

Josef had arranged his meeting with care, allowing almost two days from his arrival in Stockholm before he met the Briton and then another forty-eight hours before his encounter with the American. Negotiating drained Josef Bultova. Even the ridiculously easy two-hour session with Count von Sydon had left him too tightly wound. And now there was more than the usual anxiety. His very involvement with a prospective Nobel prizewinner was wrong, he thought. Perhaps, he mused hopefully, wandering aimlessly through St Stephen's Square into the old part of the city, some members of the Praesidium would have the same doubts. He hoped so. It would make any subsequent inquiry easier to attend. He feared there would be such an inquiry. Devgeny didn't intend allowing this negotiation to end in the success that had marked Josef's other involvements. He paused, leaning over the river wall. He always thought it sad that such a miserable, ditch-like river as the Wien had given a city a name. It was almost like cheating. He shivered, feeling the cold. When the snow melted, the river would have a moment or two of pride.

It was unfair to leave Pamela like he had, he thought, his mind running on. Long absences in a strange country would be too much of a strain on her. He wondered if the short, irritable disagreements that were breaking out between them stemmed solely from their sexual difficulties or went deeper. Perhaps they should consult a doctor when he got back.

He looked at his watch. It was identical to that which he had sold, all those years ago, on the rocking, smelling prison train. It had been an obsolete model by the time he was released and so he had had one specially made, actually sketching the design for the watch-maker. Perhaps, he conceded, picking up his thoughts of earlier that day, he was in love with nostalgia.

Josef got back to the Sacher with thirty minutes in hand, knowing Henry Stanswell would be on time. As with the American, there had already been several letters with the British publisher. Today's meeting was the culmination of tentative approaches that had spread over several months, beginning with personal approaches to Hattersley and Black in London as Josef returned from the negotiation of a wheat sale to compensate for the disastrous Russian harvest. He

49

wondered what the reaction would be to the news the novel was likely to be the Nobel prizewinner.

There was, of course, a reason other than his enjoyment of Vienna for Josef insisting the meetings be outside England or America. This was a settlement session and they were coming to him. And so they were giving a little away, even before the talking began. It was important psychology.

Josef's telephone rang precisely at the prearranged time and the Russian experienced that jump of excitement preceding any bargaining. Afterwards there would be the exhaustion, but before there was always a lurch of anticipation.

Immediately they met, Josef liked the Englishman. He had a brown gravy voice and a habit of caressing his wide moustaches and would, Josef guessed, have wartime stories of the R.A.F. He was tall and fat from self-indulgence, wearing tweeds that accentuated his size. He was used to overpowering people, Josef guessed. His white hair was long, which gave him a passing resemblance to Count von Sydon, but here the affectation fitted. There was none of the self-awareness that made the Count constantly discomforted.

Josef had booked dinner at the Frances Karna restaurant, preferring it to the Three Hussars. Throughout the fifteen-minute ride to the restaurant, they circled around the subject of their meeting like prize fighters seeking an opening.

'I trust this meeting means we've got the book,' said Stanswell, finally, after they had ordered. Josef had waited for him to begin the proceedings.

'It depends,' responded Josef. 'Our decision to publish in the West is unique. Anyone getting Balshev's book will have the coup of the year ... '

'We've already discussed that,' reminded Stanswell.

'But we haven't talked specifically about money.'

Stanswell had to commit himself before he heard the news, so that he would over-compensate in his eagerness to recover.

'We thought of £2,000 advance against royalties, assessed on a scale,' said the publisher. 'Ten per cent for the first 8,000, 12½ for the next 5,000 and 15 for any sale after that. We'll guarantee an initial print of 7,500.'

Stanswell had stopped eating, reciting the terms from a small notebook fitted inside his wallet. There was no cash in the wallet, Josef noticed, so Stanswell must be wealthy. Only rich people had the confidence to be without money. At no time did Josef carry less than £150 in sterling and dollars in his pocket, with letters of credit and drawing facilities for £5,000. Stanswell smiled, expectantly. He had a gold tooth that glinted when he smiled, like a tiny beacon.

'No,' said Josef, abruptly.

He didn't bother to look up, concentrating upon the final morsel of his venison pâté. Since his imprisonment, Josef never left food.

The beacon across the table went out.

'But Mr Bultova ... '

'Please.' Josef stopped him. He wiped his hands on his napkin. That *was* good pâté, he thought.

'I am offering you the book that is to become this year's Nobel prizewinner,' he announced, dramatically.

Stanswell looked at him in complete astonishment. This was going to be easy, thought Josef, like Stockholm.

'But ... ' tried the Briton.

'I know', continued Josef, deliberately cutting him off, 'that your advance exceeds by hundreds of pounds what British publishers usually pay in an advance. I know, too, that the percentages are not over-generous. For a Nobel prize book ... one that you could print and have available for the time of the presentation, the whole offer is ludicrous.'

It was important to maintain Stanswell's confusion.

'If Balshev is nominated, then he'll be permitted to go to Sweden to collect the award,' continued Josef.

Stanswell leapt at the uncertainty, as Josef had intended. Now it was time to appear generous.

'You said "if",' challenged the publisher.

'I'm not asking you to accept anything before a formal announcement.'

'That's very fair of you,' conceded Stanswell.

A waiter served pheasant.

'Immediately after going to Stockholm,' continued Josef, enlarging the bait, 'Balshev will be permitted to promote the book in England.'

The Russian admired Stanswell's control. The only indication of his excitement was the complete disregard of the food.

'You'll appreciate that what I'm telling you is in the strictest confidence,' warned Josef. 'For the slightest hint of this to get out would be most embarrassing.'

Stanswell nodded, half hearing, jabbing at his meal.

'I cannot commit my company to any binding contract merely on your expectation that Balshev will earn the nomination,' he opened, clumsily.

He stopped, raising a pudgy hand. Medev had had hands like that, remembered Josef. In the winter they had chapped and bled as they shouldered the trucks up the last incline before the loading bay, and Medev had wept at the pain. Poor Medev.

'I propose we prepare a document binding upon both of us and which I assure you will be honoured by my government,' said Josef. 'If Balshev does not get the nomination, then I accept your contract ... '

Stanswell smiled and the tooth flashed a victory. Poor man, thought Josef, he imagines he's won.

'But I want a second document,' continued Josef. 'As legally binding as the first. If Balshev *does* become the Nobel prizewinner, then I want an advance against sales of twenty-five thousand pounds. That sale is to be restricted solely to Britain, with me retaining the rights of negotiations in Canada. I want twenty per cent on all sales and no division of paperback payment. The full amount reverts to Balshev.'

'That's ridiculous,' protested Stanswell, his voice strained.

'For a Nobel prize book, printed in time for the presentation? I think not,' argued Josef. 'It's very modest, in fact. With simultaneous publishing, you'll make a fortune.'

'No.'

'You get a sensational book that will sell in record amounts,' stressed Josef. 'The potential is enormous.'

Stanswell shook his head, determinedly. 'The second contract isn't acceptable,' he said. 'If it becomes the Nobel prize book, it will have to be a coffee-table production. To recover anything like the outlay, we'd have to sell for three or four pounds. Maybe more. You'll have to improve your offer.'

Josef sighed. 'What *would* you accept?' he probed. Always leave an opening. That was another rule.

Stanswell shrugged, unhappy at having to list his demands.

'I'd want some of the paperback rights,' insisted the publisher.

'What percentage?'

'Sixty for you, forty for me.'

There was just a little too much hope in the man's voice.

'Eighty–twenty,' countered Josef. 'And that's a big concession. My government instructed me to retain full rights.'

'Seventy–thirty,' tried Stanswell.

Still a little too much hope, judged Josef. And the other man hadn't been able to suppress a smile at the first offer. Adamantly, Josef shook his head. 'I *can't* go below eighty,' he said, in the voice of a man being pushed too far. 'Even with that, you'll make a fortune.'

'The Publishers' Association would object.'

'Who's going to tell them?' rejected Josef.

Stanswell made a calculation in his wallet notebook.

'Both contracts will be in writing?' he asked.

I've won, decided Josef. Always, it was the best moment. Outwardly, he remained unmoved.

'Legally drawn up,' he confirmed.

'Copyright?'

'We'd insist on supervising and approving the translation, but you'd have the translation copyright, in the normal way.'

Stanswell smiled.

'Agreed,' he said, offering his hand. Josef took it. Perhaps, he thought, he was worrying unduly. Perhaps the whole thing was going to be as easy as this. In the negotiations to pump Siberian natural gas to the west coast of America, he'd argued a fortnight over one-eighth of one per cent. And won, of course.

Josef had met Herbert Blyne six years before, at a United Nations cocktail party, when the man had been a new director at Hartner, Edwin and Elper, anxious to prove himself. He had pursued Josef throughout the function, imagining a book based on Josef's life. The Russian had been offended then by the man's pushful Jewishness, his refusal to be rebuffed first by coldness and then by deliberate rudeness. Josef remembered Blyne as an artists' model for the successful American executive, diet trim, a lapel breadth ahead of fashion, a wife and two brace-toothed children in a white-painted Colonial home in Scarsdale and a mistress on 60th and 2nd.

The encounter was very different from that with Stanswell. Blyne was late calling, hoping Josef would be the first to make the approach. The Russian waited, confidently, and when the phone went thirty minutes after the appointed time, he allowed it to ring for several minutes before picking it up. Blyne was just unable to subdue the anxiety. Josef smiled, satisfied.

Blyne would have disliked discussing business over a meal-table, Josef guessed. So he invited the man to his suite. Agreeing to it as the venue was another small psychological concession. Apart from his weight, which Josef estimated had gone up by about half a stone, the American managing director was as Josef remembered. He was quite small and very dark, almost arabic, with short, nervous gestures about which he seemed embarrassed, as if to indicate apprehension showed weakness. He probably carries pills in his briefcase, too, thought Josef, and pays fifty dollars a week to a psychiatrist. They shook hands, recalled their earlier meeting, laughed about it and then sat, regarding each other.

'I knew we'd get together eventually,' began Blyne. 'I see the wheat deal came off.'

Either he reads financial newspapers, thought Josef, or he's had someone prepare a dossier on me. Probably the latter.

'I was lucky,' said the Russian, modestly.

Silence grew between them.

'I think you're going to be pleased we opened discussions,' tried Josef.

'Oh?'

'We think Nikolai Balshev is going to get this year's Nobel prize,' he said, matching the bluntness he'd practised with the Briton.

'I figured something like that,' said Blyne, unimpressed. 'All this secrecy crap and flights to Europe.'

It was a good reaction, judged Josef. He wondered how difficult it would be to unsettle him.

'But the Soviet Union are delighted at the prospect,' offered Josef.

'What's that mean?' asked Blyne, nudging the lure.

'That immediately after the presentation in Stockholm, he'll be allowed to tour the West, for personal appearances.'

For several moments, the American sat completely still,

only his hands moving around his lap in those gestures that embarrassed him.

'You mean to New York, right after the ceremony?'

Josef nodded. 'I won't let him go out on those incredible author's tours,' he warned. 'Fourteen cities in fourteen days, or anything stupid like that. But there will be some personal appearances.'

Blyne nodded slowly. He'd recovered, decided Josef, and was calculating the potential.

'You will be the only American publishing house in history to bring out, with permission and therefore with the full approval of the Soviet Union, one of their Nobel prize-winners,' said Josef. He paused, gaining effect. ' ... And that would be quite a coup for a publisher to pull off, wouldn't it?'

Blyne smiled and Josef was happy he had isolated the man's thoughts.

'There's something else, of course,' said Josef.

'Oh?'

'I would imagine', continued the Russian, 'that a publisher selected by the Soviet Union to publish one work would find other material forthcoming.'

'Are you giving me an undertaking?' demanded Blyne, excited.

'No,' said Josef.

'A hint?' Blyne was stretching almost too far.

'No,' repeated Josef. 'I'm just expressing a Russian train of thought.'

Blyne smiled. 'It wouldn't be possible to put those thoughts into some sort of written document, would it?' he pressed.

People should learn that negative questions prompt negative responses, thought Josef.

'No,' he said. 'A great deal will have to be on trust.'

'But there could be a definite contract for *Walk Softly on a Lonely Day*?'

'If the terms are right.'

'What do you want?'

'Two million dollars advance,' said Josef. 'A different-from-normal paperback division. And I retain Canadian rights.'

'Bullshit,' dismissed Blyne.

'It's not bullshit and you know it. A million was paid for a Howard Hughes phoney. *That* was bullshit. This is kosher.'

'There's nothing in it for me.'

'Now you're talking bullshit. What about the paperback rights?'

'So?'

'So I'll split with you, seventy–thirty. In the last three years there have been three cases of a paperback sale going for two million dollars plus. This book will exceed any of those. The moment you put your signature on a contract, you're into profit. And there's the investment for the future. And you know as well as I do that any publisher with access to Russian literature is being given the key to a gold mine.'

'I want to think about it,' said Blyne.

'No time. And no reason,' argued Josef.

'I can publish simultaneously with the news of the award?' Josef nodded. It was getting close.

'But there must be no advance release,' cautioned the Russian. 'If there is, the deal is off. And I'll also undertake to re-negotiate if Nikolai fails to get the award.'

Uninvited, Blyne poured himself a drink from the bar Josef had in the room, needing the time.

'We *will* work together again?' he pressed.

'I can only give you my word.'

'It's a deal,' announced the American. Again, the brief feeling of contentment wrapped itself around the Russian.

'Why allow Balshev out when you made it so fucking difficult for Solzhenitsyn?' demanded Blyne, bluntly.

Josef weighed the question, unhappy the man had to swear.

It was another indication of his uncertainty. How the obscenity of the camp, the constant, unremitting cursing until the men knew no other words and so lost yet another aspect of their self-respect had angered his father, he remembered.

'He has no political conviction,' replied Josef, simply. 'His writing is completely untainted.'

'So an unpolitical farm boy is being allowed to come to the West where nothing he will do will embarrass the Soviet Union?'

Josef looked for the sneer, but found only a statement of fact.

'Yes,' he said, admitting the cynicism. Would there be no embarrassment, wondered Josef.

Suddenly Blyne switched the conversation.

'Balshev is going to make a lot of money,' he said.

'Ah, yes,' said Josef, as if he had forgotten, which he hadn't. 'I'll want the same contractual arrangement with you that I have with Britain. I want fifteen per cent paid into my Geneva account ... '

'Fifteen?' queried Blyne. 'Shit!'

Josef produced the letter of authorization from the Ministry of Culture permitting the commission, together with Nikolai's written agreement.

'You're an expensive man,' remarked the American.

'But good,' responded Josef, laying out the documents upon which he had already written the method of Nikolai's payment into Russia through the Narodny Bank. Blyne stared at the other man. There was no conceit, decided the American, no conceit at all. One day, he thought, picking up Josef's outline agreement, that guy will make the subject of a great book.

Chapter Six

He had telephoned from Vienna, warning of his return, so there were no customs formalities. While his luggage was being loaded into the car, he rang the dacha and was surprised to learn that Pamela had returned to Moscow. Immediately, a childlike excitement at seeing her swept through him.

Like tombstones in a neglected churchyard, the apartment blocks reserved exclusively for leading government officials who shared their homes with no one were regimented with a view of Kutuzovsky Prospekt. Josef's apartment formed the penthouse on the first section, externally as drab as those that surrounded it. Inside, it rivalled the dacha for indulgence. It had taken him nearly three years to furnish it satisfactorily to suit his purpose, shopping throughout the world. It was essential, above every other consideration, that he had what no others possessed in the city. And was known to have them. With the exception of the huge sunken lounge, where the walls were lined with raw Japanese silk, the apartment was largely panelled in Norwegian pine, not because he particularly liked the style, but because it was unusually modern in Moscow.

The furniture was predominantly Scandinavian, mostly Swedish. The kitchen was almost entirely automated with electrical goods purchased in America and a book-lined study was an Aladdin's cave of more electrical equipment. Two Xerox machines had been set into cabinets. One tape recorder was so large it occupied the whole of the specially constructed side-table, and during a visit to Tokyo two years before he had purchased two miniature recorders. Since he was a man of precise records, painstakingly kept for his own protection, one was fitted into a briefcase he took on all business trips to enable him to dictate all correspondence and memoranda at the end of each day, to be shipped to Moscow in the diplomatic pouches of whatever country in which he was working.

Having created an apartment that would have been remarkable on New York's Fifth Avenue and which was consequently dazzling by Moscow standards, Josef occasionally gave carefully selective dinner parties, where he served imported wines and liquor often untasted in the Soviet capital to Party executives and neighbouring officials of whose envious gossip he was assured. Until four months ago, after the natural gas negotiations in America and before he had been entrusted with chaperoning Nikolai Balshev, he had intended inviting Uli Devgeny to one such function, aware that every other guest would know the reason and that Devgeny would be humiliated whether he attended or not. Now the gas deal, like all the other successful negotiations that had preceded it, was forgotten. Now, thought Josef bitterly as he moved away from Moscow's Sheremetyevo Airport, Devgeny's only likely visit would be to take over the place.

As the Zil moved slowly through the rush-hour traffic, the memory of the last night in Vienna, with the choking nightmare, forced its way into his mind. In needless reassurance, he unclipped the briefcase. In the specially segregated side-pockets lay the drugs with which he had restocked while he had been out of the country. He had methalaquone, librium and valium, and in Vienna had visited a chemist he had used before, to buy a greater concentration than normal of chlordiazepoxide and diazepam.

Her reaction was different from that he had expected. He

stood just inside the lounge, waiting for her to smile, but instead she frowned at him, combing her hands through her hair, dishevelled and unkempt.

'Hello, wife,' he greeted, in anticipation. She appeared to forget their word game.

'Hello, Josef.'

'Is that all?' he asked, offended by her flat greeting.

'But I didn't expect you ... look, I'm a mess.'

She wore the same jeans and shirt as that last day at the dacha, but her face had lost the well-scrubbed look.

'You're lovely,' he said, untruthfully. He stared at her, uncertain of her mood.

'What's wrong?'

'You surprised me. I wish you hadn't arrived like this, darling. Unexpectedly, I mean.'

'But I *wanted* to surprise you, once I learned you weren't at the dacha.'

'And I wanted to dress up properly, in a dress. And with my hair done. Not like this ... like some bloody hippie.'

'It was a bloody hippie I fell in love with, remember?'

'And still am?' she asked. There seemed an urgency for the compliment, he thought.

'And still am,' he reassured. He cupped her chin and kissed her. She locked her arm around his neck and held him, tightly, almost grinding her face into his.

'Hello, husband,' she said, remembering at last. Then, in a rush, she added, 'Oh darling, I'm so glad you're back.'

'You're crying. Your nose is red.'

She sniffed, scrubbing her hand over her face. 'I'm so happy to see you. I've been ... lonely.'

'I've missed you, too,' he said.

She turned away from him, sharply. 'I need ten minutes to make myself presentable to my husband,' she said.

While she changed, he opened champagne, and selected tapes on the stereo-unit recessed into the wall. She came

61

back shining from soap and rough towelling, her hair strained back into a comb, Spanish style. She wore a plain black dress, with scalloped neckline and flat heeled shoes. She pirouetted, pleased with his attention.

'Now I feel able to greet you properly,' she said. She accepted the wine, raising her glass in a silent toast.

'How's Nikolai?' he asked.

'What?'

Josef stared at her, curiously. 'I asked how Nikolai was,' he repeated, mildly.

'All right, I suppose. Why shouldn't he be?'

'Did you fight with him?'

'Of course not. Why ask a funny question like that?'

'You seemed angry at his name.'

She sat down opposite him in one of the low armchairs, taking elaborate care arranging the folds of her skirt.

'Have you eaten?' she asked. 'There's food in the freezer.'

'Did you quarrel with him?'

'No, of course not. He's just not my idea of a honeymoon companion.'

'If there had been a way of avoiding it, I would have done so.'

'I know. I'm sorry.'

For several minutes, neither spoke, each recognizing the nearness of an argument.

Pamela voiced the fear. 'Please, let's not fall out on your first night home.'

'You still haven't answered my question,' pressed Josef.

'Nikolai is like he always is,' she said. 'He needs to be told, every day, how good he is. It doesn't matter who tells him, as long as somebody does. You could train a monkey to do it. And he still smells.'

'So you don't like him.'

Pamela shrugged, holding out her glass for more wine. 'I don't dislike him. And I don't like him, either. He makes me feel uncomfortable. Like birdwatchers create hides from which to spy on birds, to learn about them, Nikolai spies on people, from behind his artificial barrier.'

'I think you're wrong,' said Josef. 'He's unusual, that's all. A sort of person you haven't encountered before.'

Pamela made a dismissive motion with her hand, unwilling to discuss the man.

'He's anxious about you,' she reported. 'He wants to know about Stockholm.'

Josef looked at his watch. He wondered if the price to prison guards had risen over the decade. Did prisoners still drug themselves with tannin and sometimes run to the wire, hoping to get shot? They never did shoot them, of course. Outside there was nowhere to go, so eventually they had to return.

'I'll speak to him tomorrow,' he said, discarding memories. He looked at her. 'Are you sure nothing is wrong?' he asked.

'Positive.' She spoke over-loudly, he thought. Some wine spilled from her glass, staining her skirt, but she ignored it.

'When did you come back to Moscow?'

'About six days ago,' she said. 'I decided I'd rather be here. At least there are things I could do by myself. And get away from Nikolai watching me.'

She suddenly brightened. 'Oh, I saw the ballet. It was fantastic.'

'The Bolshoi? How did you get tickets?'

'A friend of yours suddenly rang, the night I got back. Said he had heard you were away and had thought of me. Apparently he got the tickets for someone who had let him down.'

Slowly Josef replaced his glass on a side-table. A feeling near to nausea gripped him.

'What friend?' he asked.

Pamela picked up the jotting pad from beside the lounge telephone.

63

'Devgeny,' she read, looking up and smiling. 'Uli Devgeny. Wasn't that kind of him?'

'Very,' agreed Josef. What the hell did that mean?

'He said he'd like to talk to you when you returned. I promised you'd telephone and thank him.'

'Oh, I'll speak to him,' said Josef, absently. 'I'll certainly speak to him.'

That night they both got drunk. Josef did it knowingly, welcoming the feeling of irresponsibility like a schoolboy playing truant for the first time. He was secure in his locked apartment. No one could take advantage of him. There could be no record of any indiscretion, no memorandum to be produced months later at an inquiry. He lived constantly aware of himself, Josef thought. Every action was assessed for its effect, every word considered for its implication, like a chess master thinking perpetually five moves ahead of an opponent. Suddenly there was the need to relax. Or collapse. But even as he tried to rationalize the decision, he recognized the element of desperation. He was giving up, just a little. He *did* need to unwind. And it *was* safe. He needed sleep, too, and alcohol might help. But there had been other, safe occasions when he could have relaxed with a bottle. And the pills in his briefcase could provide rest, of sorts. Above everything else, Josef Bultova knew himself. And so he accepted the fear and its motivation. Now he was seeking oblivion, like the flotsam of fifteen years ago who had traded with him to brew their strange narcotic concoction and upon whom he had lived, like a parasite on a series of dying animals. By recognizing Pamela, Devgeny had made it quite clear he intended destroying Josef completely, moving not only against him, but against the only other person for whom he knew Josef had the slightest feeling. There was too much unknown opposition, he thought. Pamela was Josef's weakness and Devgeny knew it. Love, thought Josef, before alcohol flooded his reasoning, had little place in his life. It made him vulnerable.

Pamela got drunk because she was frightened, too. She had left Nikolai's bed in the middle of the night, long before the servants had awakened, and remained tense all day for a knowing look from whomever had had to change the bed or an expectant, over-familiar move from the writer. But the servants remained as taciturn as ever and Nikolai hadn't approached her again. She had rehearsed her belated, positive rejection but his attitude had changed that day. Incredibly, he seemed almost respectful, pulling back into his shell of reserve, speaking few words at meal-times and spending hours walking alone in the grounds. The experiment, Pamela had realized, was over. The knowledge doubled her humiliation, worse even than if they had made love again.

And her fear went beyond Josef discovering her stupidity. Constantly since it had happened, she had recalled Nikolai's boast. If he were as important as he had maintained, he had an advantage over Josef, as well as her.

'Darling,' she said, suddenly. 'How important is Nikolai to you?'

More in reflection than answer, he said, 'Vitally important. To both of us.'

He opened the second bottle of wine and she leaned forward anxiously for her glass to be filled. Drunkenness failed to extinguish the predominant fear in both of them, but it achieved one thing, the importance of which neither realized at the time. The wine, coupled with the need she felt to compensate, swamped her apprehension of sex with Josef. And it dulled his initial realization, so that he accepted what developed without the surprise that might have raised the lowered barriers. And they made love.

Even drunk Josef was the consummate, accomplished lover she had accused him of being during her apology at the dacha. He was tender where Nikolai had been gauche, forceful where the other man had been clumsy. She and

65

Nikolai had been two youngsters staring into a darkened room where they believed hidden something neither had seen before. Josef shone the light on more beauty than she had ever expected to see.

She came ahead of him, wildly, and then again with him, matching his climax. She kissed him, frenzied and imploring, not wanting to stop. But at what, for them, was the most important moment, Josef was exhausted, tired and drunk, wanting only for her to cease the demands. He forced himself to embrace her and hold her, gently, until she quietened.

'Oh my God,' she said, both disappointed and relieved. Then, much later, she said gratefully, 'We're properly man and wife.'

Josef lay beside her long after she had drifted into a contented, drunken sleep. His head ached, badly. After two hours, he took methalaquone. And then, desperately, more. His headache worsened. Sleep still would not come. He turned towards her and in the shadowy light of the bedroom made out her face, turned towards him, fur-like through a skein of hair. She was smiling, very slightly. Love, he thought, for the second time that night, was an inconvenience. An inconvenience he was uncertain whether he could afford.

Chapter Seven

Predictably, Uli Devgeny refused to see him the following morning. The secretary, a pebble-spectacled, never-smiling young man with late-clearing acne, cited pressure of work and previously arranged meetings. Josef reacted immediately and with equal predictability, leaving Devgeny's Kremlin office with the curt instruction that the Minister should telephone to discuss a mutually convenient appointment. Fighting cocks, thought the secretary, unimpressed as the plump Russian hurried out. Bloody fools, both of them. In the end, probably neither would win.

Josef decided to go to the dacha to see Nikolai, so that he could justifiably reject Devgeny's first suggestion for a meeting. The negotiator was permitted to keep a Mercedes in Moscow and he drove with the sun-roof fully retracted, unsuccessfully trying to blow away the previous night's drunkenness. He was unused to hangovers and felt awful. The night had been completely sleepless, culminating at dawn with a violent spasm of vomiting that had left him aching and sore. His eyes were red-veined and puffed from insomnia and his chin stained from bad shaving. A band of pain kept tightening around his head. There had been rumours, he remembered, that tourniquet headbands had been used for torture in some sections of the camp. He wondered if it had been true. Medev had insisted it was.

Pamela, in complete contrast, had been almost light-headed in her gaiety, disregarding an admitted headache and chattering without direction, like a bird suddenly freed from captivity, giggling at him, imagining the legacy from drink was the only reason for his moroseness.

The consummation of their marriage had lifted from her an enormous uncertainty. A person of frequently ill-considered impulses from which, once committed, pride prevented retreat, she had been deeply worried. She believed her decision to turn away from the carefully ordered life of a wealthy M.P.'s daughter in London had been one of the few to which she had devoted the consideration it justified. Russia, from the moment she had stepped ashore in Leningrad, had enthralled her. But no matter how sincere her feelings, for a single girl — particularly the daughter of a Tory Member of Parliament — to quit London for Moscow was a ridiculous hypothesis which even she, in her haphazard way, did not consider. And then she had met Josef at a British embassy reception. She had heard of him, of course. Everyone at the function had and she had been intrigued finally meeting someone about whom she had read so much. She had first thought him an unprepossessing, fat little man with glasses, immaculately dressed to disguise his shortness, but by the time the evening had ended, she was enraptured by him, her interest far exceeding the aphrodisiac of power. She had had a week remaining of her tour and he had seen her every day. She had been flattered by his attention and impressed at his easy access to everything in what she accepted with the myopia of the irrationally committed was a largely closed society. Gradually, beginning with the first and strengthening with the two subsequent visits she made within the year, the idea developed of how she could adopt a life she felt preferable to her own. The opposition from her family had been enormous and sustained. And the publicity in the West, particularly as her name was linked to that of Josef Bultova, had been terrifying. But she was determined she was in love, had withstood the publicity and laughed at the Victorianism of her father's final gesture in publicly disowning her. But although she would have argued otherwise, it was impossible for Pamela's life to exist on unsound foundations. While she had been contemptuous of her English background and the way of life it represented, she had needed its reassurance. Having spurned it, she needed a replacement. Marriage to Josef would provide that, she knew, but it had to be a proper marriage, a complete one. What had belatedly happened the previous night had made it so, she felt. Her buoyancy was even unaffected by what had occurred between her and Nikolai, which seemed to lessen in importance.

Nikolai saw Josef's car arrive and came running from the house like a schoolboy welcoming his father to the boarding school on speech day.

'Josef, my friend.'

'How have you been, Nikolai?'

'Miserable without you.'

'I thought you preferred to be without people.'

The writer shrugged a contradiction. 'I need people I trust. I trust you.'

'Wasn't Pamela company?'

'Of course,' responded the writer, immediately. 'I was sorry she decided to return to Moscow.'

The pale, inconspicuous boy smiled up at the older man and Josef felt a surge of pity for him. He was to be used by men who distained literature with contemptuous boorishness, jerked and paraded like a puppet suspended on elastic. And there was nothing he could do about it. Josef wondered if he would ever become aware of it. They went into a small chamber off the main hallway in which the Archduke had created a gun and trophy room. Nikolai had chosen the room when they had first arrived and announced it was to be his study, the room in which he would structure a sequel to *Walk Softly on a Lonely Day*. An empty typewriter, dust-marked from disuse, was on the desk, paper confettied around it, a few pieces marked by isolated jotting.

'Work not going well?' probed Josef, curiously.

Nikolai shrugged, irritated by the question. 'It's impossible to work here. You wouldn't understand. You're not an artist.'

Josef smiled at the conceit, shaking his still aching head. The open drive hadn't done any good. Nikolai pulled a chair from behind the desk and sat facing Josef, hands on his knees, once again the anxious schoolboy awaiting the end-of-term report.

'What happened in Stockholm?' he asked.

'It went well, I think.'

'Am I going to be chosen?'

Josef smiled at the naïvety.

'I don't know that. The decision is made by an impartial committee.'

'Why did you go, if it wasn't to be told the award was mine?'

Nikolai sat straight up in the chair, offended by Josef's unwillingness to make a prediction. Josef sighed. Had the young man changed in three weeks? Or was his impression clouded by the stupidity of the previous night's debauch?

'Nikolai,' he started, gently. 'There are things you don't understand about this award. There's more than the Nobel nomination involved.'

'That's ridiculous,' rejected the writer.

'I wish it were ridiculous,' said Josef. 'Believe me, I wish it were.'

'Why did you go? I want to know.'

Josef paused, halted by the imperiousness of Nikolai's demand.

'There were people to see ... assurance to be given,' generalized the negotiator.

'But the Literary Committee know the book?'

'Yes.'

'And like it? They *do* like it, don't they?'

'Yes, I believe they do.'

'It is a good book, isn't it Josef? It will become part of Soviet literature, won't it?'

Some things haven't changed, thought Josef. 'Yes,' he recited. 'It's a wonderful book. And it will become recognized as such.'

'When will we know?'

'Soon, I hope,' said Josef. He pressed his fingers into his forehead. Would the bloody pain never dissipate? He yawned.

'Now that Pamela and I are back in Moscow,' he said. 'There doesn't seem a great deal of point in your staying all the way out here ... '

He nodded towards the little-used desk.

' ... particularly as it seems to hamper your writing.'

'I refuse to share an apartment with anyone,' announced Nikolai, sharply. 'I want a place by myself. I am one of Russia's foremost writers. I have a right to certain privileges. I want you to make that quite clear.'

The boy gradually becomes a man, thought Josef. Amused at the writer's posturing, he said lightly, 'All right. I'll let everyone know.'

'You're laughing at me,' erupted Nikolai, suddenly. 'There was a sneer in your voice. I will not be laughed at.'

Josef's humour evaporated. 'And I won't be addressed like that,' he snapped. 'You stand a very good chance of having more honour and money bestowed upon you in the next few weeks than most men dream of in their lifetimes, certainly in Russia. You'll be exposed for weeks, maybe months, before people just waiting for you to behave as you did a few moments ago. As long as I am with you, entrusted with seeing no disgrace comes to you or to Russia, then you won't behave like that. And don't you forget it, for a moment.'

'Perhaps someone else should have the responsibility,' retorted Nikolai, still defiant.

'I wish there were someone else,' said Josef, sincerely. 'There isn't.'

'We'll see,' Nikolai tried, unconvinced.

'No,' corrected Josef, too experienced to be angered by rudeness. 'We won't see. We go abroad on my terms. Don't ever imagine I'm a servant, Nikolai. Never make that mistake.'

'I thought you were my friend,' complained the writer, edging towards capitulation.

'I will be,' undertook Josef. 'I'll make you one of the most famous Russians in the world. But on my terms.'

'You don't understand strain,' said Nikolai, subsiding further.

Initially, Josef could not reply. Oh God, he thought, do I understand strain. I live with it, exist on it, like a machine running on electricity. Without strain, I'd wind down and stop. How good it might be, just for a short time, to be able to wind down and stop.

'I'm not going to try to understand it,' he said, taking up the argument again. 'With me, there will be no tantrums of genius.'

The telephone concluded the argument. Both men were relieved.

'You're elusive,' rebuked Devgeny, when Josef took the receiver from the housekeeper.

'It seems to be a sudden development in both our lives,' replied Josef. Tired and ill, he felt drained by the surprising argument with Balshev. He couldn't compete today with Devgeny. The meeting had to be avoided.

'I have other duties to perform, you know,' said the Minister. He was relaxed, his attitude rehearsed. 'Sometimes I envy you, able to detach yourself completely and devote your undivided attention to just one project. You're a lucky man.'

He waited, but Josef did not respond.

'We're anxious about Stockholm,' said Devgeny. 'We thought of convening this evening, around seven o'clock.'

Pamela had been excited when he had left the apartment, happy at the thought of personally preparing their first meal together.

'I'm at the dacha, as you know,' countered Josef. 'I can't make it tonight.'

'Oh, you can, Josef,' insisted Devgeny. 'It'll only take you two hours in that rather ostentatious motor-car of yours.'

'After this morning, I find this sudden urgency surprising,' said Josef. It was a poor protest. 'And it's inconvenient. Let's meet tomorrow.'

'We can't do that, Josef. Both Illinivitch and Korshunov have gone to great personal difficulty to attend. It wouldn't be wise, inconveniencing them. I'm sure your wife will understand. Did she enjoy the ballet, by the way?'

'Very much,' said Josef, tightly. Devgeny couldn't wait, thought the negotiator. 'Thank you for providing the tickets.'

'Is she settling to life in Russia?' asked the Minister.

'Yes.'

'Good. I see she's retained her British passport.'

He wants me to know he's studied the files, thought Josef.

'Yes,' he said.

'No doubt she'll get homesick, in the future.'

'We haven't discussed it.'

'Of course not. But there'll be a time when you'll want the necessary travel documentation, won't there?'

'There could well be.'

'Quite. Well, as I said, the meeting tonight starts at seven o'clock. You won't be late, will you?'

'No,' promised Josef. 'I won't be late.'

Chapter Eight

Josef was angry at his helplessness to oppose Devgeny now
that he was using Pamela as a lever. Nikolai was not the
only one destined for the role of a puppet, he accepted,
reluctantly. His confidence, Josef realized, was being eroded.
Which was probably what Devgeny intended. It had to
stop, immediately. Soon he would begin making stupid
mistakes, errors that everyone would recognize. Then the
doubts would begin to fester. And the door would be open
for Devgeny's arguments before the Central Committee.

To attend the meeting in his present condition would be
just such a misjudgment. Immediately after Devgeny's
summons, he left the dacha and a protesting Nikolai Balshev,
driving hard and at times dangerously back to Moscow. He
needed the apartment, and its sauna, to sweat the discomfort
from him. His flurried, curt arrival interrupted Pamela in
the middle of the dinner preparations. Immediately she
saw his face she stopped, frightened, waiting tensely for the
end to her marriage. There had to be an outburst, shouted
demands for an explanation, then for a divorce. Josef was
not a man to be cuckolded, she knew. He practically ignored
her, cursory even in his apology for upsetting the dinner
arrangements. She said nothing, withdrawing herself uncertainly into the kitchen. He went without saying goodbye,
leaving her bewildered.

Because he had known Josef for so long and was aware of
the standards to which he aspired, only Devgeny, who sat
smiling, smugly, might have been aware that Josef's edited

account of his meeting with Count von Sydon was below his usual standard. They would have debated his recorded reports from Stockholm, so tonight's meeting was largely unnecessary, suspected Josef, staged for Devgeny's satisfaction.

'You didn't get a positive assurance?' demanded Devgeny. His confidence was making him careless.

'You knew that would be impossible before I went,' rejected Josef.

'But you made it quite clear how anxious we were for the nomination?'

Careless again.

'That was the point of the visit,' reminded Josef, sarcastically.

'We seem to be repeating ourselves,' came in Illinivitch.

Josef looked at him, surprised. It was unlike Illinivitch to criticize the way Devgeny was conducting a meeting, he thought. He could hardly ever recall Illinivitch speaking.

The Minister frowned, with matching astonishment.

'I'm sorry if we're boring you, Comrade Illinivitch,' said Devgeny, heavily.

'We're busy men, Comrade Devgeny,' replied the deputy. 'These meetings might proceed more quickly if there were less personal animosity.'

It was an amazing challenge to make in open committee, decided Josef, bewildered. An uncertain silence settled in the room. Devgeny broke it, as he had to.

'Animosity?' he queried, the feigned surprise too obvious. He turned to Josef. 'Are you aware of any feeling?'

Josef's thoughts were way ahead, assessing what was happening. Incomprehensibly, Illinivitch was announcing public opposition to the Minister, which was very stupid or, depending on the support he had from other members of the Ministry and the larger Central Committee, very clever. At last, thought Josef, Illinivitch was declaring himself. He found the timing odd. But it could be to his advantage, he

75

realized. If Devgeny were deposed, the constant threat would disappear. And Pamela would be safe. Obviously, reasoned the negotiator, Illinivitch would not have made his challenge without the expectation of success and the man was now inviting Josef to join him. A power struggle, with all its blood letting, appeared under way. With Josef in the middle.

'The Minister asked you a question, Comrade Bultova,' prompted Illinivitch.

Both men stared at him, waiting. It was too soon, decided Josef. By failing him now, Josef could alienate Illinivitch and make an enemy in the future. But Illinivitch might lose. And if Devgeny successfully resisted the challenge, then those who supported the deputy Minister would disappear with him. The risk, to himself and to Pamela, was too great.

'No,' responded Josef, at last. 'I have not been aware of any animosity.'

Devgeny smiled, like a man whose pet dog had just performed a trick. His teeth were disgusting, thought Josef. Illinivitch stayed completely expressionless.

'So,' said Devgeny, both hair-matted hands palm down on the table. 'Some of us have been imagining things.'

Was the relief too obvious in his voice? Josef couldn't be sure.

'Perhaps', said Illinivitch, 'some of us have not been imagining enough.'

The statement was made directly to Josef. He had been warned, Josef decided.

'Has anyone else any views?' demanded Devgeny. He was moving quickly to thwart the challenge, thought the negotiator. Battle-lines were being formed.

'What? What?' bumbled Ballenin. 'I'm sorry. I've lost the thread of the conversation.'

'Has there been any animosity between members of this Ministry since Nikolai Balshev's possible Nobel prize nomination?' urged Devgeny, formally, staring at the white-haired man.

Still Ballenin frowned, unsure. 'Don't think so,' he said, genuinely trying to contribute. 'Seems pretty straightforward to me.'

He doesn't understand, thought Josef, sadly.

'Comrade Korshunov?' continued Devgeny, contemptuously discarding Ballenin.

Throughout all the exchanges, Korshunov had sat quite still, only his eyes shifting to follow the conversation. He was as unsure as Josef which way to go.

'As the chairman has just reminded us,' said Korshunov, 'we are preparing for one of Russia's leading writers to be awarded the Nobel prize for literature.'

He nodded towards Josef. 'So far, it appears we could be moving towards such a nomination. No body of men, charged with something as important as this, can fail at times to become over-extended and behave in a manner that appears acrimonious. I don't think we should lose sight of the responsibility with which we have been entrusted or become over-sensitive to an occasionally frayed temper.'

Magnificent, analysed Josef, the cautious reaction of a man waiting to see which way the struggle would swing before committing himself. It meant that Illinivitch had spoken without Korshunov's support. Did that mean his strength came from the Praesidium?

'Points well made,' said Devgeny. The Minister made much of looking at his watch. Then, to Josef, he said, 'Is there anything else you had to tell us?'

'Yes,' said Josef quickly. 'We haven't discussed the film approaches and they will bring in more foreign exchange than any of the contracts so far agreed.'

'Always a man with close regard to money, aren't you, Comrade Bultova?' sneered Devgeny.

'A fact for which I have been praised on many occasions by the Praesidium and other Ministries for whom I have worked,' retorted Josef. He waited, but the Minister abandoned the argument.

'What is our feeling about the book being filmed by a Western company?' he asked.

'What's wrong with it being made by our State-controlled industry?' demanded Devgeny.

'Nothing,' agreed Josef, quickly, 'but if we allowed an American company to make it on location here, we would gain an enormous propaganda bonus.'

'An expert on the Western mind,' said Devgeny, still mocking. He kept snatching looks at the deputy Minister, who appeared intent on papers he had taken from his brief-case.

'What do you think, Comrade Illinivitch?'

'I would prefer it made by Russia,' replied the man.

The answer created a dilemma for Devgeny. Either way he was committed to supporting an opponent.

'I think Comrade Bultova has a good point,' said the Minister, reluctantly opting for a known enemy against an unexpected challenger. 'Anyone feel differently?'

Ballenin and Korshunov shook their heads.

'Nothing will be done without approval, of course,' undertook Josef.

Illinivitch was the first to leave the room. Quickly Korshunov and then Josef followed, each ensuring their departure was separate from anyone else. This was not a time to be seen in close contact with anyone.

The development pleased Josef. Certainly, he would be caught up in any struggle for power, but it meant that the immediate pressure would be off him. Now Devgeny's overriding concern would be to protect himself against any intrigue and his determination to destroy Josef would hopefully be relegated in importance, to be achieved later.

For the second time that day, Pamela was surprised when

Josef entered the apartment. His mood had completely altered. He was gay, apologizing without offering an explanation for his curtness earlier and lavish with his praise of her meal, which was overcooked and uninteresting. With the memory of the previous night still painful, he was careful with the wine and limited his celebration to a single brandy.

'What's made you so happy?' asked Pamela, as they sat after the meal, rotating brandy balloons in their hands.

'I'm not sure I know myself,' said Josef, unhelpfully. 'It might not even be a reason for happiness.'

Pamela was staring at him, bewildered, when the doorbell sounded. A flicker of uncertainty settled in Josef's stomach. Illinivitch laughed at the look on Josef's face when the negotiator opened the door.

'Don't worry,' he said, immediately divining Josef's thoughts. 'No one saw me arrive.'

Josef stood aside for the man to enter, the danger to Pamela rising in his mind. He ushered Illinivitch into the study. No later investigation should ever be allowed to establish the slightest connection between her and the man. Illinivitch stared contemptuously around the study.

'I'd heard stories of how you lived, but I thought they were exaggerated,' said the deputy Minister. He spoke in fluent French.

Josef sat behind the desk, staring at him. Why was it necessary for the deputy Minister to show off another language? Illinivitch fingered one of the two Xerox machines, unsure of its use, then studied the large tape recorder.

'Is it *really* necessary?' he asked. This time, the language was English.

'All the equipment is functional,' replied Josef. 'Why all the languages?'

Illinivitch shook his head in disappointment at the study and came to a chair bordering the desk.

'I get such little opportunity to use them with anyone

else,' said Illinivitch, incongruously. Flatly, still in English, he said, 'Devgeny hates you.'

'I know.'

'He thinks the time you spent in Potma affected your mind.'

Seeing the surprise on Josef's face, Illinivitch hurried on, 'Oh, he doesn't say you're insane. He means all this ... ' Illinivitch swept his hand out to embrace the apartment. ' ... and that ridiculous dacha you maintain in the country.'

Josef sat, waiting.

'It's a sign of manic depression,' diagnosed Illinivitch. 'This need to remind people that you were wronged. And of the concessions the country now has to make to compensate you, because your function is unique ... ' he paused, smiling. ' ... Quite a few people have a command of more than one language. And thousands of people suffered, Josef, not just you.'

'If I wanted an historical discussion or psychoanalysis, I could obtain it elsewhere,' sneered Josef.

'I think you should,' retorted Illinivitch, sincerely. 'If you're not careful, it's going to become a problem for you.'

'What do you want?' asked Josef, rudely.

Illinivitch smiled. 'You see,' he said, triumphantly, 'you're a negotiator, the man this country sends throughout the world on its behalf. There should be no better debater than you. Yet I criticize your attitude and immediately you relapse into rudeness, the reaction of an amateur. I said it was going to become a problem for you.'

Through his anger, Josef accepted the point. He smiled, consciously controlling himself.

'I'm sorry,' he said. 'I apologize.'

Illinivitch shrugged, dismissing the regret. The deputy Minister was tall, maybe six-foot-five, guessed Josef, and thin, so that his clothes never appeared to fit. They looked as though they had been handed down by an older, smaller brother. He was sure of himself, thought Josef, watching the man sit relaxed in the chair opposite. He'd always regarded Illinivitch during their rare, earlier meetings as the sort of man who saw safety in being the deputy, never the man in complete control who could be blamed for mistakes. The sudden change of character intrigued him.

'You were frightened to support me this evening,' accused Illinivitch, directly.

'Support you?' sidestepped Josef, cautiously.

'Come,' encouraged Illinivitch. 'No one's listening. You don't have to consider every word.'

'What have I to gain becoming embroiled in a struggle between you and Devgeny?'

'There's always got to be some personal gain, hasn't there Josef?' said Illinivitch, still contemptuous.

'Well?' prompted Josef.

'Well what?'

'You're either a fool, or very sure of yourself. Which is it?'

'It isn't likely I'm going to disclose everything to someone who wouldn't support me,' rebuked the deputy Minister.

'My support is obviously vital,' pointed out Josef.

Illinivitch nodded. 'Devgeny is finished. He's out of favour with the Praesidium, but he's too stupid to see it. His determination to get you back into a labour camp is as stupid as yours to humiliate him. He's got nothing else on his mind and he's making too many mistakes in other things. His drinking is becoming excessive, too.'

'So it's been decided to replace him with you?'

'Yes,' said Illinivitch.

'Who are the others with you?' demanded Josef.

The deputy Minister laughed. 'You don't expect names, not at this stage.'

'If he has to be purged, then the decision has been taken,' pursued Josef. 'Why try to involve me?'

'There has to be some major disaster for which he can be held responsible,' said Illinivitch, urgently.

Josef felt the return of the uncertainty he had experienced when the door-bell had sounded. It had started like that, so innocently, all those years ago.

'What sort of disaster?' probed Josef, cautiously.

Illinivitch smiled, confidently. 'It would be a great shame if anything went wrong with this Balshev affair,' he generalized. 'You're so engrossed in what might happen to you if problems arise that you've overlooked a major point.'

'What's that?' coaxed Josef.

'Who is the person who argued before the Praesidium to allow Balshev to accept the award? And who is the person who originated the idea of letting him travel to the West? Devgeny is seen by everyone in the Ministry and in the Praesidium as the man responsible.'

Josef felt relief flood through him. Suddenly something which had seemed so difficult became so easy.

'What could go wrong with Balshev's tour?' he asked.

Illinivitch adopted a look of innocence.

'We're only talking hypothetically,' he said.

'No we're not,' corrected Josef, definitely. 'We are talking specifically about manœuvring a completely unworldly man who stands a more than reasonable chance of being awarded the greatest literary recognition into a position where he and Russia will be disgraced. And through that disgrace, Devgeny can be toppled.'

'You've set it out in great detail,' complained Illinivitch. 'Have I misunderstood you?'

'That's more or less it,' conceded the deputy Minister.

'Balshev and Russia have to be embarrassed, just to remove Devgeny?' reiterated Josef.

Illinivitch stared at him, curiously. 'I've said "yes",' he replied.

'And you have the complete backing of the entire Praesidium to embark upon this course?'

'Those that matter.'

Josef looked sceptical.

'There's no risk,' insisted Illinivitch, encouragingly.

'Many times in the past,' said Josef, speaking carefully, 'I have sacrificed people, to achieve an aim I judged worthwhile. But the people were always expendable. In my opinion, Nikolai Balshev is not. We have tried to exert pressure to ensure his final nomination, but I don't think that was necessary. Certainly his work was not chosen initially because of pressure. It was selected because it was outstanding. If he wins, he will win because he is a remarkable writer. I think it is wrong to consider abandoning him, just so that another man can be removed from a position he can no longer satisfactorily fill. I know there always has to be a justification for these purges. It would be wrong to manipulate Balshev in this way. I think it is an even greater wrong to consider it, knowing the embarrassment it will cause Russia.'

Illinivitch laughed at him, unconvinced. 'After what Russia did to you?'

'It was you who reminded me earlier that others suffered as much as I have done,' said the negotiator.

'But you still suffered,' maintained the deputy Minister.

'Yes,' said Josef, keeping his careful delivery, anxious the other man should completely absorb what he was saying. 'But I'm still a good Russian. I returned to Moscow when I was twenty-one, having lived all my adult life in embassies throughout the world with my father, who was probably one of the greatest ambassadors this country ever had. And we were arrested. We had spent years in the West ... in London ... Washington ... Paris. And so we were suspect in the climate that existed in this country at that time. We were tried. The charges were ridiculous, blatantly false. It didn't matter. We were convicted. I spent my twenty-fifth birthday burying my father at Potma. The guards thought it was funny. They stood around, laughing, while I had to scratch with my bare hands into ground solidly frozen and bury without a coffin a man who had never, for a moment, lost his love of his country. Or even considered the behaviour for which he was imprisoned. I was another three years in that camp before the need was realized for common sense in dealing with the rest of the world. I spend five months of the year outside the Soviet Union. I have large sums of money on deposit in Switzerland, in New York and London. I could have defected a hundred ... no, a thousand times, to a life of luxury that would make even these surroundings seem spartan. There have been approaches even ... hints of how easy it would be for me, should I want another life. I have a great deal to offer any one of a number of countries ...'

'Why are you telling me this?' broke in Illinivitch. 'I know your history.'

'I'm telling you to make one point indelibly clear. Despite what has happened, I remain a good Russian. I won't do anything to damage my country.'

'You're a fool,' said Illinivitch, without rancour. 'And you haven't really any choice. Devgeny is determined that this operation will end with you and your wife back in a labour camp. You buried your father in one. Do you want to bury your wife there, too?'

Several minutes elapsed before Josef replied. Then he said, quietly, 'No, I don't want that.'

Why hadn't he considered how vulnerable marriage would make him? Perhaps Illinivitch was right. Perhaps his preoccupation with constantly advertising Devgeny's error was clouding his reasoning. Perhaps he really did need psychiatric help.

'Then I have given you a way out,' said Illinivitch.

'Yes,' agreed Josef. 'You have.'

Illinivitch stood, moving towards the door.

'Consider it,' he advised. 'Think about it more deeply than you've ever thought about anything ... ' he gestured

84

again to the study and to the apartment beyond. ' ... And learn to control this vindictiveness. It's destroyed Devgeny. Be careful it doesn't destroy you.'

At the door he turned, smiling. 'Don't worry, Josef. No one will ever know this meeting took place.'

Josef was smiling broadly when he went back into the lounge and Pamela responded, happily.

'You seem pleased.'

'I am.'

'Why?'

'I'm not sure,' he said, obtusely. He decided another celebration cognac was justified. As he handed her the glass, he added, 'There were great problems. But now I think they have been solved.'

'Sounds as if you've made a decision.'

'Yes,' agreed Josef. 'I only hope to God it's the right one.'

The letter had lain on the silver salver throughout breakfast, the Russian stamp and Moscow postmark uppermost. Both had ignored it, like youngsters with a childhood dare, waiting to see which one gave in first.

'Well?' demanded Sir Hudson Bellamy.

Stupid bastard, thought his wife. Sir Hudson was a barrel-bellied, brandy-flushed man who affected Edwardian suits, mutton-chop whiskers and an apparent disdain for publicity. He was the sort of M.P. every British political party maintains, like a medieval court jester, guaranteed to perform with complete predictability. He went to Chelsea football matches by Rolls and to the House of Commons by bicycle and during elections could be expected to descend more mines, drive more tractors and ascend more construction and dockland cranes than any other prospective candidate in any party. He had held a safe seat in Buckinghamshire for fifteen years and would stay there until death or party disfavour removed him, of which the former was more likely than the latter.

'Well?' challenged his wife.

Her contempt for her husband exceeded that of fellow M.P.s, which made her dislike intense. Doreen Miller had been first his secretary and then his mistress when Harry Bellamy—Hudson was a later creation of his publicity machine—had left the army with a £500 gratuity and a business sense honed by the black markets of immediate post-war Berlin. Now he had another secretary and several other mistresses and Lady Bellamy had a flat of her own separate from the Eaton Square apartment. She had a separate suite in the Buckinghamshire country house, too. Her future was more assured than her husband's, for Lady Bellamy, a diligent, observant secretary, had retained detailed knowledge of her husband's early business activities that could, even now, result in a prolonged jail sentence.

'I thought I'd given strict instructions that no mail was to be delivered to this house from Russia?' he said. He spoke ponderously, as if for the benefit of a poor note-taker.

'Shut up,' she said.

'I told you I wanted the staff instructed no such letters were to be allowed in this house,' insisted her husband.

'Harry,' sighed the woman, allowing a pause to follow his correct christian name, knowing it upset him. 'If you want to go through this ridiculous charade of erasing Pamela from your life, then *you* do it. I've no intention of cutting myself off from the girl.'

'Your daughter betrayed her own country.'

Lady Bellamy erupted into genuine amusement at the pomposity.

'Oh, you stupid bugger,' she said.

'But that man!'

'What's the matter, Harry? Angry he's more famous than you are and doesn't have to ride a bike to get his pictures in the papers?'

Sir Hudson buried his head on his chest and glowered, a Churchillian affectation he had cultivated for Question Time in the House and TV current-affairs programmes.

'You're getting impossible to live with.'

'Pity,' said Lady Bellamy. 'There's not a thing you can do about it, is there?'

'Cow,' he said, weakly.

'Only now, darling,' she reminded him, honestly. 'You fucked up this marriage, not me.'

'Is it necessary to use language like that?'

Lady Bellamy laughed at him, in feigned surprise. 'Hello,' she said. 'Another Harry Bellamy campaign? "Let's wash the English language whiter than white." You're on to a loser trying to remove "fuck" from the vernacular.'

'I'm not trying to erase it from the English language. Just yours.'

She stared at him for a full minute.

'Fuck,' she said, very deliberately. Then she stretched out and picked up the letter.

'I forbid you to open it.'

She slit the envelope with her table-knife, ignoring the shuffling as he collected the other morning mail he had already opened and prepared to leave the room.

'She's happy,' reported Lady Bellamy.

Sir Hudson pretended not to hear.

'Don't make yourself look utterly foolish,' sighed his wife. 'There's no audience to impress. She asks if you have forgiven her.'

'That's a ridiculous question.'

'Any more ridiculous than your asking me to forgive you for letting your mistress die in my bed from a back-street abortion?'

'You didn't forgive me,' reminded the M.P.

'It wasn't the first time I'd discovered a whore in my own bed. This one just happened to be dying.'

87

It was a familiar, accepted goad, like a picador driving a lance into a nerve.

'I said Pamela asks if you've forgiven her,' repeated the woman.

'You know I haven't. Nor will I.'

'Then I'll ignore the question when I reply.'

'I forbid you to reply.'

Lady Bellamy's pained expression was as theatrical as his earlier posture the cartoonists frequently seized upon.

'Oh, fuck off,' she said.

She stood at the window, looking down over the threadbare trees of Eaton Square. Minutes later he emerged, cycleclips already bagging his trousers around his ankles. A few people recognized him and watched. He mounted the bicycle, contrived an unsteady wobble and then weaved, face broken in genial smiles, up the square. Doreen Bellamy turned away like someone sickened at a blood-sports spectacle. It had been bad today, the worst for some time. Pity the swearing was so effective. She found it offensive. She hadn't realized how much she would suffer from the break with Pamela. Two and a half thousand miles away, Pamela was having exactly the same thoughts. But she wasn't as strong as her mother. She was crying, as she had almost every day for the past month.

Chapter Nine

'Sorry you married me?'

Pamela's question startled him out of his reverie. For a long time they had sat at the dinner-table, without talking. They were like old people approaching their golden wedding anniversary, thought Josef, who had used up all the conversation in their life, leaving only squabbles over memories. But they didn't have any memories.

'No,' he said.

'You don't sound very convincing.'

He sighed. These conversations had the familiarity oɪ Nikolai demanding praise.

'I'm sorry,' he said. 'Let's not start again.'

'Start what?'

It was like the opening scene of a well-known play. 'I know I've been ignoring you,' he admitted. 'But there's a lot of pressure. Please help me. Let me get this thing over and I promise we'll have a long holiday. Somewhere in the sunshine, by the Black Sea perhaps.'

She frowned, unimpressed.

'Who the hell wants to go to Georgia? Why can't we go somewhere civilized, outside this bloody country? The South of France ... the Middle East even ... '

'All right,' he agreed, urgently. 'Anywhere you want.'

'You're just saying that.'

He held his hands out, helplessly. 'What more can I say? I promise you ... anywhere you like.'

'How long will it be before we can leave?'

Again, the helpless gesture. 'I'm sorry, I don't know. There's still a lot to do with Nikolai's award. I've got to go away again, as you know ... ' He took a breath. ' ... It won't be for a few months, I'm afraid.'

'Christ.'

'Only a few months.'

'In this place, that's a bloody lifetime.'

Silence grew cold between them.

'What's wrong with me?' she demanded, embarking on another familiar path.

'Nothing,' he said, exasperated. 'I've told you, I'm pre-occupied. I'm sorry.'

'We won't ... we don't even make ... ' she stumbled.

'We make love as much as other married couples,' he insisted, curtly.

The telephone stopped it becoming a major row. She saw his face twist, almost in pain.

'What is it?'

He turned to her, as if he had forgotten she was there.

'Nikolai is drunk again,' he said. 'Go on to bed without me.'

'I often do.'

Without answering, he left the apartment, collecting the Mercedes from the basement garage. Josef had often thought that the Soviet Union's acceptance of alcoholism was the admission of a moral fault, but he supposed there was a need for approved places to which police could take the unconscious drunks. Left on the streets in the winter, they would freeze to death.

Josef sat outside, staring at the sobering-up station, feeling the fear burn through him. It was a low, block-house type building, with tiny, squinting windows, barred and set high in the walls. The punishment cells had been like that, he remembered, squat in the middle of the camp, where they could always be seen, a constant reminder. No one was ever the same when they came out. They stared with eyes that didn't see, deadened to everything except the word of command, the only thing left. Their whole being was geared to obey, so they wouldn't be punished again. Josef couldn't remember anyone who had emerged from a second term.

It was nearly midnight and quite cold, but perspiration soaked his back and his hands felt sticky when he stepped from the car and walked up the crackling pathway to the door. Inside, the light was harsh and yellow. The desk man stared up at him and again Josef felt the lurch of fear. Guards were always the same, he thought. They were rarely excessively tall, but they were still large men, with heavy shoulders and bellies that sagged over the belts upon which they carried the tools of their trade, the guns and the truncheons and the keys and small things in stiff leather pouches. Josef often wondered what the pouches contained. They probably hurt worst of all.

'Yes?'

They always spoke like that, he recalled, harsh and challenging.

'Josef Bultova.' His voice was even and unworried. He was surprised.

'Ah! Comrade Bultova.'

There were others in the room and conversation stopped. There was a discomforted shuffling and men found things to do in other parts of the building. The desk man's truculence became a fawning eagerness to please.

'A dreadful mistake, I'm afraid.'

How good it felt. Guards were actually frightened of him, cringing almost.

'We had no idea ... there was nothing to indicate ... '

'What happened?'

Josef was arrogantly demanding, enjoying their fear. The man sucked in his lips and chewed, rabbit-like. He scuffed some papers on his desk, seeking some sort of official report.

They always need the barrier of officialdom, thought Josef.

'I wasn't in charge, you understand. Some other colleagues. I have names ... '

'For God's sake, what happened?'

It was over-stressed, he knew. He couldn't stop himself.

'There is a liquor stall, about two kilometres on the south side of Alexander Park. It's the worst sort of place. Every night we have at least three drunks from there alone ... '

Josef shifted, impatiently, increasing the man's nervousness.

'The dregs get there ... down-and-outs. They've never got enough money for a whole bottle, so they hang around, pooling what they've got or stolen, until they have enough to buy one between them. Then they go into the park and drink it ... '

'And Nikolai was found with such a group?'

The man jerked his shoulders, his eyes widening, as if he were as baffled at Josef.

'It's incomprehensible,' he offered.

'Where is he?'

'I'm afraid he was put through the wash-room,' added the desk man. He took a piece of grey material from his pocket and dried his hands.

'The what?'

The man moved from behind his desk and momentarily the flicker of fear returned as the man came towards him. Then he passed and Josef followed down a bare, sour-smelling corridor. From behind doors came sounds, screams of men seized in nightmares and of moaning and of deep, animal-like snoring. The man opened a door at the far end and Josef was immediately aware of dripping. The room was an empty rectangle, with no furniture in it. At either end there was a nozzle with a screw top jutting from the wall. The whole room was rubber-lined.

'What the hell is it?' he demanded.

'This isn't a rest home ... ' began the man and immediately stopped, afraid the remark might be inferred as insolence. Josef motioned impatiently for him to continue.

'We just don't leave them to sleep it off. We try to sober them up. We take their clothes off and put them in here ... '

He stopped again, searching for another apology. Unable to find one, he scurried to the end.

' ... And then one of the men puts on protective clothing, fixes a hose to one of the outlets and hoses them around the room.'

Josef stared at him. 'You mean, helpless through drink, men are washed up and down this room by the pressure from a hose?'

The man nodded. 'The walls are padded. And the water isn't really freezing. They can't really get hurt. It's supposed to dissuade them from coming back again.'

'Where is he?'

The man led Josef to a side room where concrete bunks jutted from the floor, like decaying teeth. Josef shivered as the memory flooded over him. So similar, he thought, although in his barrack block the beds had been wooden and the concrete blocks had formed the tables around which they tried to eat. Most of the men were uncovered, spread-eagled like animals awaiting sacrifice. But blankets had been placed over Nikolai, who lay appearing quite comfortable. Gently the guard shook his shoulder and Nikolai snuffled into wakefulness. He stared unseeingly around the room, finally focusing upon Josef. He gave a shy half-smile.

'I told them to get you,' he said. 'They were very frightened when they learned you were my friend.'

He'd enjoyed it, Josef realized. Another self-indulgent experiment, to draw attention to himself. He stood, frowning around the room, while Nikolai dressed, helped by the solicitous guard and then filed ahead of them back along the corridor. In the car, Josef demanded, 'Well?'

Nikolai hunched down into his clothes, shivering.

'Doesn't this car have a heater?'

'Well?' demanded Josef, again.

'Good material for a writer,' said Nikolai, defensively.

'Not for the sort of books you're writing,' warned Josef.

It was as if Nikolai had been awaiting the remark. 'Why am I being kept away from everyone in the Writers' Union?' he asked. 'No one else can get published in Russia unless they belong.'

It was a question the man didn't really want answering, thought Josef. He was unsure of the direction that Nikolai was taking.

'You're an exceptional writer,' ventured Josef cautiously.

'That's not enough,' argued Nikolai. He was silent as they picked their way through the deserted streets towards the apartment into which the author had moved two months before. 'Are they frightened, Josef? Are they frightened that I might get into contact with some dissidents?'

Was it Nikolai's usual query, wondered Josef? Was he merely anxious for more importance to be bestowed upon him? He stopped the car outside the writer's home and turned in the seat, looking at him.

'It could be,' he said, honestly.

'No one need worry, Josef,' said Nikolai, returning the direct stare. 'You can tell them there is no need to worry.'

For the briefest moment, Josef was uncertain and then he realized what the writer was telling him.

'I'm being manipulated, aren't I, Josef?'

'We're all manipulated, one way or another,' said the negotiator. He felt tiredness reaching out for him. If only it meant sleep instead of near exhaustion.

'I don't mind, Josef,' assured the writer, earnestly. 'I mean I know. But I don't mind.'

Another opportunist, realized Josef. Like Devgeny, Nikolai was interested in nothing but himself.

'I see,' said the negotiator.

'You will make it clear ... if anyone wonders, won't you?'

'Yes,' promised Josef, wearily. 'I won't let anyone misunderstand.'

'Thank you, Josef. You're a friend.'

At the door of the flat, Nikolai announced, 'Sanya's here,' and carelessly punched the bell. Instantly a girl opened the door, looking frightened. She was plump, her hair straggled over her face. She had a dressing-gown that was too large hugged around her body. Nikolai pushed past her, straight into the bedroom, not bothering to introduce them. Josef and the girl looked at each other.

'I'm Sanya,' she identified, finally.

'Nikolai told me. I'm Josef Bultova.'

'I know.'

Each stood, waiting for the other to speak.

'I work at the Ministry,' she said.

'I thought I recognized you.'

She shivered. He saw her feet were bare. They didn't seem very clean.

'He lets me stay here sometimes.'

'Oh.'

'I was worried. We went to a restaurant and there was a scene ... he broke some glass and refused to pay for it. Then he walked out. I thought something might have happened to him.'

'He got drunk,' said Josef.

'He often does,' said Sanya, miserably.

Tonight had been entirely staged, accepted Josef. Nikolai had wanted to indicate his willingness to be a puppet but had had to clothe himself in drunkenness first, so that if Josef raised any subsequent query, the writer could claim to remember nothing about it.

'It isn't very nice, is it?' said the girl, looking over her shoulder. 'Is he all right?'

95

Josef followed her look. The apartment was cluttered and dirty, like a railway-station waiting-room.

'Yes,' he said. 'I think he's quite proud of it.'

'I wish he wouldn't do it,' said the girl. 'He seems to like people recognizing him. He performs for them.'

They were silent again, the girl with one hand against the door, Josef standing uncertainly in the corridor.

'I would invite you ... ' began the girl, without enthusiasm.

'No,' said Josef, 'it's too late.'

He turned, but the girl spoke again.

'Comrade Bultova?'

'Yes?'

'What did he say about me?'

'Nothing,' said Josef. 'He just said you were here.'

'Oh.'

She was another experiment, decided Josef, driving home. He suddenly grew angry at himself. It would have meant nothing to lie to the girl, creating some innocuous remark and attributing it to Nikolai. There had been times, he reflected, when such kindness would have come naturally. And the girl would probably need kindness, eventually.

Chapter Ten

Josef was humming as he entered the Ministry of Culture. He had an advantage and the adversary was unaware of it. Rarely did things combine so well.

He had anticipated a meeting different from the others, but even he had not expected the change that was obvious in Devgeny. The Minister was scruffy with neglect, chin bristled from careless shaving, his eyes reddened either from lack of sleep or too much vodka. Or perhaps from both. His customary ill-fitting suit was even more wrinkled than usual and his hands strayed constantly from smoothing his jacket to his face, which twitched to some perpetual irritation he appeared unable to subdue. Perhaps Illinivitch was right. Perhaps Devgeny had exhausted his usefulness, hollowed out from inside like a diseased tree, ready to fall in the first wind of opposition.

'This meeting is little more than a formality,' began Devgeny. 'We have decided we want you to go to London directly from Stockholm. And from London, to America. We've seen the letters concerning the film proposals. You are to proceed with those negotiations, too.'

Devgeny's speech was stilted and unnatural. He seems very worried, thought Josef. 'There are no doubts about the contracts so far negotiated?' he asked.

It was an important question. He was determined he could not be later accused of exceeding his authority. He directed the question to Devgeny, still according him the position of chairman.

'No,' said Devgeny. He hesitated, turning to Illinivitch for confirmation. 'We *are* content with the contracts, aren't we?'

Illinivitch nodded, smiling.

'I'll air-freight via the diplomatic bag any further documents I accept,' promised Josef. 'And you'll get the usual tape-recorded reports.'

'Oh yes,' mocked Illinivitch, clumsily attempting to remind Josef of their discussion in the apartment, as if they had some secret agreement. 'I believe you go in for electronic paraphernalia.' Josef ignored the jibe.

'Are we prepared to allow any film to be shot within the Soviet Union?' he queried, still addressing Devgeny.

Again the Minister turned to Illinivitch before replying. The deputy Minister shrugged, uncaring.

'Yes,' said Devgeny. He seemed unsettled that Illinivitch had not expressed an opinion. A feeling of embarrassment grew as everyone realized the pointlessness of the meeting.

'We wish you luck,' contributed Korshunov. Josef looked pityingly at Devgeny.

'I take it the meeting is over?' he demanded, not bothering to disguise the contempt. The Minister nodded and Josef leaned sideways to collect the briefcases. When he straightened, Illinivitch was beside the chair, staring down.

'I'll walk from the building with you,' announced the deputy Minister. Josef shrugged, putting one briefcase under his arm, between them. Illinivitch waited until they had cleared the committee room.

'Well?' he said.

'What?'

Illinivitch laughed. 'Don't be naïve, Josef. Devgeny, of course. Have you ever seen such a collapse? He couldn't even remember the reason for calling the meeting.'

Josef made an uncertain gesture, not replying. Illinivitch laughed again, a humourless sound, like an old man with bronchitis clearing his throat.

'You're a cautious man, Josef.' Still Josef stayed silent. 'I'm waiting for your commitment,' said the deputy Minister.

'I thought I didn't have a choice.' They paused outside the Ministry building. Josef's Mercedes was in the reserved parking section.

'By the way,' said Illinivitch, suddenly. 'Did you hear about Count von Sydon?'

'Who?' asked Josef.

'Count von Sydon, the man from the Nobel Foundation whom you went to Stockholm to see. He committed suicide, just after the Literary Committee selected Nikolai.'

'Oh.'

'Sad,' said Illinivitch, heavily.

'Yes,' dismissed Josef, getting into the car. 'I'll keep in touch from Stockholm.'

'Do that,' said Illinivitch.

Because it was their last night together before he left, Josef took Pamela to the Metropole Hotel for dinner. They sat, isolated in the middle of the chandeliered elegance of the dining-room, Pamela slumped with depression at the thought of being left alone again.

'Perhaps it won't be for very long,' tried Josef. Every conversation was becoming an argument, he thought, irritably.

'Then again, perhaps it will,' she countered.

If only there were outside friends, thought Josef. There had been a desperation in their pursuit of other people. Although he knew it would arouse criticism, he had even allowed some contact with the expatriate British colony, the defectors and spies whom she knew by reputation and imagined would have some aura of attraction, even though she recognized them as traitors and despised them for it. But it had been a novelty, like looking at two-headed calves at an Easter funfair. She had found them grubby, insecure little men, like junior clerks lost on a firm's outing to the seaside. Their slang vocabulary was of a decade ago, their conversation meaningless trivia involving nostalgia about favoured restaurants that really weren't very good or plays that had long ceased to run or prompt comment. Most retained their old-school ties, she had noticed, and wore suits shiny with grease and over-wear, just because there was a London or New York label inside the jacket. There was not one whom she had met whom she did not feel secretly regretted the activity that had forced them into exile. So the experiment had not worked and they had been driven back to one another and their marriage was too young for that. Maybe in ten or fifteen years it would not have created a strain. They might even have welcomed it, because by then they would have completely known each other and not needed the assurance of comparison with other people. But now their marriage needed people, like a suffocating man needs oxygen. Each felt a resentment against the other, Pamela against Josef for isolating her in a strange, even hostile country, Josef against Pamela for making him vulnerable. Tension festered until minor idiosyncrasies became major character defects. Each was ultra-polite to the other, in the way of people alert to misinterpretation, each with an almost schoolroom anxiousness to prove the other was at fault in beginning any argument. Each shied away from personal conversation, seeking neutral discussion, and always they ran into the same cul-de-sac.

'I think Nikolai's drinking is getting worse,' he said. The author was the only person they both knew well enough to bridge the gap of communication.

Pamela thought often of Nikolai's drinking, particularly at the dacha. As her loneliness increased, the memory of what had occurred there presented itself for examination like a bad photograph she would have liked to destroy if only she had had the negative, until she had persuaded herself that she had been drunk, purposely reduced to help-lessness by a man determined to seduce her. She had almost exonerated herself from guilt, imagining the incident as practically a case of rape. 'Why?' she asked. Josef shrugged. 'There's rarely a night when he isn't hopelessly drunk,' he said. 'Last night he was unconscious. I considered getting a doctor.'

'Perhaps he was lonely.'

It was the ambiguous sort of remark that could have caused another row and she had made it knowingly. It seemed important to score points. Josef refused the challenge.

'Hardly. Sanya was with him.'

'The same girl?' Pamela's question was abrupt. She tried to analyse the feeling. Jealousy? That was ridiculous.

'Yes,' said Josef. He had detected the quickness of his wife's reaction.

'Are they ... I mean, how ... ?'

'Yes,' said Josef. 'They are sleeping together.'

'Lucky girl.' It seemed too much trouble to pick up the invitation. She pecked at the remains of the chocolate cake with which they had ended their meal, needing distraction.

'Has she moved in with him?'

'I don't think so. I think she just stays some nights. Remember Nikolai has a flat to himself—that's quite a novelty for a secretary at the Ministry.'

Pamela returned to the original question. 'Certainly he *did* drink quite heavily while you were in Stockholm,' she said. 'You know how I feel about a lot of his behaviour. I felt the drinking was experimenting, too. On the two occasions we've had him at the apartment, he hasn't drunk excessively.'

Pamela had been terrified at both dinners, presenting every excuse and objection until they could be postponed no longer. At each, Nikolai's disregard of her had been almost impolite.

'Not excessively,' agreed Josef. 'But he's been fairly drunk.'

'Are you worried about it?'

Josef looked uncertain. 'He still hasn't begun a sequel to *Walk Softly on a Lonely Day*,' he said.

'I don't see that proves anything. Surely writing a book

isn't like building a motor-car? You can't expect a level of productivity every day.'

'I suppose not,' accepted Josef. 'But whenever I mention a sequel he gets annoyed, dismissing me as someone who doesn't know what he's talking about. I think he's enjoying fame too much.'

She laughed contemptuously. 'That's pretty limited, surely?'

'By Western standards,' he agreed. 'But not here. He's recognized wherever he goes ... makes sure of it even. I think he's flattered by the privileges. If it's gone to his head here, what's it going to be like in Stockholm and London?' Josef smiled, reflectively. 'I think I preferred it in the early days at the dacha. He was certainly easier to control.'

Aware that by this time the following day she would be alone, Pamela wanted to protract the evening as long as possible.

'Had a letter from my mother today. She said she might get a visa to come here.'

She seemed to expect some response from Josef, but he stayed silent.

'Could you help?' she asked.

'I'll try.' He paused. Then he said, 'You're pretty unhappy here, aren't you?'

She tensed, anticipating another argument.

'Yes,' she admitted. 'Very unhappy.'

'I'm sorry.'

She jerked her shoulders. The movement spilled cake crumbs over the table. Embarrassed, she began picking them up between thumb and forefinger and replacing them on the small plate.

'So am I,' she said. 'I didn't think it would be like this. It's like being ... like being locked up. I feel trapped here, just like those poor sods at the British colony.'

'I did warn you it would be different from what you were used to,' he reminded, gently.

'I know.'

'Wish you'd listened?'

'Frequently.' Silence built itself into a barrier between them.

'I've been wondering … ' she said, groping.

'What?'

' … Would it be possible for me to accompany you on these trips? Could we afford it, I mean?'

Josef hesitated. First a weakness. Now an encumbrance.

'We could afford it, certainly … '

'You don't want me.' Immediately the anger flared, her voice loud. Several people glanced from adjoining tables.

'That's not true,' he said, anxiously. 'And you know it. I'm as upset at these separations as you are. But mine aren't the sort of business trips to which you're accustomed. Sometimes the discussions are … ' He stopped, searching for an expression that would not offend her. ' … Well, delicate. The government wouldn't welcome the thought of your being with me.'

'So I'm going to be stuck here for ever.'

'Of course not. You've retained your British passport, so you won't need an exit visa, just the guarantee of readmission.'

'I hate this country,' she snapped, bitterly.

'You don't know it,' he said. 'You've been here barely eight months.'

'I'm miserable. And lonely.'

She really was quite immature, he decided. He wondered if she had been spoiled by both her parents or just one of them.

'Perhaps you could come on some trips,' he offered. 'Once I'd made the initial contacts and overcome most of the problems of negotiation. I'll try. I promise.'

'And mother. You'll help with her visa?'

'If I can.'

Chapter Eleven

Despite the cold, Josef insisted on driving to Sheremetyevo Airport with the car windows half down, trying to drive away the stench that still clung from Nikolai's apartment. The rooms had smelt of sweat and vomit and unwashed bodies, and had brought the memories crowding back. The barrack blocks had been like that, at first. He'd become used to it, very quickly, but his father had never been able to adjust. The old man had been physically sick the first day, Josef remembered, retching at the foulness, his fragile body arched because his stomach was empty. Never before had Josef seen his father cry. It had embarrassed him, like the first time he had seen him without his trousers, squatting over the open toilet-hole. He'd blushed then, he recalled, and walked quickly away, hoping he hadn't been noticed. The old man had to be allowed some dignity. In the end, of course, there had been nothing. In the months before his death, he'd cradled the sobbing head and put him to toilet, like a child. It had been a vow when he left the camp that never again would he allow himself in contact with such squalor and he hadn't, not until that morning. Dust had been so thick it furred everything, almost like moss, puffing up in tiny clouds at any movement. The debris of meals lay around in nearly every room, scum and mildew forming in cups and over discarded scraps of food. There was a profusion of bottles, some standing, some lopsided on the table, bleeding away their tiny residue over the yellow, stained cloth. The typewriter had been on a small table in the corner, the lid closed, paper haphazard around it. Josef had walked over and ruffled the paper. The Nobel Lecture should have been there. Twice Nikolai had assured him he was working on it. He had shuffled the paper, like cards. It had all been blank.

Distressed by the recollection that the smell had brought and angry at the man, Josef had burst into the bedroom, to find Nikolai alone and crying. He had kicked the clothes away and was lying, naked.

'I'm scared, Josef. I don't want to go.'

'You've no choice.'

His anger had made him hostile, which was wrong. But it was another performance, Josef had decided.

'I don't deserve it. We'll make an excuse. Say I'm ill. I can't do it again, ever. I've tried. Really, I've tried. But the words won't come ... '

Josef had looked down on the man, feeling a small surge of pity. He was very frail, his ribs marked out against his flesh. His penis was very small, with hardly a puff of pubic hair, Josef saw. Even in the camp, there had been the instinctive male need for comparison, Josef had remembered.

'You've written other books,' Josef had tried. '*Walk Softly on a Lonely Day* wasn't the first ... '

'But it's the one they're signifying for the award. From now on, it'll be the book by which I'm judged.'

The crying had worsened, the sobs coming in screeches. Nikolai had stretched out, trying to seize Josef's hand.

'Please. You're my friend. Help me.'

Josef had hit him, in fact harder than he had intended, for as he had swung, backhanded, to quell the hysteria, Nikolai had moved forward to reinforce his plea and come into the blow. He had spun backwards on to the bed, glaring-eyed with shock, groping at the red blotch against his cheek. The screaming had subsided into shuddered breathing, which he could still not properly control, hunched in the opposite corner of the car, as far away from Josef as he could get.

They drove through the barriers to a low building near the control tower where a small group had gathered for the farewell. Photographers from *Pravda* and *Isvestia* positioned Nikolai between lines of Praesidium dignitaries. He looked crushed and unkempt, glancing worriedly to his left and right. Josef saw the red mark where he had slapped him. It had been a stupid thing to do and he felt ashamed.

'Prepared to commit yourself?'

Josef turned to Illinivitch, by his elbow. He shrugged.

'I've given you a lot of time, Josef.'

'The wrong decision could put me back into a labour camp,' reminded the negotiator.

'You more than anyone else,' agreed the deputy Minister.

'So don't hurry me.'

'Remember, keep in touch, from Stockholm and other places.' He handed Josef a card. 'It would be better if you telephoned me at this number, rather than at the Ministry.'

Josef took the card and wedged it into his wallet.

'I hope you make the right decision, Josef.'

'So do I,' agreed the negotiator.

The flat needed no attention, but Pamela had performed the charade for two hours after Josef left until she tired of re-arranging small pieces of furniture that would be replaced in their original position the following day. She sighed, touring the immaculate rooms, touching things, examining ornaments intently, as if they contained some hidden message. She considered washing her hair and discarded the idea. She'd set aside the afternoon for that. She didn't want to rob that part of the day of its activity. A fortnight-old copy of *Newsweek* lay on the table. She resisted the temptation. Tonight. After supper. She decided on a walk. In fact, she had determined upon it before Josef had left, but relapsing into the game she played with herself, she had pushed the decision to the back of her mind, so that it could arrive fresh. The concierge looked at her expressionlessly as she approached the exit from the apartment. Pamela smiled and said 'Good morning' in Russian. The woman continued to stare, just slightly deflecting her head in acknowledgment. Sour old cow, thought the girl. Outside the apartment, she turned left. One hundred and twenty steps to the main junction, she reminded herself, like a blind person. Consciously, she lengthened her stride and reached it in one hundred and eighteen. A miscount. Tomorrow she'd have to count it again to see which was right. Another game. Two hundred steps before reaching the next turning. This time she walked normally. Two hundred steps later, she reached the intersection. No mistake here. No need for a recount. She found herself approaching the giant Gum department store, as she'd known she would the moment the walk had occurred to her. It was the place Western visitors knew, because it was in all the guidebooks. It was convenient when photographing the Kremlin became boring. She might meet somebody there. Somebody to talk to. Perhaps she'd become really friendly and invite them back to the apartment for lunch and then they could spend all afternoon gossiping about London or New York or wherever they came from. In the evening there would be washing up to be done. Her hair could be put off until tomorrow. It would be good to have something planned for the next day. Happy at the fantasy, she bustled into the store, looking around expectantly, as if she had an appointment.

The tourist season was virtually over, so the store was not as crowded as it was in the summer. Most of the people were Russian, she decided. There were a few who could have been European, but they all seemed intent and assured, with none of the uncertainty of casual visitors. Probably from an embassy. No point in trying to become friendly with embassy personnel. They certainly wouldn't accept a casual invitation to lunch in a Russian apartment, definitely not when they discovered she was the wife of Josef Bultova.

She encountered the two Americans on the far side of the ground floor, in the children's section. They were giggling over matryoshkas, the traditional wooden dolls, where one is lifted to reveal another replica, until the family are uncovered. Both women were deep into plump middle age, white, carefully ridged hair clamped under freshly purchased Russian winter hats, heavy coats obviously bought from America and inadequate for the Russian winter. Fur boots, an attempt to match the hats, swathed their feet and the lower parts of their legs. Pamela thought they looked like an illustration from a Goldilocks and the Three Bears book she had had as a child.

'For three dollars, it's got to be a bargain,' said the slightly older of the two. She made a calculation on a presents list. 'And we can afford it, easily.'

'They're authentic,' stupidly agreed the second, moving towards the conviction of her companion.

'Don't look,' snapped the first woman. 'But we're being approached.'

The unconvinced one immediately looked around wildly, then locked her attention back on to the dolls.

'What!'

'There's a Russian woman, across the counter. She's watching us.'

'Don't be silly.'

'I'm not silly. She is staring at us. Remember what they said at the embassy.'

'What shall we do?'

'Ignore it. That's what they said. And refuse to sell any money, no matter how good the rate.'

Each was trying to talk without moving her lips.

'I don't see ... '

'For God's sake, Anne. Don't you remember what the

counsellor said. They get friendly, then trap you into some indiscretion.'

Pamela hurried from the store, actually colliding with a man at the entrance in her anxiety to get out. Disregarding the need to occupy time, she continued to hurry, even running the last few yards to the apartment block. The concierge stared at her bustled arrival, still expressionless.

Pamela slipped the burglar lock into place immediately she entered the apartment, leaning back against the door, breathing heavily. Safe, she thought, quite irrationally. I'm safe. She checked the time. Eleven forty-five. She opened Josef's wardrobe-like liquor cabinet, poured a sherry and then carried the bottle with her to the writing table in the bedroom.

'Dear mother,' she wrote. 'I'm still very happy here. Moscow stays as fascinating and interesting as ever. I met two charming women from Des Moines today. They came to lunch. Guess what they told me ... '

Chapter Twelve

Bad weather delayed the Aeroflot flight for seventy minutes and despite the warmth of the V.I.P. lounge, the welcoming committee were clearly disgruntled. Nikolai was almost mumbling his fear, clutching child-like at the negotiator's arm as if afraid the older man would abandon him. He shuffled through the formal greetings, hand extended before him, his head nodding like a puppet to every word that was said, twitching slightly every time a flash-bulb exploded. Josef was unwilling for an airport press conference, but knew they had to give one. He compromised, pleading that Nikolai was travel sick, which was hardly an exaggeration, and insisting the encounter should be limited to ten minutes. The conference room was packed, heavy with cigarette smoke and pebbled with discarded coffee cartons. Josef and the author sat on a slightly raised dais, staring out unseeing into the glare of television lights. A disembodied voice asked, 'How does Comrade Balshev feel at winning the Nobel prize?'

Josef made the pretence of a muttered conversation with Nikolai, then turned back to the room, grateful at the easy opening.

'Honoured,' he replied. Then, feeling modesty was appropriate, he stupidly added, 'And surprised. He feels there were others more deserving.'

'Who for instance?'

The question rasped from the back of the room, an unpleasant Bronx drawl. 'Eldon,' the questioner identified himself. 'United American Wire Service.'

'There was an American writer, we believe,' said Josef, attempting diplomacy for the benefit of the questioner.

'What about the Chinese?'

Josef squinted, trying to isolate the man. He had tried to steer the discussion away from the other nominee.

'What Chinese?' he fielded.

'Didn't you know there was a Chinese nomination — a book by Lin Tsai-Fu?'

Josef hesitated, feigning to consult Nikolai to gain time.

'No,' he replied. 'We hadn't heard that. But then, the consideration of the Literary Committee is confidential.'

'Despite which you knew about the American,' came back Eldon. 'How would you feel about a writer from Peking getting the Nobel prize?'

The last part was careless, asked by a man who felt too confident.

'Ask me when it happens,' dismissed Josef, curtly. 'Next.'

'What does Comrade Balshev think of women's lib?' asked a short-haired woman in the second row.

Again Josef, relieved at the lightness of the inquiry, pretended to speak to the writer. Then, smiling, he said, 'Unlike the West, the Soviet Union has always regarded woman equally with men. Comrade Balshev recommends it as another example the West could learn from the Soviet Union.'

'What does Comrade Balshev feel about being allowed to accept the prize when Alexander Solzhenitsyn was not? And what compromises did Comrade Balshev have to make to be allowed this concession?'

Josef snapped up at the question. The pleasantries were over, he thought. The query had been put in Russian, so the buzz continued throughout the room.

'Translation,' somebody demanded, from the back of the hall.

'Certainly,' agreed the questioner. He stood up, quite

close to the girl with the short hair. He wore a crewcut and large oval glasses, like a barbered panda. A Finn, judged Josef, as the man repeated the question in carefully enunciated English, pleased at the attention.

'Yeah,' concurred Eldon. 'How does he feel about that?'

The delay had given Josef the opportunity to think. He gained more time in apparent conversation with Nikolai. The author was staring at him. It was the first question he had understood and he was frightened.

'Comrade Balshev knows of no compromise,' began Josef. 'Because none was sought. The decision not to attend the ceremony was Comrade Solzhenitsyn's alone ... '

'Because he was afraid he would not be readmitted to the Soviet Union,' shouted the persistent American.

'You appear better-informed about the affairs of the Soviet Union than we are,' responded Josef. 'We have no knowledge of why Comrade Solzhenitsyn refused to come here.'

It was becoming an argument, a snappy exchange of which he had been afraid.

'Why are you, a spy, accompanying Comrade Balshev?'

The question was in English again, from a sallow man in the front row.

Josef laughed. 'I was asked to accompany Comrade Balshev because I speak several languages and have a knowledge of the West. Stories of my being a spy are ridiculous.'

'Weren't you in a labour camp once, like Solzhenitsyn?' asked Eldon.

'I was unaware Comrade Solzhenitsyn had been convicted of any criminal offence ... '

' ... He wasn't.'

The interruption came from several points and Josef stumbled. It had been a bad reply and now he was compromised.

'But what other reason could there have been for his imprisonment?' he said. Again, it was a poor recovery.

'You tell us,' said the sallow man in the front row. 'You were wrongly accused, weren't you?'

'Yes,' replied Josef, quickly. 'And as soon as the injustice was uncovered, I was released under the properly established legal system of my country.'

'Jesus, doesn't it make you sick,' said Eldon, to the assembled journalists.

Abruptly, Josef stood up. 'There have not for several minutes been any questions asked of Comrade Balshev,' he said, tightly. 'So I assume you have enough information. I thank you for allowing a sick man to bed early.'

'No.'

The protest echoed from several parts of the room. Josef remained standing, urging Nikolai to his feet. As he bustled through the room, steering Nikolai between flowerbeds of camera flashes, he got momentary satisfaction seeing several reporters turn angrily upon the American.

Nikolai was silent in the embassy car that took them to the Grand Hotel. Josef ignored him, locked in his own thoughts. It had been a disaster, he judged, a pointless slanging match that would be turned into damaging stories throughout the world. Worse, the whole accent would be upon him, with little reference to Nikolai. It was an appalling start.

They had adjoining rooms, with communicating doors. Josef put the younger man immediately to bed, overriding his earlier decision to insist upon nightly baths. Less than five minutes after he had given Nikolai two seconal from his own medicine supply, the author was asleep, occasionally jerking in the grip of some dream, whimpering often. For several minutes, Josef stood at the linking door, watching him in the half light. Poor man, he thought.

Sandwiches and coffee had already been delivered to the suite, so he was surprised at the second knock. It was light and very hesitant. Perhaps, he thought, the waiter had failed to get a bill signed. He opened the door, carelessly, then stopped.

A complete stranger stood facing him, smiling hopefully.

'Yes?'

'Hello,' said the man.

'Yes?' repeated Josef.

'My name is Endelman, James Endelman.' He stopped, expectantly. Then, when Josef did not respond, he prompted, 'Perhaps you've heard of me?'

'The photographer?'

The man smiled at the recognition. He looked over Josef's shoulder, awaiting an invitation into the room. Josef regarded the man, avoiding the courtesy. Endelman was very tall, almost as tall as Illinivitch, but while the Russian had difficulty with his height, Endelman capitalized upon it. His clothes were perfectly tailored, Josef noticed appreciatively, so that the man was a commanding figure, not the oddity that Illinivitch appeared. The photographer's shirts were obviously hand-made, too, patterned and coloured to accentuate the suit. The shoes were genuine crocodile.

'It's very late,' said Endelman, offering the rejection that should have come from Josef.

'Yes, it is,' said the negotiator. The hostility was wrong, he accepted, but the strain of negotiating was pulling at him, familiarly. Endelman was among the top three or four photographers in the world, he knew, the three-times winner of the Pulitzer prize for his coverage of the Biafran war, the Israeli–Arab six-day conflict in 1967 and Vietnam.

'I'm sorry about the time,' continued the photographer. For someone so well known, he was unusually deferent.

'The press conference was earlier,' snapped Josef.

'I know. I was there. Quite a brawl, wasn't it?'

'Then I don't see ... '

Endelman stood back slightly, accepting that he was going to have to conduct the conversation in the hallway. He handed Josef a letter. He seemed amused at the Russian's rudeness, which Josef found unsettling. It was a short note from Blyne. Endelman, he wrote, had a commission for a complete portfolio for worldwide syndication. It meant exposure in *Paris Match*, *Stern*, *Oggi*, plus *Cosmopolitan* in both England and America. He was also preparing a complete portfolio on the tour for major American promotion.

'You'd better come in,' said Josef, reluctantly.

Endelman followed him into the suite and sat uninvited in one of the large armchairs. He was very relaxed and elegant, thought Josef.

'How can I help you?'

'By allowing me to accompany Nikolai and yourself throughout the tour,' said Endelman, directly.

Josef stared at him, amused. 'You mean actually travel with us?'

'Yes,' said Endelman.

Josef smiled at the naïvete. 'I really don't think that's possible.'

'It would provide a fantastic collection of pictures.'

'It probably would,' conceded Josef. 'But it's not a practical request.'

'Not when the Soviet Union has obviously decided to milk this tour for all the publicity it can provide?' said Endelman, presciently.

Josef found the man disquieting. Oddly, he experienced the same uncertainty that he sometimes found with Nikolai, which was ridiculous, he thought. It would be difficult to find two men more dissimilar. The deference that Endelman tried to indicate was false, Josef decided. He felt Endelman was a very determined man.

'It's hardly a decision I would be permitted to make,' hedged Josef.

'Blyne contacted the Ministry in Moscow,' reported Endelman. 'I had several meetings with the Russian ambassador to the United Nations in New York. He thought it would be possible.'

'I know nothing of that,' said Josef. Why had Devgeny withheld that information, wondered Josef. He couldn't see the advantage of doing so. And obviously Endelman would not lie, because the statement was so easily checked.

'You could call Moscow,' urged the photographer.

Publicity, or what Moscow regarded as publicity, was the point of the tour, thought Josef. And the man came with Blyne's recommendation, which was a factor to be taken into consideration.

'I'd have preferred to have discussed this in Moscow,' he said.

'They know, believe me.'

'I'll inquire,' promised Josef. 'But decisions are made slower in Moscow than they are in New York.'

'I'm a perpetual optimist,' said the photographer. It was like someone unfolding himself when he stood up, Josef thought.

'I'll contact you tomorrow,' said Endelman.

'That'll be far too soon.'

'It'll be a way of keeping in touch,' pressed the other man.

'As you wish,' said Josef. 'You'll be wasting your time.'

'Not if it's finally productive, I won't,' countered Endelman.

He was the sort of man who always had to have the last word, thought Josef.

'Until tomorrow,' smiled Endelman, at the door.

Instinctively, Josef knew it would be wrong to allow Endelman the involvement he wanted. There were already sufficient difficulties, he decided. Why had the approach been kept from him in Moscow? And why hadn't the publisher sent to him a copy of the request to the Ministry? He had sent copies of all other correspondence.

Josef booked telephone calls to the Russian capital and New York, then drank his cold coffee and nibbled the sandwiches, which had become soggy. As he ate, he replayed the press conference from the briefcase tape upon which he had recorded it. Finally he shrugged, the decision made. Briefly, he dictated his customary nightly report into a second recorder, added Endelman's request, then summoned an embassy attaché to include it in the diplomatic pouch to Moscow.

After he had gone Josef stretched, realizing how tired he was. Perhaps tonight he wouldn't need the pills. He answered the telephone immediately, anxious not to disturb Nikolai. Lines to Moscow were down, the operator insisted. There was no chance of a circuit that night. He had promised he would call Pamela. She would never accept that it was impossible to get a connection, so there would be another row when he spoke to her the following night. He was becoming exasperated at the constant bickering.

The American call came within thirty minutes. Blyne was ecstatic. Advance subscription was unprecedented in their history. They intended a Dutch auction for the paperback rights and anticipated a record there, as well. Every major film company had contacted him, urging him to use his influence in any subsequent meeting they might have with Josef. The publisher seemed surprised the negotiator wanted to talk about Endelman. The man came with his full support, as he had said in his letter to Josef in Moscow. So his mail was being intercepted, Josef accepted. Blyne was bemused at Josef's reluctance.

'But what do you know about him?' asked the Russian.

'What sort of question is that?'

'Can I trust him? If he's allowed to get as close as he wants, there'll be some pictures I *won't* want him to take.'

'The man didn't win three Pulitzers and achieve his reputation without integrity,' argued the American. 'He's not going to risk getting thrown out on his ass, is he?'

Josef replaced the receiver, dissatisfied. Blyne, he realized, was swamped under a tidal wave of success. Devgeny and Illinivitch appeared locked in their own struggle. Which left no one to be objective, apart from himself.

Josef pulled the briefcase towards him, to close it. And stared down. There, in the corner, neatly wrapped in one of of the napkins that had come with his supper, lay the last of the sandwiches, automatically hoarded. Angrily, he threw it back on to the tray. It missed, collapsing on to the floor in a pile of bread and ham pieces.

Dear God, he thought, will it never stop? Consciously, he reached for the sleeping tablets. He would never, he knew, be tired enough.

They were at breakfast in the Eaton Square flat, the only time they encountered each other long enough for prolonged conversation.

'I'm going to get a visa to visit Pamela,' announced Doreen Bellamy, defiantly.

She hesitated as she saw him prepare to speak.

' ... And for God's sake, don't say you forbid it.'

Sir Hudson closed his mouth, deciding upon persuasion.

'It will be embarrassing for me,' he said. 'I'll be a laughing stock in Westminster.'

'That's probably an exaggeration,' she said. Then, sincerely, she added, 'I'm not doing it to embarrass you. I genuinely want to see Pamela again.'

'The Russians are bound to leak it,' said Sir Hudson, reflectively. 'I know I'm on their black list for all the anti-Soviet speeches I've made.'

'Crap,' sneered his wife. 'That's a line from the publicity machine.'

'They *will* leak it,' he insisted, with slightly less conviction. The woman made a 'so what' gesture.

'I don't suppose it would be any good if I sincerely asked you not to go?' he asked, quietly.

'No,' she retorted.

For a moment, they sat in silence. Lady Bellamy went back to her newspaper, using it as a shield.

'I've something to tell you,' he said.

His wife looked up, irritated.

'I've got to go into hospital, for an operation.'

'What for?'

'Exploratory,' he said. 'It might be prostate.'

'Poor dear,' she mocked, unsympathetically. 'That'll ruin your sex life, won't it?'

'Sometimes,' said Sir Hudson, seriously, 'I lay awake at nights, imagining how wonderful life would be without you.'

Lady Bellamy looked at her watch theatrically.

'It's late. Shouldn't you run along?'

Wordlessly, he moved towards the door.

'Don't forget your cycle-clips,' she called, without looking up from the paper.

Chapter Thirteen

Pamela had run to the telephone, imagining the call from Josef. The voice had confused her. Her immediate reaction was that it was a practical joke. Then she realized it could not be. Only friends played practical jokes. They both accepted the problem of identification and finally Pamela agreed it would be better if they met there, in the apartment. The call completed, she stared down at the phone. Had she done right in agreeing to the meeting? She shrugged. Why not? She suddenly realized that it was the first person to whom she had spoken in the past forty-eight hours. Or was it fifty-six?

She laughed, aloud. Someone to talk to. She glanced around the apartment. Nothing needed doing. She was a mess, though. She showered, washed her hair and then fluffed it into a style reminiscent of London, rejecting a brightly patterned dress for one of severe black wool, broken only by a diamond brooch high on the left shoulder.

Promptly at the arranged time, the doorbell rang. Pamela stood in the middle of the room, waiting for the second ring. Even then, she moved slowly to answer it.

'Hello,' said Pamela.

'Hello,' said the girl. She was a little taller than Pamela, hair bobbed short, mannishly almost. She wore no make-up and Pamela noticed that her nails, visible as she held her handbag nervously before her, were badly bitten. Pamela judged the dress she was wearing would be her best one. It was mottle tweed and badly cut, the seam some way off her shoulders. It was too long, as well.

'Come in,' invited Pamela, standing aside.

'Thank you.'

Attractive voice, thought Pamela, unless the huskiness was caused by nervousness. A broken front tooth made her lisp slightly.

'Do sit down,' said Pamela, gesturing towards the long settee before the fire. Had there been a patronizing note in her voice? Of course not. Anyway, her flawed Russian would disguise any offence.

'So you're Sanya,' said the English girl.

The Russian sat with her handbag clutched on her lap, legs tight together. The low heel of her left shoe needed repairing, Pamela saw. And she had fat knees.

Sanya nodded, half smiling. 'You know of me?'

It was a hopeful question.

'My husband mentioned your name.'

'Oh.' She sounded disappointed.

'Would you like something to drink? Some sherry, perhaps,' gushed Pamela.

'Thank you,' said the girl, who had never tasted it.

Pamela served the drinks, smiling happily at the encounter. She was conscious of Sanya's attention to the dress and the brooch. The apartment obviously overpowered her, too.

'I hope you weren't angry at my calling,' said Sanya, repeating the telephone apology. Aware of Pamela's faulty Russian, the girl was speaking slowly. Considerate, thought Pamela.

'Of course not,' she assured. Calculated from the time she had said goodbye to Josef, it was fifty-six hours since she'd engaged in any conversation, apart from unresponsive greetings from the concierge.

' ... But really, there was no one else I could ask.'

Nervously, the girl sipped her wine. It caught her breath and she gulped, just avoiding the cough.

' ... You'll think me silly ... ' groped the girl.

'No, please,' said Pamela. The other girl was extraordinarily plain, thought the Englishwoman. And naïve. Perhaps that was what had appealed to Nikolai, the attraction of somebody as unworldly as himself. The thought distressed her. Had that been her original attraction for the writer?

'Have you heard from your husband?'

'Yes,' lied Pamela, immediately. 'I've had several telephone calls. Everyone is excited about Nikolai's book.'

'I'm glad.' It was said without conviction. She finished the sherry and replaced her glass. Immediately, Pamela refilled it from the decanter she had carried to the low table between them.

'We fought,' Sanya suddenly blurted out, looking away from Pamela. 'We fought and he threw me out ... '

She gestured to the iodine-like stain of a disappearing bruise on her left cheek.

'He hit me, too. My tooth broke. I have weak teeth.'

The girl sipped her drink, embarrassed at the admission. She'd be quite attractive with longer hair, thought Pamela. Her nails would have to be manicured, of course. And her clothes fitted properly.

'Would you help me?'

Pamela frowned. 'How?'

'The next time your husband calls. Can you ask him to give Nikolai a message? Say I'm sorry. And ask him to contact me.'

'*You're* sorry?' echoed Pamela. 'I thought he hit *you*?'

Sanya smiled. 'But I want him back.'

'So you're prepared to plead?'

Now the Russian girl frowned. 'I'm not actually pleading. But I would, if I had to.'

'But ... ?'

' ... I love him,' said Sanya, simply, anticipating the question.

Pamela blushed. 'I'm sorry,' she said.

'What for?'

'For not understanding,' said the Englishwoman, gently. How frequently she apologized, she thought.

'Nikolai says that you and your husband are his only friends.'

'Oh,' said Pamela.

'He's very shy,' said Sanya, as if Nikolai needed a character reference. 'That's what makes him drink. I wish he wouldn't. He's only cruel when he drinks.'

'Have you asked him not to?'

Sanya nodded. 'He says rude things to me.'

They were silent for several minutes and the Russian girl became embarrassed again.

'Will you get your husband to persuade Nikolai?'

'Yes,' promised Pamela.

But Nikolai wouldn't call, she thought. She wondered if Sanya knew it. She must be very desperate. Would she plead for Josef, Pamela wondered. It was an uncomfortable question. She wasn't sure of the answer.

Sanya looked at her watch. 'I've occupied too much of your time.'

'But you haven't finished your sherry.'

'I must go.'

'Have you another appointment?'

Sanya hesitated, half rising from the chair.

'No,' she said. 'But I'm intruding ... '

She gestured towards Pamela's dress. 'You are going out.'

'Why don't you stay for supper?' invited Pamela, hurriedly. It couldn't end so soon. Sanya was on her feet.

'But I couldn't put you to such inconvenience.'

'Look,' said Pamela, emotion clogging her voice, 'you're the first person I've spoken to in two days. I'm practically going out of my mind with loneliness ... '

She extended her hands.

' ... Please.'

The acceptance speech was the way to turn Nikolai back into the focal point of the tour and recover from the abysmal airport press conference, Josef knew. He obtained the lecture that Solzhenitsyn had prepared but never delivered and the response that Hemingway had had read to the Foundation in 1953. Nikolai studied both, then timidly stop-started his attempt to match them.

'I can't do it, Josef.'

'You've got to,' rejected Josef, refusing the writer the self-pity he was seeking.

After five hours, it was still incomplete. Nikolai sat, exhausted, unable to continue. There would be time the following day, Josef decided.

Initially, it was easy for Josef to disguise the delay to the official reception, because Nikolai was not ready. Then the author appeared, dressed in his hired evening clothes, and the postponement became more obvious. Twice, the embassy driver appeared, seeking instructions. Finally, after the third deferment because of bad connections, Josef transferred the call he had booked to Pamela to the building where the reception was being held. He drove in silence, annoyed the solution had not occurred earlier. Personal mistakes angered him.

The greetings were effusive, but Josef detected the annoyance. To work on the speech, he had refused to allow Nikolai on two sightseeing tours the Foundation had organized and he knew that was being interpreted as impoliteness.

Every other Nobel Laureate was already in the room when they entered the chandeliered chamber. People turned towards them and Nikolai winced at the attention. They edged through the officials and Ministers, Josef methodically memorizing the names and constantly apologizing for their late arrival. Nikolai's face was waxy with sweat. A waiter approached, assorted drinks on the tray. Nikolai looked inquiringly to the older man. Josef handed him champagne, then took a glass himself. They were surrounded by the Literary Committee. Josef's head moved like a June spectator at Wimbledon, translating and inventing responses from the near-unspeaking author. Josef detected frowns of uncertainty at Nikolai's cowed demeanour.

'Good evening.'

Josef turned to Mikhail Sukalov, the Russian ambassador to Sweden. He had been a friend of his father's, Josef remembered. He had not come forward to defend him at the trial, but he hadn't lied for the prosecution, either, and in the atmosphere of the time, that had amounted to friendship.

'I'm sorry I wasn't able to meet you at the airport,' said the ambassador.

'It didn't matter.'

'I'm not sure,' said Sukalov. They stared at each other for several moments, then Sukalov added pointedly, 'You were late.'

'Unavoidable,' said Josef. Over the ambassador's shoulder, Josef saw Nikolai replace his empty glass and take another from a passing tray. Aware of Josef's attention, Nikolai ignored his eyes, over-attentive to some stumbling point a member of the Literary Committee was making in bad Russian. Josef recalled the man's name was Lev Krantz. Jewish, he had decided when they were introduced. And ashamed of it. Medev had never been embarrassed by his race. He had been a proud man, recalled Josef, boasting of the life he would eventually make for himself in Israel.

'This is a great honour for Russia,' said the ambassador, putting on cocktail-party conversation like a favourite cardigan.

'Let's hope it doesn't become a disaster.'

'Could it?' queried Sukalov, directly.

'Easily.'

'Do you need help?'

'I don't think so,' rebuffed Josef, too used to relying only upon himself.

'I was sorry about your father, Josef,' said the elderly man, making the gesture. 'Often, I wondered if ... '

'They were difficult times,' broke in Josef, selecting the platitude. He didn't want the old man to become embarrassed. An official appeared at Josef's side.

'Telephone,' said the man. 'Moscow.'

Josef turned towards Nikolai. Ten yards away, the writer took another drink from the tray. Was it the third or fourth? Josef had lost count. The author appeared relaxed, smiling easily. A little champagne spilled from his glass as he turned back towards Krantz.

'It must be urgent,' urged Sukalov, curiously.

'Watch Nikolai, will you?' asked Josef.

The kiosk was stuffy and clouded with cigarette smoke. He edged the door open and was immediately aware of laughter from the reception. Turning back into the box, he heard a snatch of Russian, the ringing tone and then, faintly, Pamela's voice. Immediately they were connected, the line faded, only one in every four words discernible. Josef wondered if it were caused by a listening device. It was a ridiculous, stilted conversation, shouting at each other, using single words for sentences, repeating themselves again and again. Josef was conscious of the attention of people passing outside the box as he yelled to make himself understood. He grew irritated by the need for such an inconsequential conversation. Marriage, he decided, was definitely a nuisance. Again that thought. He felt ashamed, like noticing the gradual breasts of a girl not yet sixteen. Abruptly, dismissing the fear of upsetting her, he concluded the conversation, refusing to emphasize his love. It had been stupidity to worry about the call and leave Nikolai alone, he thought, as

126

he hurried back to the reception. At least the telephone difficulties had prevented an argument. The ambassador was beside Nikolai, stone-faced, staring around for assistance. Nikolai was now quite drunk, laughing at remarks he didn't understand, his jacket and shirt flecked with spilt champagne. Two embassy attachés had eased themselves alongside the author. He was slack-mouthed from alcohol, leaning against one or the other of the two flanking Russians. Accomplished diplomats, they were conversing with people around them. Many people in the room had noticed, Josef realized.

'What happened?' demanded Josef.

'I was talking with the Swedish trade minister, when Balshev began dropping glasses. The man's behaving like a fool,' said Sukalov defensively.

'Thank God there aren't many who can understand Russian,' said Josef.

'He wants a lavatory,' interceded one of the two attendant Russians.

'Take him,' ordered Josef. 'Even inside a cubicle.'

Distastefully, the diplomats edged Nikolai towards the door.

'Your concern is too obvious,' warned Sukalov. He was a tall, white-haired man, elegant in evening dress, an odd, malacca cigarette-holder held between them, like a demarcation line. Long ago, Josef remembered a picture of the man with his father. It had been at a Washington reception for Roosevelt, just before his father had become ambassador there.

'I'm terrified of the acceptance speech,' confessed Josef.

The author returned from the lavatory. He had been sick, Josef knew. His face was yellow-looking. And wet, of course. Why did he perspire so much, wondered the negotiator. Fear, he supposed, even through drunkenness. The writer was almost comatose when he reached them, unaware of what was going on around him. He was guided unprotesting on a slow farewell to the door. In the embassy car, he slumped, eyes closed until they almost reached the hotel. Suddenly, he lurched forward and vomited on to the floor of the vehicle.

'Oh God,' said the ambassador. He wound down the window, straining out. Nikolai had to be almost carried into the hotel, the two attachés walking with their arms locked behind him. Before they put him to bed, Josef insisted they bathe him.

Sukalov and Josef went into the adjoining suite, an embarrassed atmosphere between them, like friends who discover they are sleeping with the same woman.

'I pity you,' said Sukalov, as Josef poured him vodka.

'I pity myself,' said Josef, with equal sincerity. The ambassador turned, ignoring the drinks for the moment.

'Is it that important?' he asked, stopped by the tone of Josef's voice.

'Yes,' said Josef.

'Then I really pity you.'

For the first time for several days, Josef relaxed. He leaned back, closing his eyes. If he felt so tired, why couldn't he sleep? No one could feel as he did and lie, sleepless, for hour after hour each night. How good a holiday would be. A fortnight — a week even — just sleeping and relaxing somewhere nobody knew him. Just a few days of blissful anonymity. Just good food. Walks maybe. And sleep. Normal, easy sleep. No nightmares, no blocked, strangled breathing. No sleeping pills. Oh yes, and Pamela. Of course. Pamela.

'Are you all right?'

Josef opened his eyes. 'I'm sorry,' he apologized.

Sukalov shrugged.

'It's a strain ... ' began Josef, but Sukalov raised his hand, stopping him.

'I don't want an explanation. And I mean that.'

'It's nothing that could embarrass you,' assured Josef.

'I still don't want an explanation.'

My father would not have said that thought Josef. He would have recognized somebody in need of help. He would have come forward at the trial, too, not held back as Sukalov had done.

'It hasn't gone well, so far,' admitted Josef.

'I know.'

'I'm not sure I can do it.'

'That isn't something you should say to me,' cautioned the ambassador.

'Will you report it?'

'No. So you're lucky, but you're not thinking enough, Bultova. If it's important you're making too many mistakes.'

'And I could die because of it,' said Josef. Immediately, the theatricality of the remark embarrassed him.

'Rubbish,' threw back Sukalov. 'No one would have behaved as you did tonight, abandoning someone like Balshev, if his life depended on it.'

More than a nuisance now, thought Josef. She was a danger to his life. A risk of a labour camp again. The barracks with beds like shelves; cold, mist-layered landscapes; brick trucks on their never-ending circle. Swill; whips; and guards, laughing, jeering guards. Had Medev managed to die? He'd wanted to, Josef remembered. Towards the end, he'd spoken constantly of dying.

'I made a mistake,' confessed Josef. Admitting errors was a relief. Sukalov was a good man, he decided.

'Your father died because he made small mistakes.'

I'll never make that error, thought Josef. I'm aware of so many difficulties I'm building phantoms out of shadows.

One of the attachés came through the linking door, interrupting them. He looked damp and irritable.

'He wants a sleeping pill,' reported the man.

Josef took some seconal from his briefcase and handed it to the attaché.

'It's going to be difficult for you, personally, elsewhere,' predicted Sukalov.

'I've realized that,' assured Josef. The Washington ambassador had been one of the chief prosecution witnesses at the trial.

The second attaché came from the adjoining suite and said Nikolai was asleep.

'I suppose you'll have to report this,' said Josef.

'If I don't,' said Sukalov, nodding towards where the man had disappeared. 'One of them will. It will sound better, coming from me.'

Endelman must have been waiting in the lobby for the ambassador to leave, Josef realized. The telephone went within five minutes of the diplomat's departure.

'It's Endelman,' announced the photographer.

'I know,' said Josef. The other man had a soft voice, inclined to sibilance.

'How is he?'

'Better, thank you.'

'Good. He was very drunk tonight, wasn't he?'

Josef could not remember seeing the photographer at the reception.

There was a pause. Then Endelman offered, hopefully, 'I don't think too many people noticed.'

'I'm glad,' said Josef. The man was trying very hard to be sympathetic. Josef wondered if it were a trick, like remembering names.

'Have you heard from Moscow yet?'

'No.'

'Oh,' said the photographer. The disappointment sounded very genuine. 'Have you spoken to Blyne?'

It was a clever guess that he would have called New York.

'He wants you to come with us,' said Josef. 'Perhaps I'll talk to Moscow this evening to try to get a decision.'

'I'd appreciate that,' said Endelman.

After the call, Josef dictated his nightly report, then paused, wondering about the photographer. Was Endelman one of the small mistakes about which Sukalov warned? In the pocket of his evening jacket he detected a cube of cheese affixed over a piece of pineapple. He pulled out the fluff-flecked canapé surviving from the reception, carefully removed the debris from the lining of his jacket and nibbled it, enjoying the faint flavour of the fruit. The nightly account finished and despatched, he searched his pockets in case he had hoarded more than one piece. He hadn't, he realized. Pity. They were really quite nice.

It took an hour for the call to come through to the number that Illinivitch had given him. Very carefully, he outlined Endelman's request, refusing to be cut off by the deputy chairman's interruptions that he had considered the overnight contents of the diplomatic pouch. It was all right, Illinivitch assured him. The Ministry felt it fitting that one of the world's best-known photographers should record the tour and accordingly every facility should be made available. Josef's doubts were dismissed almost flippantly.

'Why wasn't it discussed before I left Moscow?' demanded Josef.

'Devgeny,' replied Illinivitch, immediately. 'He knew you'd realize your mail was being intercepted and be unsettled by it. He wants you to know you're expected to fail and be constantly worried, so that you'll make more mistakes. Your only hope is to support me openly.'

It was wrong, decided Josef, when the call had finished. Instinctively, he felt that the inclusion of Endelman would create problems.

Chapter Fourteen

Nikolai's artificial groans disturbed Josef before seven a.m. The writer was very child-like, he thought. Nikolai was lying on his back when Josef went into the room, his eyes closed but obviously not asleep.

'What's the matter?'

Nikolai moaned, slowly opening his eyes and squinting against the light.

'It's no good, Josef. I shan't be able to go to the rehearsal. I'm too ill. I've even vomited blood.'

'Oh,' said Josef, unsympathetically.

'Call a doctor,' demanded the writer.

Josef ordered coffee and orange juice in the room and had showered by the time it was served. He returned to Nikolai's suite carrying the larger of the two briefcases.

He offered coffee to the prostrate author, who grimaced and turned his head away.

'Leave me alone, Josef.'

'Nikolai,' said Josef, gently. 'You've got a hangover. Probably a bad one. But you deserve it.'

He opened his briefcase and handed Nikolai three paracetamol tablets.

'These will get rid of the headache,' he promised. Nikolai took them, staring at the orderly arrangement of bottles and phials inside the briefcase. Josef took another bottle from its holder.

'This will make you feel more confident about the receptions and the rehearsals,' he added, handing the writer two of the chlordiazepoxide tablets he had acquired in Austria.

Nikolai smiled up at the negotiator.

'Thank you, Josef,' he said. 'You're a true friend.'

He gulped the analgesic tablets, waited for thirty minutes, as Josef instructed, then took the chlordiazepoxide. An hour before their first appointment, Nikolai was more relaxed and confident than Josef had ever seen him.

Josef had telephoned Endelman, telling him of the overnight decision by Moscow, and the photographer arrived at their suite at nine. Nikolai was taking the bath upon which Josef was now insisting, so Josef served coffee while they waited.

'I'm glad it's worked out,' said Endelman.

'I'm surprised,' admitted Josef. 'But I don't like the idea. So let's understand one thing. If it becomes awkward, the arrangement ends.'

'Sure,' agreed Endelman, easily.

He doesn't think I mean it, thought Josef. Nikolai was surprised and at first retreated into his shell of reserve. But gradually, as the day developed, with Nikolai being introduced to other Nobel Laureates, Josef noticed the writer smiling more often at Endelman's efforts to communicate. The photographer had made a joke, in the hotel suite, of his Russian, which Josef thought quite good.

'Jimmy and I have made a pact,' announced Nikolai, at lunch. 'He's going to speak to me only in Russian and I'm going to reply only in English. That way we both improve our language.'

Just like the arrangement between himself and Pamela, thought Josef. He looked over the writer's head, to Endelman.

'See,' said the photographer. 'I told you it would work.'

Josef didn't return the smile. Again the thought returned that Illinivitch's decision was wrong. He wondered if it had been made by the Ministry or by the deputy Minister alone. If the Ministry had been involved, then there would be an official record.

The afternoon rehearsal in the concert hall was strange, like a funeral without a body, Josef thought. He had anticipated Nikolai's request and brought more chlordiazepoxide which he had given him as lunch was ending.

It was the first time Josef had seen Endelman work. He was very professional, decided the Russian. None of the Nobel Laureates, encased in their own nervousness, seemed aware of him.

The ceremony dictated that Nikolai be officially conducted into the hall by two members of the Literary Committee. Lev Krantz, whom Josef recalled from the reception at which Nikolai had got drunk, was one of his attendants. The other was a man called Noedstrom, whose christian name Josef had missed. Names were becoming a problem for him, he realized.

For nearly two hours they went over the ceremony, beginning with the entrance from the Oxtorgsgatan, into the committee rooms and then, after the trumpet calls and royal hymn that would indicate the arrival of the royal party, the entry through the centre doors to their places on the right hand side of the platform. There were cocktails after the rehearsal. Nikolai, Josef noticed, moved immediately to Endelman and the two became immersed in conversation, apparently oblivious to people around them.

Krantz smiled and came up to the negotiator, nodding towards Nikolai.

'He seems better today,' he said.

'I'm afraid he was nervous the other evening.'

'They often are,' said the Swedish Jew. 'I have known many literary winners. Always they are frightened. Writers are private people. They shouldn't be exposed to public view.'

Josef nodded, but could not think of a reply. Ballenin could get on well with the man, he thought.

'It is a sad occasion, this year,' filled in Krantz.

'Oh?'

'You are unaware of our tragedy?'

'I'm afraid ... ?'

'This year we are avoiding the salutatory oration that would have come from Count von Sydon.'

'Oh yes,' recalled Josef. 'A sad loss.'

'Indeed,' said Krantz. 'You never met, I suppose?'

'No,' said Josef. 'Never.'

'A remarkable man,' said Krantz. 'Really remarkable.'

Nikolai, thought Josef when they got back to the hotel, was an enigma. His moods swung like a pendulum from one extreme to the other and Josef was unable to decide how much was genuine. A great deal of Nikolai's behaviour, he thought, was calculated, like a man glancing sideways into a shop-window reflection to gauge his appearance. The early part of the day had gone without difficulty and Nikolai had built an icing-sugar confidence from it. As they prepared for the ceremony, Josef heard him whistling in the adjoining room. The negotiator went through the linking doors, into Nikolai's rooms. The writer swirled in his hired evening-dress and Josef realized he had bathed for the second time.

'How do I look?'

'Magnificent.'

'Will I look as good as Endelman?'

Josef stared at the writer curiously. Was he jealous of the American photographer?

'Every bit as good,' assured the negotiator.

'I want another pill,' announced Nikolai.

'No,' rejected Josef. 'You've had three. Already that's too many.'

Immediately the fragile confidence began flaking away. 'In two hours time I've got to stand on a stage and deliver the most important speech I'll ever make in my life. I'll be representing Russia. We both know I can't do it without help. This will be the last time, I promise,' said Nikolai.

He was right, of course. This was the highlight of the tour and nothing could be permitted to go wrong. Nikolai had written the address, finally, but Josef was still apprehensive of it. He couldn't afford a public disaster.

'The last time,' he warned.

'I promise.'

As Josef returned with the capsule, Endelman arrived, with champagne. 'Our own celebration,' said the photographer, 'Before the razzamatazz.'

He worked hard at being liked, decided Josef. Even in the formalized clothes, Endelman still looked outstanding. Josef saw Nikolai admiring the other man. Endelman uncorked the bottle, poured and handed round glasses.

'A toast,' he announced. 'To success. The only thing worth having.'

Josef drank, with feeling. 'Don't let's forget luck,' he added.

They separated at the concert hall, Nikolai going with his two attendants and Josef moving into the main body of the hall. Endelman had a place next to the negotiator and had arranged with the ushers to be seated late, after recording the arrival of the royal party and the assembly of the laureates and their families in the side chambers. Television and film lights glared down, whitening everyone into invalids and making the hall ridiculously hot. Josef twitched damply in the starched formality. He was aware of attention from several parts of the room and it increased his discomfort. Limited recognition was all right, necessary even. But he disliked the sustained exposure. He wanted discreet boardrooms and measured arguments, the tension of nuance and concession. Not this. Not pressed down by a spotlight, squinted at like some malformed freak at a country fairground.

Expectation was seeping through the room and encompassing people, like water overflowing from a flooding stream. The doubts about Nikolai's lecture would not recede.

The address was something that should have been created slowly, over a period of weeks, not scrabbled together in the time they had spent on it, like a message left for a tradesman. A Nobel lecture became a piece of history. By his words today, Nikolai was standing up, throwing open his coat and saying, 'Look at me; this is what I am.'

Josef was horrifyingly aware it could become a case of indecent exposure.

The trumpets sounded and everyone stood. How small the king looked, thought Josef. They remained standing as the Nobel Laureates entered, bowed to the royal party and then sat upon the platform. Nikolai looked small and crushed, like he had when they had left Sheremetyevo airport. Josef tried to catch his eye, but realized he was too far away. Endelman was in the front of the hall, Josef saw. Nikolai noticed him and smiled, gratefully.

The photographer moved back and edged in beside Josef. 'He seems all right,' he whispered.

Because Count von Sydon's speech had been cut, the ceremony moved straight on to the presentation addresses from the members of each academy. They were in Swedish, followed immediately by translation into the language of the respective winners. Tensely, Josef listened as Krantz made his speech, then heard the words in Russian, stilted and formal. Nikolai was actually walking across towards the king before Josef fully realized it was him, moving quite steadily, with none of the hesitation that Josef had feared. The applause rippled and then grew and there was a dazzle from the photographic enclosure as the king handed over the gold medal, the diploma and the assignation of the prize. Although slight, the king still dwarfed the Russian, who stood attentive, looking up into the man's face as if he understood the words being spoken, each holding one edge of the memorial scroll while the cameras recorded the historic moment.

137

Then Nikolai turned away, searching for the podium that had been pointed out that afternoon. Twelve steps, Josef remembered warning him, just twelve steps and you're there. Steadily, the writer paced his way forward to the lectern and stood, looking out, hands either side and pinned down by the lights. He seemed more alert than nervous, thought Josef. Recalling the airport press conference, Josef was glad about the lights. Nikolai would be unable to see the people laid out before him in serried, identically dressed rows, like the ornamental lawns in French châteaux. Occasionally there was a muffled, embarrassed cough, but otherwise there was complete silence. Josef strained upwards, curiously. Nikolai was looking slowly right and left, like a consummate actor gaining effect from silence. It must be nerves, decided Josef. He must be standing there, unable to force the words beyond his lips. The coughing seemed to be increasing and there was the scrape of feet being scuffed over the floor as people shifted, as if in sympathy with the lonely man's discomfort. Nikolai cleared his throat and the sound was picked up by the microphones. The room became silent.

'Many men,' the writer began, 'have stood where I stand today, the award I have just received crowning a lifetime's work ... '

The words came a little too quickly, like small boys at playtime tripping over one another. Nikolai was staring towards the part of the hall where he knew Josef would be. The negotiator smiled, even though he knew the author would not be able to see the encouragement.

' ... Many have said they feel the honour undeserved, because modesty in moments of great recognition is expected. Modesty, I fear, is the conceit of many men. Risking the nomination of my own criticism, I declare a feeling of humility, a fear that the works for which I have today been accorded the greatest recognition that can be given to a writer are undeserving ... '

He stopped. He was speaking slower now, with better delivery. Again Josef was reminded of an actor.

' ... Forgive me my moment of conceit ... ' added Nikolai, after just the right pause. There was a murmur of polite amusement. Josef sat bemused by the change in the man.

' ... It is customary, in Nobel Lectures from writers, for much to be said of art. I admire those men who find themselves able to discourse so freely and so easily upon such a subject. I will not talk to you today about art, for I do not feel competent to do so. In the conceit of modesty, I suppose a man can be forgiven for believing the Nobel prize befits him to lecture others on how his work should be received or performed. I do not feel that confidence. I do not feel I can declaim upon an art in which I believe myself to be an amateur ... '

It was going amazingly well, decided Josef. Now Nikolai's voice was strong and evenly pitched. There was, of course, the difficulty of translation, but sufficient people seemed able to understand. Josef had noticed several head-together conversations, always followed by approving nods. Josef saw Sukalov looking at him and smiling. Josef wondered how long his contentment would last.

' ... I feel to the art of literature like an ant crawling around the base of a giant oak ... '

Once more Nikolai cleared his throat and appeared to straighten on the podium.

' ... Every year ... ' he began, coming to that part of the lecture about which Josef had so much concern. He coughed and stopped. Around him Josef was aware of an intensifying of interest as people suspected a problem.

' ... Every year,' Nikolai began again, 'the awarding of the Nobel prize for literature arouses world-wide interest. That is to be expected. This year, the award has created even greater interest. That is to be expected too. Because I am Russian ...'

Even those unable to understand caught the feeling that

139

swept the room, a tightening that seemed to go through the people, as if a wire to which they were all attached had been turned by one notch.

' … I am aware of that interest. I stand before you today an oddity, a man different from his fellows, from his countrymen, like someone with two heads, each facing myopically towards the other. I am aware, too, of the reason. Another Russian, a short time ago, was accorded the honour that has been bestowed upon me today. For reasons which no doubt seemed compelling to him and for which I extend no criticism, he chose not to travel here to accept it. I could find no such reason. But I respect his feelings, for in my conceit of modesty, I regard him as a far better writer than I shall ever be. Many of you will have read of the lecture that my fellow Russian had intended to deliver here. In it, reference was made to a Russian proverb—"One word of truth outweighs the whole world." It provided a title for the lecture when it was published in the West … '

Josef was conscious of Sukalov's wide-eyed stare. Other people, aware of Josef's identity, were looking at him. There was utter silence, that hollow nothingness that preludes the acceptance of disaster.

'Upon my arrival here, I was asked what concessions I had made to enable this trip to be undertaken. I replied "none". That is my word of truth. Against me—and therefore against my work, which I resent—there appears to be growing criticism. It is a criticism by default. "The writing must be suspect," runs the argument, "because the man has no political motivation. He is not at war with his country." Is it necessary for a man to be a politician before he can be a writer? Does a man need to suffer the humiliation and the deprivation of a prison camp before he can encompass the cruelty of man to man … ?'

Sukalov looked frightened, Josef thought.

' … In the Soviet Union, there is undoubtedly much that

140

can be criticized. Mistakes have been made. And will be made again … '

Sukalov was bent, whispering into the ear of the First Secretary, gesturing towards Josef.

'People have suffered. And—perhaps regretfully—will continue to suffer … '

Nikolai hesitated again. This time, the cough had the edge of nervousness. Even blinded, he appeared able to detect the feeling from those before him. Haltingly, but then with growing confidence, Nikolai continued.

' … The world was once a large, inaccessible place. Now it is small. Borders are now merely drawings on a map. Is it the function of all writers to turn lines on maps into insurmountable barriers? To establish the system which now exists in the People's Republic of China, twenty-six million people died. Should China be isolated? In Australia, the native aborigine has become almost extinct under white rule and now exists—but barely—in squalor unparalleled in the world. Should Australia be isolated? One hundred and thirty years ago, the American government, then, thank God, unaware of a place called Vietnam, adopted a policy called "manifest destiny". It was, according to their legislation and even religious guidance of the time, destiny that the white man should occupy the continent and that the American Indian should perish if he objected. Should America be isolated? In South Africa, no black—or kaffir, to use their own word, which sounds offensive, like spitting— may walk a street without a pass, a document that herds him, like cattle, into settlements which, like those in Australia and those in America of one hundred and thirty years ago, are always in the worst parts of the country, the places where the white man does not want to be. Should South Africa be isolated? During a holocaust that should be the shame of mankind, in the Katyn Forests of Poland, in eighteen terrible hours, an entire intellectual stratum of Poland was destroyed in the name of Nazism. In every Ministry in the West German government today, there are men who were Nazis, still holding positions of office. Should West Germany be isolated ... ?'

Nikolai stopped, his throat ragged. He sipped from some water somehow concealed below the lectern. Josef couldn't remember it having been available at the rehearsal. The shuffling and coughs were growing now. The audience were like people at a traffic accident, unwilling to involve themselves in a minor tragedy, standing back waiting for the person next to them to step forward. It was working, Josef thought.

' ... A writer is like a man who has undergone a cataract operation. He can see, where others are blind. He enjoys beauty, but always sees the ugliness. Because I do not write about ugliness—political ugliness, personal ugliness, human ugliness—it does not mean that I am unaware that it exists, that I cannot see it. But I view things of beauty in a particular light, in better perspective. I have been gifted, if that is not too pretentious a word, with a way of portraying beauty. To include ugliness would be to smear mud on my view of beauty. I repeat the proverb from my country—"One word of truth outweighs the whole world." With apologies to its unknown creator, I borrow from it—"A vision of beauty illuminates a moment." '

Only Josef, who knew the lecture, was aware it was over. Nikolai stood there, transfixed, awaiting reaction. Silence sat on time, stretching it from seconds into minutes. People were gathered in groups, three or four clustered around one who was able to provide a translation. The applause started first behind Josef, sounding a long way off and then picked up nearer, to his left and grew, like a snowball rolling down a hill, increasing in its size with every turn. And then it echoed through the hall, sound building on sound, and Nikolai stood at the rostrum, blinking at the ovation. He was staring towards the photographers, Josef saw.

Sukalov fought through the crush at the reception preceding the banquet. Nikolai was damp, his shirt sticking to his body, but with the half-shy, half-confident smile of somebody who believes he has done well but is not quite sure how. His face was red.

'I never want to witness something like that again,' said the ambassador. 'That could be disastrous.'

'No,' disagreed Josef. 'I know the Western mind. Nikolai will be lionized.'

'But Moscow ... '

'He said nothing about Russia that hasn't been publicly conceded in exploding the myths of Stalin and Krushchev. Less, in fact. Yet from a world platform, he has jangled the skeletons in half the cupboards of the world. No one can level at Nikolai the accusation that he is politically naïve. Neither can he be accused of not being aware of his own country's mistakes.'

'Very clever,' admitted the ambassador, without feeling. 'The only reservation is that everyone must interpret it as you have.'

'They will,' promised Josef, confidently. 'Those that matter, anyway.'

'But they weren't his views, Josef,' guessed Sukalov. 'They were yours. What's going to happen to Nikolai when he gets exposed to the television talk-shows and newspaper interviews?'

'It just won't happen, will it?' rejected Josef, smiling. 'My job is to protect him.'

'I always thought writers were supposed to have integrity.'

'What does that mean?' asked Josef, curiously.

'Is Balshev so eager for the honour he's prepared to say whatever he's told? I already thought he might know he was being manipulated—now I'm wondering if he isn't a willing puppet.'

'Show me a truly independent man, Comrade Sukalov, and I'll name a new religion after him,' said Josef.

'It's time for me to circulate,' said Sukalov, the professional diplomat. He fitted the ambassador's smile into place and moved away. Endelman and Nikolai looked towards Josef.

'James said I was magnificent,' opened Nikolai, stepping off on a predictable path. 'Was I magnificent, Josef?'

'Yes,' conceded the negotiator. 'There were times when I felt you were enjoying it.'

'I was,' admitted Nikolai.

'I felt proud of him, too,' said Endelman.

Josef noticed that Nikolai was not bothering with the tray of drinks passing within arm's reach, content with the half glass of champagne that he had held for the past fifteen minutes. Suddenly Nikolai giggled, like a child with a secret, and raised his glass to the photographer.

'We must toast Jimmy,' he said, to Josef. 'Without him, that speech wouldn't have been possible.'

'Don't,' said Endelman, his face serious.

'Why not? Josef should know. He's my friend. Aren't you my friend, Josef?'

The negotiator looked at Endelman. 'What did you give him?' he demanded, quietly, a suspicion confirmed.

'They were quite safe,' said the photographer. 'Just "uppers".'

'James is going to come and live with us,' announced Nikolai. 'Seems ridiculous that he should stay elsewhere. He's moving in tonight.'

'Oh.'

'And Josef.'

'What?'

'See he's included in all the other reservations, will you?'

The author turned as Josef was about to reply, moving off to join Sukalov, who greeted him apprehensively.

Endelman smiled at Josef. 'Sorry about that,' he said.

' ... Endelman.'

The photographer looked directly at Josef, the easy smile slipping away.

'Less than eighteen hours ago, I made it clear to you that I objected to the facilities you were being allowed. I made it equally clear that I would withdraw those facilities if you became a nuisance. Even I didn't foresee you'd be pumping the man with drugs.'

'Is that your prerogative then, Mr Bultova?'

'Get out, Endelman,' said Josef. 'Don't bother even to say goodbye to Nikolai.'

'I don't think it's altogether up to you.'

He turned to where the writer was standing, amid a group of people from the Literary Academy. Nikolai saw the look and came over, smiling. Had they rehearsed it, wondered the negotiator.

'I've been told to clear out, Nikolai,' announced Endelman.

Nikolai laughed and Josef knew the writer's announcement had not been the casual admission it had seemed, but contrived to create the confrontation. Josef stared at the writer. Having broken through the eggshell, the baby was anxious to fly, he thought.

'But I don't want Jimmy to go, Josef. So I won't allow it.'

He raised his voice, darting glances to ensure people were watching. Krantz, fearing a repetition of the earlier reception, frowned.

'Nikolai,' said Josef, his voice quiet. 'I'm running this tour ... '

'There's no need to whisper,' interrupted Nikolai, his voice higher. 'I agree you run this tour. And you will continue to do so. You will run it exactly as I wish. And I wish Jimmy to stay.'

He turned to the photographer. 'Let's circulate,' he said, heavily. Obediently, Endelman moved off in the writer's wake.

Sukalov hurried over. 'What in God's name was that?'

'Growing pains,' identified Josef, angry at the public humiliation.

'Is he determined to wreck this damned tour?' demanded the diplomat.

Josef shook his head, gradually recovering.

'He's not sure what he wants to do. Except get everyone to look at him.'

'He's certainly succeeding in that.'

'Unfortunately,' said Josef, 'most of them are laughing.'

Because she had not been available, as people should be in times of illness, they were rude to Lady Bellamy at the clinic.

'Cancer?'' she echoed, in the consultant's office.

'And a weak heart.' Perhaps her indifference was caused by shock, he thought. It happened sometimes. The man was prepared to make allowances.

'He knew little pain. It was only under anaesthetic that we really learned how extensive it was. We knew his heart was weak, but we didn't realize that the operation would last as long as it did. He died without regaining consciousness.'

'Fancy,' she said, like someone commenting upon a cricket score.

Chapter Fifteen

They were necessary to him, so Josef knew exactly the amount of tranquillizers, drugs and sleeping pills he carried in his case. It was two days after the ceremony, when they were packing for London, that he realized some had been stolen. His control over Nikolai had diminished as Endelman's had grown, and Josef was anxious not to make an unfounded accusation that would allow Nikolai another opportunity for contempt. Three times he counted the contents of each bottle. There were ten valium and librium tablets missing, eight methalaquone and fifteen capsules from each of the bottles containing chlordiazepoxide and diazepam. He sat for nearly fifteen minutes, staring into the repacked briefcase. He would have to challenge the man, of course. Nikolai would expect the accusation. To avoid it would be making a bigger concession than losing yet another argument. He accepted he would have to lose because of Nikolai's growing awareness of his own importance, like a child showing off at his own birthday party.

'Nikolai,' called Josef. The separating door was open.

'What?'

'I'd like to see you.'

'I'm here.'

'In here, please, Nikolai.'

'I'm busy, Josef.'

The negotiator detected Endelman's smirk of amusement as he entered the adjoining suite. He had the briefcase in his hand.

'What have you done with the pills you took from my case?'

'You see!' said Nikolai, triumphantly, turning to the photographer. 'I told you he'd notice them.'

He turned back to Josef. 'We had a bet. Jimmy said you wouldn't realize it, but I knew you were cleverer than that.'

'Give them back to me,' said Josef, extending his hand.

Nikolai laughed at him.

'But I need them, Josef. I like the sensation. We mix them with the amphetamines that Jimmy has and the sensation is tremendous. Much better than sex.'

Josef sighed, helplessly. More stage management, he thought. Why was it so important for insecure people to prove themselves?

'I want you to stop taking pills,' he said. 'And I want those back you haven't yet taken.'

'You're making yourself look ridiculous,' said the writer. 'I've made it quite clear how this tour is going to be conducted. You really must stop telling me what to do. Pills do me good. I can meet people. Without the confidence they give me, I might make mistakes and that would reflect badly upon Russia. We neither of us want that, now do we?'

He'd assimilated sarcasm very well, thought Josef. He looked at Endelman, who shrugged.

'Jimmy's on my side,' said the writer. 'It's no good looking to him for support.'

'It can't cause a lot of harm,' offered the photographer.

'That's bollocks and you know it,' said Josef.

Nikolai glanced at his watch. 'You'd better hurry, Josef,' he said. 'The car is due here in thirty minutes and we don't want to miss the plane, do we?'

Stanswell organized the London reception well. The arrival press conference was as large as that in Stockholm a week before, but the questions were less demanding. The newly confident Nikolai volunteered answers for Josef's translation and on several occasions groped replies in English. There was a large section of book critics who dealt solely with the novel on its artistic merit and even the political questions were easily answered. No one probed Josef's association. The London ambassador, Dimitry Listnisky, was at the airport with a small delegation. He was withdrawn and barely courteous, recognizing the politics and unwilling to become involved with them. Josef had expected an embassy reception, but the ambassador said nothing. He wondered hopefully if the diplomats in America would similarly ignore him. It was hardly likely, he thought.

They travelled into London in a fleet of limousines, Stanswell in the same vehicle as Josef and Nikolai.

'I did well, didn't I?'

'Yes,' agreed Josef, wearily.

The portly publisher looked at Josef questioningly.

'He appreciates the welcome you've arranged,' lied the negotiator. Stanswell smiled, pleased.

'There's a Foyle's lunch,' said the publisher. 'And a dinner for selected critics. Some paperback publishers will be there, too. Incidentally, we want to publish the Nobel lecture. I suppose you'll print it in Russia, to keep the copyright?'

Josef nodded. Even the professional pride in negotiating a good price seemed an effort. He determined on a holiday as soon as he got back to Russia. He mustn't forget the promise to telephone Pamela, he thought.

'We thought of five thousand pounds. And twenty per cent, like we agreed on the novel, with you retaining the paperback rights.'

Josef nodded. He could probably get another one thousand pounds, he knew. Why bother?

'Fine,' he said.

Stanswell seemed surprised. 'Good,' he said.

'I will have a suite at the hotel, won't I?' demanded Nikolai.

'Yes,' sighed Josef.

'And Jimmy?'

'He's on the same floor.'

'You're doing very well, Josef.'

'I know you aren't keen,' interrupted Stanswell, 'but there's been an approach from the leading television talk-show here. I said I'd let them know after discussing it with you.'

'He has virtually no English,' pointed out Josef. He recalled his earlier decision not to allow Nikolai to undergo such exposure. Beneath the conceit and drug-induced euphoria there was still a nervous, frightened man, he thought. Such exposure would still be a strain.

'They said his lack of English didn't matter. They'll record it and run translations beneath when it is finally shown.'

'I'd insist on the right to edit anything I didn't like. And I'd be there myself, of course.'

'They seemed keen for you to appear, as well.'

Josef frowned. Another fiasco, like that in Stockholm? He turned to Nikolai.

'How do you feel about going on television?' he asked.

Nikolai straightened, turning his head almost into an imagined photographic pose. Christ, thought Josef.

'I'd like it,' he said, immediately. 'I shall look good. Jimmy is going to take me to some tailors he knows here, so that I can buy something better than these pieces of sacking.'

There were more cameramen at the hotel and Nikolai preened, delighted at the attention. He was pleased with the Savoy suite, bustling from room to room, shouting at the discoveries. He played with the television, turning to Josef.

'I shall be very good,' he predicted again, clicking from station to station. 'Tell Stanswell to agree.'

They ate that night at Stanswell's London home, an exquisitely furnished mews house off Montpelier Square. Nikolai insisted that Endelman accompany them and

Stanswell acquiesced immediately, assuring them it would cause no inconvenience. The request disturbed Josef. He was becoming increasingly worried at the growing influence Endelman appeared to be having upon the writer. But he had to concede the advantages. In Endelman's company, Nikolai never drank excessively. He looked across the table and smiled at the thought. As it came, Nikolai had been sipping from a water glass. It was a good evening. It became, for Josef, the most pleasurable occasion since he had embarked upon the tour. He enjoyed Stanswell's company. Two critics who were there he found pleasant, too. One had a flawed command of Russian and joined in the writer's conversation with Endelman, whose control of the language, forced as he had been to speak it almost continuously for a week, had improved. Listnisky attended, to Josef's surprise, but stayed aloof. Every word, Josef knew, would be reported back to Moscow. They left before ten p.m., going straight back to the hotel. His name was called as he was collecting his key. He turned to face an attractive, blonde-haired woman, perhaps a well-preserved forty-five, but certainly looking younger.

'You don't recognize me,' she challenged.

'I'm sorry ... ' began the negotiator, then remembered the photograph on Pamela's dressing-table.

'Forgive me. Lady Bellamy.'

'I hope you don't mind my lying in wait for you like this ... I saw your arrival on television ... '

'Of course not,' assured Josef. 'I was just going to telephone Pamela. Why not come and speak to her?'

He introduced the woman to Nikolai and Endelman and they travelled up in the lift together, a self-conscious group.

'Nightcap?' he offered at the door of his suite. Nikolai shook his head.

'Jimmy is tired. So am I.'

'Do you want a sleeping tablet?'

'No thanks,' said Nikolai, grinning. Then he added. 'You don't want me to become an addict, do you?'

'He seems a nice boy,' offered the woman, as they entered Josef's suite.

'Your daughter isn't very keen,' sidestepped Josef. He had had a well-stocked bar installed in the suite and joined her with a brandy. He was told the Moscow call would take thirty minutes.

'I've been trying to telephone Pamela for the last two days,' said the woman. 'But there's been no circuit.'

'Was it important?'

'Her father died.'

'Oh,' said Josef. Her announcement was one of complete detachment. 'I'm sorry,' he said, automatically.

She shrugged, discarding the pleasantry.

'We didn't get on.'

Josef said nothing.

'In fact, we hated each other. We stayed together for his public image.'

It was not the confession to make to someone at the first meeting, Josef thought. He didn't think he liked the woman. She finished her drink and looked at the glass, pointedly. Josef refilled it, his back to her. She smiled up at him when he returned with the drink and he almost faltered, seized by the thought that she was trying to flirt. He felt sorry for her. Was it incestuous, he wondered, to sleep with one's mother-in-law?

'I've come to ask a favour,' she said.

He waited, suspiciously.

'Don't look frightened,' she said, coquettishly. Josef was curious at the reason for her stupidity. Was she worried about her failing sex-appeal, he wondered.

'What?'

He was conscious of the curtness and she seemed to detect it. The smile became uncertain.

'I'd like Pamela to come and visit me,' she said.

'She's too late for the funeral, surely?'

'Of course,' agreed the woman. 'But I'd still like her company.'

Josef thought of his wife's unhappiness just before his departure.

'Have you heard from her how she likes Russia?' he questioned.

Lady Bellamy hesitated before answering. Then she said, 'In every letter she tells me how wonderful it all is.'

The scepticism was obvious.

'But you don't believe her?'

'No,' said the woman.

The conversation had run into a cul-de-sac. Josef poured her a third drink.

'Are you frightened?' she asked, behind him.

'Of what?'

'That she wouldn't return?'

Josef shrugged. 'I don't know,' he answered, honestly.

'So she isn't happy?'

'No,' he admitted. 'Russia is different from what she expected.'

'So there's little chance of your letting her come home?'

'Pamela has already asked me,' he replied. 'She wants a visa for you to come to Russia.'

'That would be nice,' she said, without enthusiasm.

'Another brandy?'

'Please.'

The same invitation was being extended two and a half thousand miles away as Pamela tried to protract an already over-long dinner. Sanya had eaten in the apartment for three nights, and for the past two hours the English girl had argued the pointlessness of the other girl returning home when there was a bed in the apartment. As it was snowing, the offer had some validity. But Sanya hesitated, unsure. She felt stifled, as she did when the elder sister with whom she slept in their cramped, two-family apartment pulled the blankets over her face. Always Pamela hovered, offering the flat or her Western clothes or the use of her jewellery as bribes, like an elderly aunt fearful of abandonment by a daughter who had already sacrificed too much.

'You'll be frozen to death,' said Pamela, reinforcing the argument.

'It isn't far.'

'In this weather, it is.'

'My parents will worry.'

'Telephone.'

'We haven't one.'

'Isn't there a concierge with whom you could leave a message?'

Sanya felt the blanket moving higher and higher. 'No,' she said, definitely. 'I must go.'

'Nikolai might phone,' threw out Pamela, desperately.

Sanya looked at the other woman, pityingly. At first she had feared the English woman's interest might be sexual and had tensed for the approach, but it never came, not even when Pamela had insisted she try on her clothes, which they both realized would not fit without alteration. The only reason for the effusiveness, Sanya concluded, was genuine, soul-aching loneliness. If only, Sanya reflected, she wouldn't try so hard.

'I don't think it's likely Nikolai will telephone, do you?'

As if in rejection of the argument, the telephone rang. They both looked at it, surprised. Pamela's uncertainty immediately registered with Josef and he became apprehensive.

'What's the matter?' he asked.

'Nothing,' said Pamela, recovering. 'Sanya's here.'

Josef frowned. Had the woman been planted by Devgeny, he wondered. He explained to Pamela that her mother was

154

with him, then connected them. He poured another drink, thoughtlessly, while they spoke, juggling the suspicion in his mind. It was possible Devgeny would try to get someone that close, he thought. He tried to recall the girl, realizing he could not properly imagine what she looked like. There was only a misty outline of a scruffy girl, who was too fat, with ragged hair. Pamela appeared to have accepted the news of her father's death with the casualness with which Lady Bellamy announced it. Gauged from one side of the conversation, they were embroiled in plans for one to visit the other, chattering with the excitement of sixth-formers planning a school outing. They were great friends, Josef realized. He wondered if Pamela would develop like her mother. Would Pamela return to Moscow, once allowed out? Perhaps. Then again, perhaps not. He took the doubt further. Did it matter? He tried to imagine it would, but found it hard to create the inner emotion. The only thought was that Pamela's departure would make him less open to attack. It was, he realized, a reaction of utter selfishness. But one of great practicality.

'She wants to speak to you,' announced Lady Bellamy, offering the receiver.

He felt inhibited by the woman's presence and his conversation was formal, embarrassed almost and he actually lowered his voice when she demanded whether he loved her. But that only came at the end of the conversation, after a long account of what a good friend Sanya had proven to be. As if she had mentioned it before, which she hadn't, as far as Josef could recollect, Pamela asked him to remind Nikolai to establish contact with the girl. It would be best, Pamela said, for Nikolai to call the flat. Sanya was usually there. Josef frowned, quite sure the author had forgotten completely about the girl. With the assurance to phone again before he left for America, Josef replaced the receiver.

'Thank you,' said Lady Bellamy. 'That was marvellous.'

Josef wondered if she were drunk. Why does everyone drink so much, he thought, reflectively. A world of uncertain people, afloat on a sea of alcohol. The idea amused him. The thought of a drunk, he concluded.

'Well,' he said, fearing another hole in the conversation and keen to bring the meeting to an end. 'I'll see what I can do about a visa.'

The woman glanced at her watch, an artificial gesture.

'I'm being dismissed,' she said, anticipating a denial.

She *was* slightly drunk, decided Josef. And she was still flirting. Poor woman. She looked at him expectantly, awaiting the contradiction. Instead, he said, 'Have you got a car?'

She seemed unsettled by his anxiety to get rid of her. He was treating her rudely, he knew.

'Yes,' she said. Perhaps realizing she had behaved badly, she straightened, trying to create a distance between them.

'Well,' she said. 'Thank you. And I'd appreciate what you could do about a visa. Either way.'

Josef thought it would be better if Pamela came to London. He did not think he would enjoy a prolonged period of Lady Bellamy. He saw her to the lift, accepting the discourtesy of not travelling to the foyer with her. The woman disconcerted him. It was almost a feeling of nervousness, he thought. It would be necessary for there always to be a barrier between them.

In Moscow, Pamela had turned from the telephone, provided with a full hour's further conversation by the call. Sanya would have heard her mention Nikolai's name. She could fabricate that part of the discussion further and ensure the Russian girl's interest. She'd have to stay now.

The lounge was empty. She glanced into the dining-room. Empty too. The bathroom, she decided, sitting down to await the girl's reappearance. It wouldn't be a lie to promise Nikolai would telephone, Pamela convinced herself. Curiously, she glanced along the passageway leading to the bathroom. Sanya was taking a long time. Finally Pamela walked lightly towards it, listening, then tried the door. It opened into a darkened room. Quickly, panicky now, she ran into the bedrooms calling the other woman's name. She returned to the lounge, arms tight at her side, striving for control.

'Damn,' she muttered aloud, furious at not hearing Sanya's departure. 'Damn, damn, damn.'

Although she tried very hard, she couldn't prevent herself crying.

Josef was surprised it was only eleven-fifteen. He thought Pamela's mother had been there much longer. It was an undesirable effect, he thought, to appear to occupy more time than one actually did. He hesitated after dictating his nightly report, then ended with the request for an exit visa for his wife.

The daily account finished, he looked around the lonely hotel suite, then stared from the window. A tug sobbed, unseen on the river. He could vaguely see the water, wandering slowly by. The Thames never seemed to be in a hurry, thought Josef. But the Moskva did. Perhaps it was anxious to get away. Along the embankment below, cars scuttled like frightened beetles, as if they were trying to escape from something. He went back into the room, glancing at the linking door, then remembered Sanya's message to Nikolai. He opened the door, listening for any sound from Nikolai. The apartment was buried in deep silence, but as he turned he saw a ruler of light beneath the bedroom door. He smiled, sympathetically, then collected sleeping tablets from his briefcase. Gently, he pushed the bedroom door open, whispering 'Nikolai' in case the author had fallen asleep with the light on. There was movement from the bed.

'Nikolai,' repeated Josef, louder. 'I've got some tablets.'

Nikolai seemed to jump under the covers, then emerged,

157

mole-like. He was staring, surprised. How white he looks, thought Josef. The negotiator smiled, extending his cupped hand.

'Pills,' he offered.

'Get out.'

It was a scream, high pitched, the sound of an animal in a trap.

'Nikolai? What ... ?'

'Get out. How dare you.'

'I only thought ... '

'You're spying on me ... '

'Nikolai, don't be stupid ... '

Josef moved towards the bed.

'Go away,' shouted Nikolai, the rejection cracking into hysteria.

Then Josef saw other movement and stopped. He felt himself blush. Oddly, the reaction embarrassed him. They stared at each other, author and negotiator. Far away, a car horn squealed. One of those scurrying beetles hadn't got away in time, thought Josef.

'Please get out,' said Nikolai. He wasn't shouting now and there was dampness in his voice.

'I ... ' started Josef, but then the other movement increased and Endelman's head came into view. He shrugged himself into a near-sitting position, then looked expressionlessly at Josef before reaching to the bedside table for a cigarette. A forced gesture, judged Josef, to cloak his nervousness.

'Bastard ... ' erupted Nikolai. He would cry soon, Josef knew.

' ... Hadn't you better hurry back?' sneered the writer. 'Won't this be something to whisper into that bloody recorder of yours, so that those fools at the Ministry can get a wet dream about it? Would you like to know what we've done ... who did what to whom ... ?'

'Stop it, Nikolai,' said Josef. It would be wrong for the man to cry, he thought.

Nikolai sat up further, so that the clothes fell away from him. He was still thin, ribs stepped out through his skin. It wasn't only his face that was white. His body was, too, almost unnaturally. Nikolai saw him looking and his control slipped further.

'Curious, Josef? Want to see more ... ?'

He tried to thrust the clothes away, but Endelman gripped the edge of the sheet, preventing it. The writer laughed, a jagged, uneven sound.

'I'm the passive one, Josef,' babbled the author. 'He does it to me ... '

'Shut up,' shouted the photographer. His hand was shaking, spilling the cigarette ash.

'Oh no,' snapped Nikolai. 'Josef's interested in sex, aren't you Josef? It's not easy for him. His wife's frightened of it. She winces when he touches her and they have long conversations about how sorry they are and how much they really love each other ... '

Endelman reached out, putting his hands upon the naked Russian's shoulders as if to physically restrain him, but Nikolai shook him away. All control and reason had gone now. The only motivation was to hurt.

'Have you made it yet, Josef? Have you finally got her to open her legs and perform her wifely duties ... ?'

'Nikolai ... ' tried Endelman, again.

'It isn't too difficult, Josef. Just feed her a little wine, like I did. And make her feel sorry for you. I cried. I really did. It was a magnificent performance. She really liked it. "Poor Nikolai," she said, when she kissed me. She cried, too, after she'd opened her legs. It was the most wonderful thing that had ever happened to her and she said so. That's the trick, Josef. Wine and sympathy. Don't ... '

Endelman hit him, swinging his arm sideways in a wide

arc, slapping the author full in the face. Sitting with no
support, he slammed backwards with such force that he
almost bounced back up again in the same sitting position.
The pain and surprise unlocked the gates and he let out a
wailing, sobbing cry.

Endelman looked up at Josef. ' ... I'm ... Oh God ... ' he
stammered. Then he said, angrily, 'Oh fuck.'

Throughout the diatribe, Josef had stayed immobile, his
face completely without expression. He felt a numbness and
then, inexplicably, the fear that had washed over him as he
and his father had been hustled through the camp gates, then
forced to stand for an hour before the other prisoners, awaiting the commandant's inspection. At last he moved, going
carefully along the furniture, opening drawers and cupboards. Both men were watching him, Nikolai through his
cupped hands into which he was sobbing. Finally, Josef got
to the bed. He hesitated, hand half forward as if touching
something contagious. He motioned Endelman away from
the pillow and looked beneath it. The bed smelt of warmth
and use and perspiration. Endelman's chest was very hairy,
like his arms, he noticed, wondering if it scratched. Josef
went around to Nikolai's side of the bed, jerking the pillow
from underneath his head. Crushed now, Nikolai edged
away, appearing frightened.

'What are you doing?' muttered Nikolai.

'He's looking for my cameras,' guessed Endelman. 'If
you were photographed in the compromising position that
you're in now, you'd be ruined.'

The photographer smiled at Josef. 'There ain't any
cameras,' he guaranteed.

The search completed, Josef turned and walked from the
room, quietly closing the door behind him. He stopped, just
inside his own suite, breathing deeply. He detected something in his hand and looked, curiously. The sleeping pills
were soggy with perspiration and disintegrating. He washed

them away in that bathroom, conscious of a growing sensation, not nausea, more like the feeling of hunger after a day without food. He began retching, but found he could not be sick. He ran water into the basin, then scooped it into his face. He walked uncertainly back into the living-room, jumping at the sight of Endelman. The photographer was wearing Nikolai's bathrobe and was barefoot. Men's feet and legs were ugly, thought Josef. It had often occurred to him in the camp, as the men shuffled around the barrack block just before lights out.

'There's no need to worry about pictures,' began Endelman.

'Oh.'

'I'm homosexual, Josef. Happily so. And so is Nikolai. It's very obvious. At least, it was to me, in Stockholm. I'm attracted to him. I wouldn't do anything to hurt him.'

He spoke in little squirts of sentences, still nervous. There was nothing Josef could say.

'You'd be disgusted if I said I was falling in love with him, wouldn't you?'

Never, thought Josef, would he be asked a more bizarre question.

'Not disgusted. Perhaps unable to understand.'

'I think I am falling in love. So there's even more reason why I wouldn't hurt him. There won't be any photographs ... not of the wrong sort, anyway ... '

Josef stayed silent.

'Don't make difficulties, will you Josef? Nikolai knows his strength. He says he'll make a scene, at the lunch and on the television show. And he'll refuse to go to America. He knows you couldn't really make him go, not if he didn't want to.'

'Another ultimatum?' said Josef, wearily. 'I accept. Or else.'

'I suppose so,' agreed Endelman, mildly. 'But don't misunderstand me. I'm not threatening you. I'm just passing on what Nikolai's said.'

Josef sat down. Endelman had a large vein on the inside of his left leg, he saw. Later it would probably become varicose and need surgery.

'It might be better,' he argued, 'if I announced an illness, cancelled the tour and went back to Russia.'

Endelman pulled the bathrobe around him and tightened the cord.

'You couldn't really, could you?' said the photographer, conversationally. The feeling of unreality hovered. 'Nikolai knows the importance to Moscow of this tour. It's pretty unusual, after all. To suddenly rush back to Russia would create just the sort of publicity you're trying to avoid.'

'True,' conceded Josef. Suddenly, he laughed. 'This is stupidly civilized,' he said.

Endelman laughed, too. 'There's no reason why we should shout, is there?'

Instead of answering, Josef said suddenly, 'I could have you killed, you know.'

'I suppose you could,' said Endelman. 'Russia would murder to protect someone as important to them as Nikolai.' He was silent for a moment. 'Will you?' he asked.

'No.'

'It wouldn't enable the tour to continue, would it?' said Endelman, realizing the decision was dictated solely for that reason.

'No,' said Josef.

A man used to balanced arguments in which he usually had the major bargaining points, Josef accepted the strength of Endelman's position. Without the photographer, Nikolai would wreck the tour. And it had to go on.

'I mean it, Josef. There'll be no scandal.'

They had about ten days to visit both London and America, assessed Josef. Perhaps after half that time, if Endelman's involvement proved dangerous, he could curtail it without the reaction that Endelman was correctly predicting. There was no compromise for which he could argue, Josef concluded. Nikolai's narcissism, surfacing like a cork on water, would too easily extend to a public revolt, he knew.

'What do you say, Josef?'

Again that smile. Everyone enjoys winning, thought Josef.

'It's "yes", isn't it?' conceded the negotiator.

Endelman's smile broadened.

'Good,' he said. The photographer put out his hand. Josef looked at it, then up into the photographer's face.

'Don't be ridiculous,' rejected the Russian.

'Oh,' said Endelman.

'I've no other choice,' said Josef. 'If there were one, even if it meant some physical harm to you, I would take it, without the slightest hesitation. I don't like being beaten. So be very careful. I can't allow this tour to break down yet. But as each day passes, your threat diminishes. I'd rather have the conjecture stories than I would have the filth to get out.'

'I've given you my assurance ... ' broke in Endelman.

'Let me give you one,' cut off the negotiator. 'If you cause me the slightest harm, then I'll hurt you. I'll hurt you physically or materially. Or maybe both.'

'You're not a very nice person, are you Josef?'

The negotiator considered the question for a moment.

'No,' he admitted. 'No, I'm not.'

Josef threw the pause up, preparing the jibe like a conjuror flourishes his cape before a trick.

'Shouldn't you go back? I expect Nikolai will be waiting.'

Endelman smiled and shook his head sadly and Josef wished he hadn't said it.

'There's another thing,' said Endelman, remaining seated. Josef waited, questioningly.

'It was a lie about your wife. Nikolai was just trying to

163

hurt you ... he was saying the first thing that came into his
head ... the worst thing he could think of ... '

Perhaps Endelman had some kindness, considered Josef.
'Oh,' he said.

'Honestly. Nikolai regrets it now. He'll apologize,
tomorrow ... '

'It's not necessary,' said Josef.

'Oh it is. It was an awful thing to say ... '

'Yes,' agreed Josef, softly. 'It was. Unfortunately, it was
true.'

The full Praesidium had listened intently to everything that
Devgeny had said. Frequently he had paused, for argument,
but nobody had offered any. It was going well, the Minister
thought. He paused now, building up for the moment of
his final remark.

'I think,' he said, gauging the moment. 'It can be judged
as absolutely appalling.'

He sat down, looking for reaction. Everyone seemed to
be awaiting response from somebody else.

'Not quite,' tried Illinivitch. 'Certainly things have been
bad. But the only public criticism came from the initial press-
conference. Since then all the comment has been pretty
favourable.'

Devgeny bridled at the challenge.

'That drunken scene at the Stockholm reception was
witnessed by dozens of people,' retorted the Minister, quickly.
He shuffled through a file, extracting a report. 'It clearly
states here that Balshev was at one time dropping glasses
and behaving stupidly close to a large number of journalists
and that Bultova was nowhere to be seen ... '

'But no damage was caused,' insisted Illinivitch.

'How much longer do you think Balshev can go on being
permitted to behave as he is doing without it becoming
public knowledge?' demanded Devgeny.

No one took up the question and Illinivitch began reading the papers spread before him. Devgeny smiled, triumphantly. When he returned to his office, Devgeny considered again Josef's recording that had arrived that morning. Because of Josef's current work Devgeny had insisted that every decision concerning the man should be made by him and not allowed to dissipate through other Ministries. Complete control was important because victory had to be absolute. He listened several times to that part of the tape in which the negotiator sought exit permission for his wife, reminding the authorities that with a British passport, all she needed was the assurance of re-entry. Alongside was the written application from Lady Bellamy to visit the Soviet Union in the event of her daughter being unable to leave, together with the embassy confirmation of Sir Hudson's death that Josef had mentioned.

So Bultova wanted to get his wife out of the Soviet Union at the same time as himself, thought the Minister. He laughed at the naïvety of it. He would have expected something more subtle from the man. Quickly he dictated a refusal to guarantee Pamela's re-entry, then another memorandum refusing Lady Bellamy a visa. He poured a celebration vodka, considered the measure, then added to the glass. It would be very soon now, he told himself. Very soon.

Chapter Sixteen

The Foyle's luncheon was an overwhelming success, insisted Stanswell. Rarely could he remember an author having greater impact than Nikolai. The young Russian almost bubbled with effervescent confidence, which surprised Josef slightly. He hadn't detected any more pills missing.

Nikolai and Endelman had shopped that morning. Begrudgingly, which Josef realized was becoming a constant attitude of mind, he admitted that even though ready-made, the suits were better than those Nikolai had brought from Russia. Before changing for the lunch, Nikolai had showered. It was the second time that morning, Josef had noted.

At their first meeting the following morning, they had stared at him, barely concealing their apprehension that he would pick up the argument. They are not as confident as they pretend, thought Josef. He said nothing, which actually appeared to increase their discomfort. During the morning and then at the meal, Josef had been tense, alert for any overt campness between them. Neither made the slightest movement that could have aroused suspicion.

In the afternoon, there was a publicists' picture session, which Nikolai enjoyed with his growing delight in being photographed, and in the evening a dinner in the private boardroom of the *Sunday Times*, which was carrying a profile of the author in their Sunday colour supplement. Lord Snowdon took the pictures, after the publicity session. Nikolai presented him with an autographed copy of *Walk Softly on a Lonely Day*, a gesture that had surprised Josef.

'Thank you,' he said later, to Endelman, knowing the idea would never have occurred to Nikolai.

Endelman had shrugged. 'I realized you have a lot of things on your mind and might not have thought of it.'

Slowly, realized Josef, his self-assurance was being worn away, like a piece of marble eroded by the tiny, continuous irritation of water. Just as the lunch had been successful, so it was impossible to fault Nikolai's behaviour at the dinner. With prompting from Endelman, he even managed to make a speech of thanks in rusted English.

'Another of your ideas?' asked Josef, as they were going home.

Endelman nodded. 'I thought it would be appreciated,' said the photographer, deprecating as usual.

Nikolai and Endelman walked almost challengingly along the corridor leading to their suites, paused, and then both entered Nikolai's rooms. Nearly inside, they paused as if on cue.

'Good night,' they said, in unison.

'Good night,' said Josef, very controlled. He heard them sniggering as the door closed.

Alone in his rooms, Josef poured a brandy and sat in front of the window, staring out at the Shell building. It was quiet from the adjoining suite. Embarrassingly, he realized he was straining to catch sounds, like a Peeping Tom.

He felt hollowed out and expended, like an old man at the departure of a busy life facing years of empty retirement. Apart from the negotiations over the film contract, he had nothing to do. The negotiator wondered if either Nikolai or Endelman had thought deeply about the shortness of their relationship. In a fortnight's time, maybe less, it would be over. And when that moment came, Nikolai would be monumentally difficult to control, decided Josef, accepting that his retirement would be short. His mind slipped sideways. Had he and Pamela ever been as happy as they appeared, he wondered, laughing at private jokes, anticipating each other, anxious to be the first in some expression of tenderness? Perhaps, he decided. Perhaps in the very beginning, during the courtship or in the early days, at the dacha. Immediately, the contradiction came. It hadn't been the same. The attitude between him and Pamela had been politeness, an anxiousness not to offend, like casual acquaintances eager to impress each other. Suddenly Josef tried to engender some emotion, tears or anger or hatred for what had occurred between Nikolai and Pamela. There were no tears, of course. They had all been used up years ago, before he had forged the impenetrable compartments in which he housed all emotion. Certainly there was anger, but not the feeling of a husband betrayed, but of a man made to look ridiculous. He would have felt exactly the same, he was sure, had he suddenly realized at the Foyle's lunch that the zip on his fly had been undone and that people were laughing. He groped for hatred. That would be the logical reaction, he accepted. Against Nikolai. And against Pamela. The feeling of hollowness, a vacuum in which nothing lived, was the only emotion. And that, he knew, wasn't an emotion. That was just emptiness.

It took only minutes to dictate the nightly report. An account of complete and genuine success, he reflected. Moscow should be impressed by the coverage planned by the *Sunday Times*. He took another brandy to the bedside table, swallowed three sleeping tablets, ignoring the danger of mixing them with alcohol. He noted the dosage on the pad, so that he would have a reminder if he awakened and then lay waiting for unconsciousness to come.

Lady Bellamy was summoned to the family lawyer's office a fortnight after her husband's death. The solicitor, Henry Pottinger, had acted for Harry for twenty years and didn't like her, she knew. His unsympathetic voice was dry and brittle, like twigs crackling underfoot in June.

'This is a little unorthodox,' he announced, as she sat down. 'But I'm afraid your husband made an unusual will.'

Pottinger must have been aware of their marital difficulties, she thought. He would have had to draw up the allowances for Harry's other women.

'Your husband was a rich man, an extraordinarily rich man ... ' he began.

'How much did he leave me?' she asked, shortly. There was no point in protracting the meeting.

'Nothing,' announced the lawyer. 'Three other women get it.'

Lady Bellamy laughed openly. 'Oh, the bastard,' she said. 'He really did hate, didn't he?'

'I'm afraid he did,' agreed Pottinger.

'How sad it must have made him,' reflected the woman. 'That he couldn't be around for all the publicity. He liked publicity.'

'I suppose you could challenge it,' offered Pottinger. He was still loyal, realized Lady Bellamy. The interview wasn't dictated by kindness. The man wanted to know if there would be a fight over the estate.

'Challenging the will would only involve unnecessary legal costs and put off the inevitable publication of Harry's opinion of me,' she said, realistically. 'A court case would be too dirty.'

'So you definitely won't challenge it?' he confirmed, relieved.

'No,' she said. She wondered if her Moscow visa would arrive in time for her to be out of the country. She'd have to hide somewhere.

'There's another thing,' said the lawyer. He shuffled papers, wedging half-rimmed spectacles on his nose. She could never understand why men wore such ridiculous glasses.

'The will ends,' he read out, ' "And to my daughter,

Pamela, whom I love and whom, through stupidity, I wronged, I leave two hundred thousand pounds in the hope that I can bring her more happiness in death than I brought her in life. And, now dead, I seek from her the forgiveness I could never ask when alive." '

Pottinger looked over his spectacles. 'It's in a trust fund,' he added, helpfully, a man of detail. 'Set up years ago. The money's very safe from duty.'

For a moment, the lawyer thought the woman was going to cry. She swallowed several times and the first attempt to speak failed.

'Hate is such a stupid thing,' she said, finally.

Chapter Seventeen

The television recording went perfectly, as Nikolai's public appearances increasingly seemed to. The author appeared completely confident and indulged in the affectation of stumbling replies in English, to the delight of the interviewer. They regarded it as something of a coup getting Josef on the same programme and the interviewer was awed by his legend and consequently the questions were soft and unabrasive. Moscow could only be pleased, Josef had decided. It seemed a recurring thought. Always, there was a desperate hope associated with it.

The negotiator entered the hospitality suite relaxed, escorted by the producer, Harriet Brindley, a bolster-bosomed woman wearing an ill-advised trouser-suit, given to smoking small cigars and trying to impress people with her outrageousness, which she practised assiduously.

'Magnificent,' she judged, handing Josef a whisky. She, like the interviewer, was impressed at Josef's reputation, laughing nervously at the end of sentences, agreeing too readily with his half-expressed opinions.

'You think it went well then?' queried Josef, politely.

'Undoubtedly.'

Nikolai and Endelman were in the centre of a small group of people across the room. The author was embarrassingly patronizing in his over-politeness to everyone, thought Josef. The interviewer, a carrot-headed young man whose name Josef had half heard as Deakon was braying with nervous laughter, shoulders jerking at whatever Nikolai said. Josef felt sorry for the man.

'I see it's caught on in your country, too,' said the woman. She grabbed two more glasses from a passing tray and handed one to Josef.

'I'm sorry?'

The producer nodded towards the laughing group.

'Grass,' she said.

As Josef looked across, he caught the eye of both Nikolai and Endelman. Very slowly, Nikolai took a cigarette to his lips and Josef saw that it was crumpled and badly made. As he withdrew the cigarette, Nikolai gave a small wave and he and Endelman laughed. Endelman shrugged a 'don't blame me' gesture. Harriet talked on, unaware of the shock effect of her announcement.

'I think it should be legalized, for Christ's sake,' she continued, with the vehemence of liberalism. 'A bloody sight more harm is done by booze than by a little harmless pot. Cheers.'

'Quite,' said Josef, recovering. 'Good health.'

The bastards, the arrogant, conceited bastards, he thought. Another challenge. He wondered if, drug-fogged, they would flaunt their homosexuality. It had been a long time since anyone had dared laugh at him.

'There's no medical danger, you know,' insisted the woman. Two weeks before she had had a forum of free-thinking doctors on her programme.

'So they say,' replied Josef. He wanted to end the boring party and get them both away before they made some noticeable mistake.

'Is he queer?'

The question was like a cold hand reaching deeply into Josef's stomach. He turned to the woman, subduing the panic. Her perfume was being defeated by body odour.

'What an odd question,' avoided Josef. 'Why do you ask?'

There must have been some gesture he had missed. Or maybe a remark when he was concentrating upon the interviewer. What was his name? He'd forgotten.

'No reason,' shrugged Harriet, dismissively. 'Deakon is, that's all. I thought it might be a mutual attraction. They seem to have some way of spotting each other. And he seems pretty taken with Nikolai.'

'I think he's just impressed,' tried Josef, desperately. 'Deakon is young. I shouldn't imagine he's met a Nobel prizewinner before.'

Josef found her habit of uttering disconcerting remarks irritating. He had to get over to the group.

'Shouldn't we join the others?' he said. He couldn't afford rudeness. The recording could still be edited, he realized, into a harmful programme. 'Nikolai might need some assistance. His English still isn't that good,' he added, with forced innocence. The bastards, laughing at him. The group opened at their approach and Nikolai smiled.

'My mentor,' said the author, showing off his new English word. Everyone smiled and Josef wondered if Nikolai had shared their joke against him. The author seemed alert and in complete control of himself. No one was smoking now and there was no evidence of any stubs. Josef presumed they had been pocketed.

'We must go soon,' said Josef.

Nikolai sniggered.

'Why, Josef?' he replied, the Russian so rapid that even Endelman would have had difficulty in following. 'Frightened I might make a scene?'

'Stop it Nikolai,' warned Josef, at the same speed. 'I won't be made to look a fool.'

'But the role fits you so well, Josef.'

'Come now,' interposed Deakon. 'No one can understand a word.'

The interviewer moved his hands about a lot when he spoke, and Josef saw his nails were coated with clear varnish.

'Forgive us,' he apologized, reverting to English.

173

'Jeremy has invited us to a party,' announced Endelman indicating the interviewer.

'We're going,' confirmed Nikolai. There was an edge of defiance in his voice.

'It will be all right if other people come, won't it?' asked Josef.

The interviewer and the producer both misunderstood. Harriet smiled, hopefully, and Deakon, imagining the arrival at a party with a Nobel prizewinner and Josef Bultova, beamed.

'Of course,' he said. 'I was going to invite you ... '

'Two people from the embassy,' enlarged Josef. He saw Endelman bending towards the author.

'Oh,' said the interviewer, deflated. The woman buried her face in her whisky glass.

'No,' said Nikolai. He spoke in English.

'Then you don't go,' replied Josef, in Russian.

Nikolai reverted, too, his English no match for his anger.

'I will not be treated like a child,' he said, falling back on a familiar protest. 'I'm going.'

'And two attachés will go with you.'

'I don't want them. It's not going to be that sort of a party.'

'Are you out of your mind? Do you think I'm going to let you loose among a load of homosexuals? For Christ's sake, Nikolai, start behaving sensibly.'

'I'll make a scene,' pouted the writer.

'Go ahead,' invited Josef. 'And I'll slap you, like the child you are. And the whole room ... and Endelman, the person you are trying to impress with your independence, can witness the weeping collapse of the great Nikolai Balshev, a Nobel prizewinner and fool.'

'Don't talk to me like that.'

Josef just stared at him.

'You wouldn't dare hit me, not in a TV studio,' protested Nikolai.

'Because of the publicity? Don't be stupid, Nikolai. They want the interview they have got, not a scandal. I'd insist on walking from here with the film they've just shot. Remember, I reserved the right to censor anything I didn't like. To prevent losing their film, they'd overlook a tantrum.'

'I don't believe you.'

'Try it.'

The tension stretched between them, ready to break. It engulfed the others in the room, like a January draught through an ill-fitting door.

'I can't get out of it now,' said Nikolai and Josef relaxed slightly.

'I can make an excuse.'

'Everybody knows we've had a row.'

'These sort of people live on rows. It seems natural to them.'

Sure of himself now, Josef turned back to the interviewer. 'I'm sorry,' he said. 'Nikolai had forgotten there are other things to do before we leave for America tomorrow. I'm afraid we're going to have to turn down your invitation.'

Deakon shrugged, smiling wryly.

'So you won,' he said, resigned.

'Yes,' said Josef. Why not admit it? It couldn't cause any harm. Regaining control gave him a twinge of satisfaction.

Deakon looked at Endelman, who sighed.

'Sorry,' said the photographer. 'We'd have enjoyed it. It's too bad.'

The embassy car was waiting for them and initially no one spoke. Nikolai sat between them in the vehicle and Josef was conscious of the author pulling away, trying to avoid physical contact.

'You made me look a fool,' complained Nikolai, again. 'So I tried marijuana. Is that a crime?'

'Leave it alone, Nikolai,' said Endelman. 'Josef is angry with us.'

The author sniggered at the mockery. They refused to be unsettled by the silence, whispering and even giggling to themselves.

'My room,' Josef announced, as they exited from the lift on the fourth floor. He glanced at the note Reception had handed him as he collected his key. The embassy wanted him. Not as much as he wanted them, he thought.

'Splendid,' jibed Nikolai. 'Josef's got a lovely cocktail cabinet. We can all have lots to drink. Drink isn't harmful, is it Josef? It's only drugs you are frightened of.'

He hurried ahead and Josef was reminded of a court jester, skipping to the crowd. Jesters were sad people, he thought. Inside the suite, Nikolai continued to attempt command, pouring and serving drinks with polite bows. They were still laughing, decided Josef.

'How long does the charade go on?' he inquired, trying to project the weariness into his voice.

'Josef's bored!' exclaimed Nikolai to Endelman, and then swinging back to the negotiator. 'Are you bored, Josef? Oh dear.'

Endelman was sitting rigid-faced, refusing to react to Nikolai's prompting.

'Stop it, Nikolai,' said Josef. 'It's finished.'

The writer dropped into a chair, then leaned forward, his elbows on his knees, head in his hands, like an eager pupil listening to his teacher. The ridicule was very practised, thought Josef.

'Josef is making threats,' narrated the writer. 'It's so silly, Josef. You know that. You were lucky tonight that I didn't want to go to that fool's party. Don't think you're in control again.'

Josef put aside his glass, untouched.

'I made it quite clear to both of you,' he began. 'That I could never allow anything that could publicly endanger this tour ... '

He nodded towards Endelman, then continued talking as if he were not in the room.

'Endelman was a mistake,' he said. 'The Ministry approved it, but I should have argued. I was always unhappy at the suggestion. There was something odd about it … '

'Josef is justifying himself,' jeered Nikolai.

'It was even more stupid for me to have done nothing when I found you in bed together.'

'Were you frightened, Josef … of what I would do? Is that why you wouldn't act?'

Again Josef ignored him.

'Tonight everyone in that bloody room except me knew you were smoking marijuana.'

'Poor Josef. He's upset because he's too unsophisticated to realize what's happening,' prodded the writer.

'The woman even guessed you were homosexual,' he said.

'So what?' dismissed Nikolai. 'I don't see it's anything to be ashamed of.'

Josef sighed, tired of the author's baiting.

'Be quiet, Nikolai,' he said, contemptuously. 'It's stopping, now. From this moment, I'm resuming control. You'll do as I say.'

Again he nodded towards the photographer.

'He's going,' he announced. 'Tonight. He's either going properly, by himself, or I'll get people from the embassy to throw him out.'

Nikolai tried to speak, but Josef waved him to silence.

'There'll be no scene,' he predicted. 'It will all be done in a very calm manner.'

For the first time, he addressed Endelman directly.

'Do you remember what I told you, when you came to my room after I found you together?'

The photographer nodded.

'I meant it,' said the negotiator. 'In fact, I would quite enjoy the thought of you getting hurt.'

'Have you finished?' asked Nikolai. The banter had gone from his voice. He was staring directly across the room and Josef knew it was the moment of complete challenge.

'It *is* over, Josef,' said Nikolai, picking up the negotiator's expression. He paused, sipping from his drink. He didn't need it for courage, realized Josef, but to extend his enjoyment of what was happening.

'I've tolerated you, Josef,' he started again. 'I've tolerated you because I needed your experience and your guidance. But I told you in Stockholm what your role was to be.'

Josef sat without any feeling. The victor of this encounter would be in charge for the remainder of the tour, he knew. Nikolai, after another sip, was speaking again.

'From now on, Josef, your only function will be to see everything goes smoothly. I will do what I like, with whom I like. I've resented every moment of your overbearing arrogance, every rebuke you've ever given me. I've counted every slap ... '

He smiled, pleased at the look on Josef's face.

'I know just why I've been allowed to come out of Russia. I know I'm a performing monkey, impressing other countries that Russia can have artists as well as square-shaped men in uniform. I know how frightened everyone is that something will go wrong. And I know just how powerful that makes me.'

He stopped, unable to avoid the smirk. He knew Josef was worried.

'If I want pills, then Jimmy will get them for me. If I want grass, he'll get that for me too. Just like he'll get anything else.'

Josef rose to the invitation, realizing too late that it had been manufactured.

'Anything else?'

'Marijuana is quite tame, really,' said Nikolai. 'I like horse much better.'

Josef turned to Endelman, for explanation.

'He wanted heroin ... to try it and see what it was like. He said he wanted every experience ... ' muttered the photographer.

'You mean ... ?'

Endelman shook his head. 'He smoked it, that's all.'

Josef reflected on the incongruity of the sentence, then said, 'I thought you cared for him.'

'You don't understand ... ' began the photographer, but Nikolai gestured him to silence, determined not to sacrifice the stage.

'Really, Josef, I've rarely known anyone more unaware of what's going on around them. Tonight isn't the first time that Jimmy's been told he can get out. I told him, days ago. He might love me. I never said I loved him. He, like you, stays because he's useful. He's as efficient in some things as you are in others.'

Josef shook his head in disbelief.

'I'm a genius, Josef. That's what everyone keeps saying. No one expects normal behaviour from a genius.'

Josef realized that Endelman was weeping and felt contempt for the man. Medev had cried a lot, he remembered. And so had his father, in the end. But each had good reason.

'So there it is,' concluded Nikolai. 'Without me, there is no triumphal tour for the mighty Soviet Union. So from now on, it goes completely as I direct.'

He drank deeply and the liquor caught his breath. He almost choked. Josef waited, hopefully, but the writer recovered. There was no sound in the room now except Endelman crying.

'Well?' demanded Nikolai.

The transition was remarkable, Josef conceded. Could it only be a few months ago that he had been the shy, stumbling person at the dacha, preferring the loneliness of an insect-veiled lake to contact with even two people.

'It was a good try, Nikolai,' he said, evenly. 'I admire your sudden courage. Strangely, I even think it's genuine. Even in those early days, at the dacha, I knew you were hiding some aspect of your personality, but I never guessed it would emerge like this ... '

The writer was frowning at him, apprehensively. He had anticipated a different reaction. Endelman had stopped crying and was looking, too.

'Endelman goes tonight,' reiterated Josef. 'If you want to destroy yourself, you'll do it in the Soviet Union, not here or in America, where the whole world can see. I'm cancelling the rest of the visit. We're going back to Russia, tomorrow.'

Nikolai shook his head, but the smile was fading.

'You won't do that, Josef.'

'I will,' pledged the negotiator.

He went to the bureau and telephoned Listnisky, but before he could speak, the ambassador began talking, explaining the difficulty of contacting Josef earlier. The American President was giving a reception specifically in honour of Nikolai Balshev in four days. Moscow was delighted and Peking was furious. So enthusiastic were the Praesidium that someone from the Ministry of Culture was flying to Washington to attend.

'What's his name?' asked Josef. He felt so tired. It was like a weight, pressing down.

'Illinivitch,' replied Listnisky. 'Do you know him?'

'Yes,' said Josef.

'Marvellous, isn't it?'

'Yes.'

'What did you want me for?'

'Nothing,' said Josef. 'Forget it.'

From the conversation, Nikolai knew Josef had not carried out his threat. He smiled, waiting for Josef to capitulate.

'You'd better get to bed,' said Josef, looking straight at him. 'We've got a long flight tomorrow.'

Neither moved.

'Both of you,' added Josef, in final defeat.

Chapter Eighteen

New York was the ordeal Josef had feared. The Russian suffered badly from jet lag and the numbed, cotton-wool feeling was washing over him as the aircraft taxied into the arrival pier at Kennedy Airport. Endelman and Nikolai had consciously ignored him throughout the flight. He had been relegated to the role of organizer and they acted out their private game and accorded him the politeness of a servant. Josef had endured it, content that neither seemed anxious to draw attention to themselves. Apart from snide criticism of the in-flight film, they had behaved perfectly, spending most of their time playing chess on a pocket set that Endelman had produced.

The Russian delegation to the United Nations was waiting, headed by Valery Semyonov, the ambassador. A Devgeny man, Josef knew, who would be a constant threat. The Russians carried the traditional bouquets, which Nikolai and Endelman greeted with laughter.

Semyonov frowned.

'Welcome,' he said.

Josef nodded. The photographers were backing away before them as they walked down the finger towards the huge lounge in which Blyne had arranged the first press-conference.

'How has it gone?' asked Semyonov, pointedly.

'Well, I think,' replied Josef.

'Oh.' The ambassador's reaction conveyed doubt. 'Moscow seemed a little surprised you weren't staying at the mission,' continued Semyonov. 'There's plenty of room at East 67th Street.'

The refusal had been another demonstration of Nikolai's independence.

'The whole point of the trip is exposure,' responded Josef. 'We thought the Pierre would be more convenient.'

'And much more luxurious. You enjoy luxury, don't you, Comrade Bultova.'

'Yes,' agreed Josef, annoyed at the man's posturing. He felt incapable of mental finger-wrestling.

'We've arranged a reception for tomorrow night,' said the ambassador. 'At the United Nations. I hope you'll be able to fit it in with the other more important arrangements.'

'I'm sorry the arrival of Russia's Nobel prizewinner is such a chore for you,' said Josef. 'I'll rebuke Moscow when I get back, so they can avoid troubling you in future with such triviality.'

Semyonov jerked round, but Blyne gushed out to greet them, smothering the ambassador's reply. The room was banked with television- and film-lights and crowded with people and noise. The conference became the longest they had had to endure, but Nikolai was used to them now, replying with growing frequency in English. Rarely did he bother to consult Josef. The conceit before a camera or television lens was almost embarrassing, thought Josef. The questions, as always, ranged from the intelligent to the ridiculous, but there were no probes about his involvement and Josef knew that Semyonov, who stayed pressed against the wall, near the entrance, would be unable to select anything incriminating from it.

Josef was saddened by the visible neglect of New York as they drove into the city. The snow had been churned to slush and tiny mountains of grime were massed around the bases of the office and apartment blocks, so that skyscrapers stood with dirty knickers around their ankles.

Favoured interviewers were allowed to travel with them in the cavalcade of hearse-like Cadillacs, so that it was not until they reached the Pierre that Josef had the chance of any real conversation with the American publisher.

He needed help, Josef accepted. It was impossible from Semyonov, from whom he had parted at the airport with frosted promises of later contact. Any revealed weakness would be played back immediately to Devgeny. So that only left Blyne. The publisher bustled through the connecting door from Nikolai's rooms, still crammed with photographers, his face rutted with smiles.

'Marvellous,' he enthused. 'Absolutely fucking marvellous. What about the President's reception? Would you have guessed? Would you have believed it was going to be like this? I tell you, this is going to be mammoth, just mammoth.'

Josef looked into Nikolai's suite. The writer was twisting and posing for the cameras. Just like a model, thought Josef, a female model. Endelman stood sulkily in the background.

'You don't look like the guy that's pulled off the coup of the century,' said Blyne, carelessly.

'This trip', warned Josef, slowly, 'has every likelihood of collapsing into an unmitigated disaster.'

Blyne, who in his excitement had been wandering the sitting-room, unable to keep still, stopped and frowned.

'Did you know Endelman was homosexual when you wrote that letter of introduction?' demanded Josef.

Blyne humped his shoulders, uncaringly. 'You know how it is with these guys,' he dismissed. 'They swing one way, then another. So what?'

'So now Nikolai is doing it that way, that's what. And he's smoking marijuana and heroin and stuffing Christ knows what pills down his throat. He got that from Endelman, too. In London, yesterday, I decided to cancel this part of the tour completely and get straight back to Russia. I'm here solely because of the Presidential reception.'

'You can't be serious.'

'You know damned well I'm serious.'

'Shit.'

'And for God's sake stop swearing like a schoolboy whistling in the dark,' snapped Josef.

Blyne's nervous hands moved, as if he were trying to shape words out of the air.

'That's not all,' enlarged Josef. 'Nikolai knows how important he is. He's treating me like dirt. And Endelman only stays because he's good in bed and supplies the drugs.'

Blyne sat down, the exuberance leaking from him.

'It can't be that bad ... ' he began, but Josef stopped him.

'I'm terrified,' he said, honestly.

Blyne made more hand movements. 'But what can we do?'

'I wish to God I knew,' replied the Russian.

An American whom Josef recalled seeing heavily involved in the airport press-conference came through the linking doors and smiled, innocently.

'Isn't it great, Herbie?' he said.

Josef stared at him, then looked to Blyne for an explanation.

'This is Matheson,' introduced the publisher. 'Harvey Matheson ... speaks Russian ... edited Nikolai's book.'

Josef nodded, still looking to Blyne for guidance.

'We're on the same side, for Christ's sake. We're going to need help,' said the publisher.

He had stopped swearing, Josef noticed. He was glad. He found the habit irritating, as his father had. Medev had never sworn, he recalled. The Jew had been a very unusual man.

Matheson looked questioningly from one to the other. He was very slim and fair. And young, not much more than twenty-eight, judged Josef. Yale, decided the Russian, or maybe Harvard, bought into the publishing house by parental money or influence. Or both.

'Nikolai is a fag,' explained Blyne, quickly. 'He and Jimmy are daisy-chaining together. He's also into drugs. And if we're not careful, this whole thing is going to come around our ears.'

The young American looked over his shoulder, to where Endelman was now dispensing drinks and then back to Blyne.

'So what do we do?' he asked, immediately. Josef looked at Matheson approvingly. He had accepted the difficulty without any of the artificial surprise to which Blyne seemed prone.

Josef shrugged. 'Stay with him pretty closely,' he said, talking as the thoughts came to him. 'Try and anticipate the scenes before they develop. He likes attracting attention. If anything goes wrong, he'll react like a petulant child.'

'And I thought this would be perfect,' reflected Blyne, bitterly. Matheson wouldn't have said that, thought Josef.

'What about the studio?' asked Josef.

'I've arranged meetings later this afternoon,' said Blyne.

'What will happen to Nikolai?' asked Josef. It was too soon for negotiating, he thought. He should have given himself time to recover from the flight.

'I thought he'd be tired ... getting over the flight,' offered Blyne, uncertainly.

'I can't leave him alone,' said Josef, simply.

'They've flown in from the West Coast,' urged Blyne, imagining the Russian was going to cancel the appointment. 'The director has even come from Europe.'

'I could stay with them,' suggested Matheson. 'Maybe go to P.J.'s or Elaine's, do the tourist bit. It would keep them occupied until you're through.'

Josef shook his head, reluctantly. He was so exhausted that words were slipping away from him, like fish he could see in a stream but not catch. He kept pausing, groping to express himself.

'I don't like it,' he said.

'Look,' said Blyne. 'You won't be away more than a couple of hours.'

'It could only take minutes to foul up completely,' argued the negotiator.

'If you act frightened, they'll realize it and try to make it worse,' reasoned Matheson. 'You're the audience they are playing to.'

He really was intelligent, thought Josef ...

'What do you think?' he asked Blyne. The oddness of the question immediately registered. He tried to remember the last time he had asked anyone's advice. It had been Medev, he recalled, during those first weeks in the camp, when he was trying to save his father as much hardship as possible.

'Seems logical,' said Blyne.

'Josef!'

Blyne and Matheson turned to the negotiator at the shouted demand from the adjoining suite.

'Come and watch the cabaret,' invited Josef.

He pushed into the other rooms. The photographers had gone, leaving Nikolai and Endelman alone. Endelman was staring out over the grey, snow-wrapped view of Manhattan, his back to the room.

'Have you properly met Herbert Blyne, who's publishing the book here? And Harvey Matheson, who edited the American edition?' began Josef, politely.

'Edited?' picked up the writer, ignoring Blyne and looking at the younger man. 'My books don't need editing.'

'I agree,' said Matheson, in flawless Russian. 'It was the easiest thing I ever had to do.'

Endelman looked crumpled and tired, thought Josef, without his customary elegance.

'I have to see some film people this afternoon,' Josef said to Nikolai.

'I'll want to approve the script,' said Nikolai, immediately.

187

Everyone knew the writer's complete ignorance of film making.

'Of course. Whatever you say.'

He saw Blyne frowning. He was unsure whether the publisher's expression came from his own easy acquiescence or Nikolai's arrogance.

'You,' said Nikolai, to the publisher, who jumped at being addressed. 'What other arrangements are there?'

'Nothing for this evening,' replied Blyne. He was having difficulty controlling himself, thought Josef. 'Tomorrow there's a breakfast meeting at the Algonquin with the *New York Times*. You've got lunch with the editors of *Kirkus Reviews* and *Publishers' Weekly* and in the afternoon a publicity tour, a taped television show and two recorded radio pieces. In the evening, there's the reception at the United Nations.'

Nikolai nodded. Josef wondered if the writer would risk making himself look ridiculous by challenging the schedule, as he had the film, but he said nothing. Matheson seemed embarrassed by the performance.

'I'm sure you're not tired,' opened the young man, directly addressing Nikolai.

'Of course not,' rejected Nikolai, a predictable reaction. He turned to Endelman. 'We have ways of staying awake, don't we Jimmy?'

The photographer remained looking out of the window.

'Good,' said Matheson. 'While Josef is with the film people, I thought we might look at New York. See a few of the bars.'

'I'd like that,' said Nikolai. He reverted to Russian, but spoke slowly, so that Endelman could understand. To Matheson, he said, 'It would make a pleasant change to be with people whose company doesn't promise to be un-utterably boring.'

The writer pouted in theatrical campness and Blyne stared in disbelief. Endelman had turned and looked at the writer sadly.

'Bring your camera,' Nikolai ordered Endelman. 'I want some pictures of myself around New York.'

He turned to Josef. 'Be here when I get back, won't you?' he commanded.

The trio swept out and Blyne stared after them. The publisher laughed, an empty sound.

'It's got to be a joke,' he said.

'I wish it were,' said Josef. 'If it weren't so serious, it would be pitiful.'

'Jesus H. Christ,' moaned the publisher. He sat on the arm of a chair, shaking his head. 'Have you told your people what's happened?'

'No.'

'Shouldn't you?'

'What good will it do?' asked the negotiator.

'They might decide, even now, to take him back.'

'Not when they've sent the deputy Minister of Culture to attend a Presidential reception.'

'If it's any consolation,' said Blyne, smiling reluctantly. 'The book is breaking records. I don't think there's been a seller like it.'

Josef looked unimpressed. 'There isn't any consolation left on this trip,' he said, bitterly.

He was too tired for film meetings. Fatigue kept snatching at him, insistently. Increasingly, his concentration had wavered as he talked to Blyne, so that the words ebbed and flowed. He showered and still felt exhausted. Reluctantly, he opened the briefcase and stood examining the neat rows of bottles. He had always disdained their help in direct negotiations, carrying them only for insurance. Apart from his fear of dependence, it would be like cheating himself, admitting a weakness, and Josef always hesitated to concede any weakness. He selected a phial of benzedrine. Today was an exception, he thought. It would be impossible without them.

The company had taken a conference suite two floors

above his. They were already assembled when he entered, and Josef paused, just inside the door, staring round. It was artificial, he thought. People were arranged around the room and at tables and on easy chairs as they might have been rehearsed for a film-set. Smiling, he moved further into the room and the man around whom everyone else was placed stood in greeting. Josef decided that Richard Watts looked more like an accountant, which he probably was, than a film-company president. He was a thin, short man, with rimless spectacles and a small, clipped moustache. The appearance was calculated, Josef thought. As the man carefully enunciated the introductions, Josef realized that he practised the affectation of the very powerful, showing over-deference to everyone. Josef felt he was being patronized, but was unoffended. He never objected to discussions with people who felt the need to portray imagined roles. The director, who sat immediately on Watts's right side, was Sheldon Burgess, a fleshy man with a sagging, American stomach and a monk's cap of hair. The stomach, Josef knew, was misleading. Burgess had worked for fifteen years in Europe after being blacked by every Hollywood studio for refusing to testify before the House Un-American Activities Committee. From Rome he had won two Academy Awards, was under nomination for a third and was now making American film companies pay for his exile by demanding three times what any other working director was being paid. Josef supposed he should feel an affinity with the man. He didn't.

The Vice-President was introduced as William Wasnet, a tight-faced, watchful man, for whom Josef felt a hint of recognition. Normally, thought Josef, Wasnet, who was head of production, would conduct such negotiations rather than be a witness. Another studio vice-president and chief lawyer, Edward Artman, sat with a file of documents on his lap and a gold pen in his hand, as if it gave him identification from the others. The remaining people, who because they either sat or stood apart from the inner caucus Josef presumed were of lesser importance, were identified only by name, without any titles. Josef disregarded them, as he knew Watts intended.

'It's a wonderful book, Mr Bultova. A great book,' began Watts. Behind him, the chorus nodded and smiled agreement. It was sad, thought Josef.

'I'd like very much to film it,' added Burgess, as if the President's views needed endorsement. Burgess had a small voice for a man of his size and seemed embarrassed by it. His hand fluttered around his mouth when he spoke, as if to disguise the source of the sound.

Outside it was getting dark. Lights on several skyscrapers were being left on, Josef saw, so that they made the shape of a Christmas tree. Belated doubts at allowing Nikolai out into New York in Matheson's charge began to tug at him.

'My government have obviously considered the film potential,' reacted Josef.

'Mr Blyne told me you've gone to particular trouble to retain the copyright in the Soviet Union,' said the President.

Watts would always prefix a name with 'mister', decided Josef.

'A business precaution,' pointed out Josef, talking to Artman. 'There have been instances of Russian works of art being badly treated because of vague, uncertain copyright.'

'I give you my personal undertaking', promised Watts, portentously, 'that you would have no argument about the artistic merits of any film my studio made. I personally guarantee that.'

'My government would ensure there was every safeguard,' assured Josef, unimpressed. It was a bad choice of words.

Burgess frowned. 'What does that mean?'

Josef smiled at the concern. It was nearly six o'clock, he noted. Nikolai had been gone nearly an hour. The time-lag to which he had not bothered to adjust would increase the affect of alcohol. Perhaps he'd be exhausted, needing sleep immediately he returned to the hotel.

'Any contract would have clauses clearly setting out the degree of interpretation allowed in the script,' he said.

'Censorship,' protested Burgess.

'It would ensure proper co-operation,' insisted Josef. He had planned the negotiation on the plane journey from England but had not envisaged a meeting like this.

'I don't imagine the other studios would raise objections,' he offered. It was almost a clumsy threat.

'Other studios?' asked Watts. The men around them registered the concern that would be expected.

'Paramount, United Artists, Universal... most of the independents. In fact, there are few people not interested.'

'Perhaps you'd better tell us what you have in mind,' said Wasnet. The production chief would definitely have been more of a negotiating adversary, thought Josef.

'For *Walk Softly on a Lonely Day*,' began Josef, deciding to list the demands before the encouragement towards their agreement, 'I would want outright payment of two million dollars. I would also want ten per cent of the gross. It would obviously be a studio financed film, with no outside money. I would want the contract to stipulate quite clearly that the ten per cent came from the world-wide gross before any other deduction whatsoever.'

He sat back, looking at them, and they returned his stare, waiting, not believing he had finished.

'Too much,' protested Watts, as Josef had known he would. The man had spoken immediately, without thought, like someone reciting an expected reaction. Josef saw Wasnet and Artman frown.

'But you haven't allowed me to finish,' complained Josef closing the door behind the other man. Watts looked uncomfortable, embarrassed by the premature response.

'You must already know', expanded Josef, 'that the book is outselling anything that can be remembered in American publishing history. The Presidential reception can only heighten that interest. The success of this book is going to be incredible.'

'You're telling us nothing we don't already know,' said Watts, irritably. He was annoyed at being so easily drawn by Josef.

The Russian smiled. How wonderful it was not to feel tired. He wondered how long the Benzedrine would last. He would have to take another if it became a protracted day. It wouldn't be at all difficult to become dependent, he thought.

'This property has assured publicity value,' said Josef. 'You can guarantee a box-office return before you announce the stars.'

He stopped, giving Watts the opportunity to challenge the point. The President frowned suspiciously. He needed a script, thought Josef.

'Further,' continued Josef, 'my government is prepared to allow the film to be shot entirely on location in the Soviet Union, the first time such a facility has ever been allowed a Western film company. For the scenes involving the Second World War, the Red Army will be made available.'

He stopped again, allowing the details to settle. In nearly every negotiation in which he had ever been involved, he found people became confused and allowed more concessions than they intended if they were made a series of offers.

'They are interesting suggestions,' agreed Watts, guardedly.

'I'm still not clear about the degree of control,' said Burgess.

'Only upon interpretation,' insisted Josef. 'And for your protection, I will agree to it being written into the contract that I co-operate with you as technical advisor, able to give decisions on the spot. That might prevent costly production delays ... '

'You would be prepared to be technical advisor?' queried Watts. The promotional value of Josef's association was registering. An uncertainty went through the men in the room, as if they had all been holding the same terminal when the electricity switch had been turned on.

'There's a catch,' insisted Burgess, voicing the common doubt.

Josef indicated the lawyer. 'Everything would be put into contractural form,' he guaranteed. 'Until Moscow's formal approval, you would pay nothing, apart from a nominal, binding figure.'

'It would put you into the position of a censor,' insisted the director.

'Don't you agree the book translates into film terms remarkably easily?'

'Yes,' said Burgess, warily.

'The dialogue needs little alteration?'

'No,' conceded Burgess.

'Then what major alteration do you envisage?'

'At the moment, none,' admitted the director. 'But I don't fancy being in the middle of Russia, unable to shoot because we can't agree on a scene or a part in the script.'

'Then why don't we extend the contract so that you pay nothing and commit yourself to nothing until agreement upon the script is reached?'

'Your terms appear remarkably reasonable,' queried Wasnet, taking up Burgess' apprehension. 'Some people might think too reasonable.'

Everyone was hunting the flaw, like a child's party game. And they'd never find it, thought Josef. If the Praesidium decided to purge him, then the precautions he was taking in establishing a connection with the film in Russia would be meaningless. But if the criticism stopped short of that, then it became an insurance policy. A very frail one, he accepted, but a reason nevertheless for him to be allowed continued involvement with the book.

'It would make the production of an epic, prestige film extremely cheap,' pointed out Josef.

Watts waved his arms, embracing everyone in the room. 'I'd like to discuss this further,' he said. Because he was personally involved, nothing could go wrong, decided Josef.

'Of course,' Josef accepted. He paused, then added, 'I'm only going to be in America a few days, as you know. I intend establishing an agreement before I return to Russia.'

'I see,' said Watts. He could not determine how or why he was being pressured.

'So perhaps I can expect an answer by tomorrow afternoon,' Josef finished. He turned to the lawyer and carefully restated the offer and the terms. Artman already had them listed correctly. Another professional, judged Josef.

'Before we went to Russia, the whole thing would be agreed. There would be no censorship?' reiterated Burgess, his mind refusing to move beyond the only difficulty he could isolate.

'It will be written in terms we both accept before the contract is signed,' reassured Josef. And then, he added mentally, altered if the occasion arose. They could always be coerced into agreement, rather than have their entire film seized. Within the Soviet Union, it would be easy to blame a nebulous authority.

Josef stood. They had gone as far as they could, he knew.

'Tomorrow, then,' he reminded, shaking hands with Watts and nodding farewells to the others.

Watts was disconcerted by the encounter, decided Josef, as he returned to his suite. The knowledge pleased him. He had not liked the man. He hesitated, stopped by the attitude. Since when had he allowed personal feelings to intrude in any negotiations? He moved restlessly in the corridor, awaiting the elevator. He had made a mistake in his eagerness to become associated with the film, he decided. They had become suspicious because he was willing to sell it too cheaply. He had been arrogant, almost presenting them with an ultimatum, he told himself. Offered differently, it would have appeared the naïvety of someone ignorant of film dealing, which they would have taken advantage of. Instead, irritated by a man he might never see again, he had had to prove himself the stronger. Surely, he thought, his self-confidence wasn't being eroded to that degree.

Blyne was waiting impatiently outside his suite, his pacing reminiscent of Josef's doubt minutes earlier. He stood, holding the lift, as the American hurried towards him.

'Trouble,' announced Blyne. The publisher was succinct and factual, never once swearing. It had apparently begun well, he said. Matheson had taken them to Jack Dempsey's and P. J. Clarke's, and then Nikolai had complained of tiredness, so Endelman had suggested something to make them feel better and Matheson had made the mistake of objecting. By the time they got to Elaine's, the young editor had become the butt off which the other two bounced their private jokes until finally Matheson became the joke himself, their captive comedian.

'At Elaine's,' recorded Blyne, 'there was a group of Endelman's fag friends. Harvey says they just stood around, taking the piss out of him.'

'So what happened?' asked Josef. The benzedrine was wearing off now and exhaustion was coming at him as if it had been hiding behind some invisible wall.

'They just waited until he went to the men's room and when he came back, they'd gone,' said Blyne as they drove away from the Pierre.

They stopped at a red light and the publisher looked sideways at Josef.

'Somewhere in this city', he said, 'there's this year's Nobel prizewinner, doped to the eyes, running shotgun to a handful of closet queens.'

The lights changed and Blyne moved off northwards.

'Fuck,' said Josef, needing the word.

'Somehow,' judged the publisher, 'that doesn't seem enough.'

Blyne was driving up Second Avenue. He made a left, then two rights, coming up outside the yellow awning of the café on 82nd Street. He parked, ignoring the hydrant. Elaine's was crowded. Just inside the door there was the crowd of ignored tourists, patiently awaiting a table in the back room. The 'club' table for Elaine Kaufman's chosen few was deserted, just inside the door, but the other ten tables were occupied by the grateful. Everywhere was an atmosphere of Italian food and pretention. Blyne, who was known and therefore unimpressed, went immediately to the bar. Matheson sat there, disregarding the drink before him. He saw them approaching and turned fully and Josef felt sorry for the man.

'Where is he?' asked Josef.

'A party,' said Matheson.

'Where, for fuck's sake?' asked Blyne. Josef forgave him the obscenity. The young editor shrugged and Blyne pulled him around on the bar stool, so that he had to face them.

'Okay,' said the American. 'So you fucked up ... ' he jerked his head towards Josef. 'If he couldn't stop Nikolai, how the hell do you think you could? Let's dump the self-pity.'

'But I let you down,' insisted Matheson, looking back to the bar. He wasn't as drunk as he wanted them to believe, decided Josef. But he needed the excuse of drink to make the maudlin apology. Would he ever meet a completely honest man, Josef wondered.

'Where did they go?' demanded Blyne, as impatient as Josef. He and Blyne were remarkably similar, decided the negotiator.

'They talked of a party,' repeated Blyne. He turned to Josef. 'Nikolai is horrible,' he said. 'He really is a shit. Why does he treat everyone like that?'

'Because he doesn't know any better,' replied Josef, irritably. It had been the worst mistake yet to allow Nikolai loose in the city, he decided. He was amazed at his own stupidity.

'Where's the party?' insisted Blyne.

'Riverside, somewhere,' said Matheson, jerking his shoulders.

Blyne disappeared among the crowd and Matheson stared into his glass. It was largely melted ice, Josef knew. So he'd been wrong about Matheson, like so many other people. It would take a long time, Josef knew, for him to regain his confidence. Blyne returned within minutes, impatiently gesturing them outside. Sleet had begun to fall in great, shovelling gusts, driving along the street and banking up against every obstruction, collecting against the debris of earlier snowstorms. Their car was still against the hydrant, ice gathering in steps against the windscreen.

'Verdi Square,' said Blyne, as he began to drive. 'A model named Sheri Anderson.'

He was proud at having found out, Josef knew. Beside him, Matheson shivered. The benzedrine had completely left Josef now. It was as if a great gap had been channelled out of his head, so that tiredness had rushed in to occupy it, like water filling a hollow on the seashore. Words were coming to him, but he couldn't catch them all, like a clumsy conjuror. By the time they arrived, the sleet had become snow. The wind scurried along the street, sowing it into drifts. It was almost as cold as Potma, thought Josef.

'Sheri Anderson's party,' said Blyne, to the desk porter as they entered the apartment block.

The porter looked worried. 'You cops?'

'No,' assured Josef, immediately. 'We're not police. Please. Where's the party?'

The man frowned, still unsure. Blyne reached across in an awkward handshake and under the cover of the desk, the man examined what the publisher had given him.

'No,' he agreed, smiling. 'You ain't cops. Twenty twelve. Top floor.'

'I'd like to make it quite clear,' said Matheson, fuzzily, as the elevator ascended. 'That I am most sincerely sorry for what has happened.'

The other two men ignored him. If he were Blyne, decided Josef, he'd fire the younger man.

The three of them stopped uncertainly outside the apartment. There seemed to be several sources of music, all overlaid with the sound of people. Blyne and Matheson turned to Josef for guidance, so the Russian pushed through the open door. It was very dark. Red and blue shades had been arranged around the lights already brought down to their lowest illumination, but in three places hard, strobe lights had been fixed, with oscillating spheres in front of them, so they kept catching faces in grotesque grimaces. People had learned the trick and were performing to it, flicking in and out of the light, artificially distorting their faces in an obscene magic lantern. They were all women's faces, Josef saw. One light was arranged so newcomers had to pass through, giving those already there the opportunity of seeing each arrival. Beyond the revolving light, the room opened into a lounge, where other shapes moved to music which seemed to come from every side. To the right was another room, where people also moved, apparently dancing. Couples were isolated around the wall, arms entwined, hands groping buttocks and thighs. There were couches, too, arranged around the outside of the room and there were people on them. Some were copulating, he decided, skirts hoisted waist-high. They were on their backs, Josef saw, in the normal love-making position. He had always thought homosexuals would have to do it differently, animal-like. He stared, curiously, wondering how it were possible. The apartment was very hot and the smells flickered with the light. He recognized the incense and then saw the joss-sticks smouldering in their holders around the room. There was a sweeter smell, too, which he knew must be marijuana. There would be other things, of course. He passed several people standing quite alone, their eyes fogged in some private dream. No wonder, thought Josef, the porter had been so frightened of the police. He moved further into the apartment, dodging the strobe light, edging around the locked, dancing couples, trying at the same time to avoid those who overflowed in their abandon from the couch.

'Fuck me,' said Blyne, instinctively.

'Any time, lover,' echoed back to him, from the left-hand wall.

There was a giggle and Josef detected a shift of interest. He could see now, providing he avoided looking directly at the revolving light. Many of them were quite beautiful, he thought. Some were quite heavily breasted from what would be silicone injections, but all were slim-waisted and svelte in full-length evening gowns. Most had long, shoulder-length hair. Blonde seemed a favourite colour, he thought. Only their faces were a mistake, decided the Russian, harshly painted to draw attention, like old butterflies desperate to mate before they died.

An enormous shudder went through him. Again, as when he had discovered Endelman and Nikolai together in London, he was engulfed with the feeling of coldness that had permeated his body at Potma, numbing him, until it became almost impossible to think. He began peering closely at couples, trying to locate Nikolai. Once he thought he had found the photographer and actually pulled the figure away from someone in a pink evening-gown, slashed to the navel, before realizing the mistake.

'Later, sweetie,' encouraged the one in the gown. 'There's enough for all.'

Matheson failed to duck the strobe. It caught him and he tried to shy away, blinking, but the person operating the light followed him, like a searchlight.

'Fresh blood,' shouted the operator.

'Straights,' identified another voice. 'Sheri's imported some straights.'

'Where? I must see. Where?' demanded a third.

'What a lovely Christmas present! Oh, she is a *sweetie*,' said someone else.

The light jumped, picking up Blyne, who ducked like someone caught doing something wrong.

'They're shy,' accused the first. 'Pull your skirts down, girls.'

'Oh bollocks,' erupted Blyne, annoyed at being made to look foolish.

'Learn to live with them,' someone said on Josef's right. 'We all have.'

Josef saw a hand reach for the switch and the lights were turned up. From several couches there were scuffles of people disengaging and isolated protests.

Josef jerked around as someone touched his arm. She was extraordinarily attractive, he thought, a black girl, her small-featured face framed in the flared bush of an exaggerated Afro.

'Hi,' she said. 'I'm Sheri. Welcome to fun city.'

'I'm looking for Jimmy Endelman, the photographer,' said Josef. His throat felt closed and dry and the words scraped out, so that he felt ridiculous. 'Is he here?'

'I guess so,' said the model, carelessly, nodding her head towards the second room. 'Last time I saw him, he was balling in there. But it's party rules that the hostess tastes the new fruit first.'

She smiled, running her tongue sensually over her teeth and then reached out, to take his hand. Josef snatched away, repelled by the thought of physical contact, an over-reaction that he immediately regretted.

The model stopped smiling. 'It's another party rule that we don't allow people with bad manners,' she said.

Behind him, Josef heard a sound, then a tiny, artificial scream as Blyne slapped somebody's hand away from him.

'Sheri, darling. What is this?' protested a brunette who had accosted Matheson. 'Going rough is fun sometimes, but they've got to have *some* finesse.'

A frightened look flickered over the model's face. 'Who the hell are you?' she demanded.

Josef pushed by, making his way into the second room, and Blyne shouldered after him, but the model stopped Matheson, repeating her question.

It was a bedroom, Josef realized. The divan had been pushed into a corner and several couples lay there. It was darker here, with no probing lights. Couples were dancing in cleared space, locked together and swaying to the music, hands inside each other's clothing, mouths fluttering.

Nikolai was in an armchair, wedged near the bed, oblivious of anything around him. He was without jacket or tie and his shirt was open to the waist. Josef stood over the writer, looking down. There were bitemarks on the man's stomach, he saw, and he smelt, sexually. Now, Josef realized, he had retreated beyond the sensation of sex. There was a lot of noise coming from the main room, Josef heard. The music gasped to a halt and there were shouts and several screams, theatrical and posed.

'Help me,' he said to the publisher.

They got the unprotesting writer upright and began searching for his clothing. His tie was caught under one of the seat cushions. Josef had to half roll a couple over on the divan to retrieve the jacket. They moved, then returned to their original position, without interrupting their motion. Josef draped the jacket around the writer's shoulders and pulled him from the chair. Nikolai stood and smiled at Josef and the publisher.

'Hello,' he said, distantly.

'He's blocked out of his mind,' diagnosed Blyne.

As they turned, Endelman emerged from the bathroom, buttoning his sleeve over his arm. He smiled and waved. He was deeply under the influence of some drug, Josef accepted. 'Don't go,' he protested.

'We can't leave him,' said Blyne. Dancers were pulling

apart, looking at them, Josef could hear Matheson shouting from the next room. He reached out, grabbing the photographer by the shoulder and shoved him towards the main room, after Blyne and Nikolai.

'Pigs,' someone said, from behind and immediately the word was picked up.

'A raid,' confirmed another, echoed immediately by a third. There were screams again and renewed shouting.

'Don't push,' said Endelman. 'Want to stay.'

'Get out,' commanded Josef. He felt an overwhelming need to hit the man.

A figure wearing woman's panties and a black suspender belt, trailing a skirt by the hand, fled through the door in front of them yelling, 'It's a bust. We're being raided.'

Matheson stood in the middle of the main room, holding his face where he had been scratched. Blood was edging out through his fingers.

'Cops. Oh, my God. The police.'

'I've got a wife. For Christ's sake, let me out.'

'Bastards,' screamed the model. 'You bastards.'

Hysteria bubbled around them, like froth on a beer glass.

'Stop it. We're not police. Stop it,' shouted Josef. A man ran past him, pushing him sideways. He was missing a shoe, Josef saw.

Nikolai was still smiling when they got outside. The man with one shoe was at the end of the corridor, frantically stabbing at the lift button. He turned, saw them approaching and whimpered. He looked around for an escape route, then burst through the door marked 'Fire'.

In the elevator, Josef put Nikolai's coat on him properly. From the indicator board came a cacophony of demands from above as the panic spread and people tried to leave the top floor.

Outside it was snowing heavily, drifts banking high against the building. But the wind had dropped, so there was a stillness over everything. Blyne turned frowning towards Josef at the sound of the party when they emerged. They squinted upwards, realizing that the windows had been thrown open far above. Snow fell into their faces, making it difficult to see. The noise was abnormal, Josef thought, everyone trying to outscream each other. They were halfway across the road, towards their car, when there was a louder shout than the others and both Josef and Blyne stopped, halted by the desperation in it. They sensed rather than heard the sound, and half ducked, instinctively. Then there was the impression of a shape and the strained scream that came from it as it plunged down out of the whiteness. The body exploded against the ground with a plopping sound, staining the snow with a huge splash of red. A blonde wig had fallen away from the body and seemed crouched, like a small dog. The homosexual had been wearing blue, Josef saw. Satin, he thought. He couldn't see any shoes. Perhaps they had been lost, like the frightened man with a wife.

'Hurry,' said Blyne. 'The police won't take long.'

Nikolai began laughing in the car, an insane, unreal sound. Josef had to hit him twice before it stopped. Even then, he hunched in the corner of the car, sniggering.

Pamela waited four days before trying to contact Sanya, wanting to show by her silence that she would not be treated so discourteously. Four days, she decided, was sufficient. When she telephoned the Ministry, she was told Sanya was not available. So she wrote. There was no reply.

On the Sunday Pamela went to Sanya's apartment block, a frightening contrast to her own. It seemed to move with people, like a hive. The occupants stared openly at her and one woman actually stretched out, in curiosity, recognizing the coat as Western-made and wishing to touch it. Pamela pulled away, nervously. The tendency of the Russians to touch always upset her. An unsmiling, fat woman answered the door. Enunciating her Russian carefully, Pamela asked for Sanya. The woman shrugged, called over her shoulder and then walked away. Several minutes passed and then it was opened again. Sanya looked at her, surprised.

'I thought you might be ill,' said Pamela.

'No. I'm all right.'

'I telephoned.'

'I know.'

Pamela waited for her to continue, but the Russian girl said nothing more.

'Did you get my letter?'

'Yes.'

Pamela shivered, but Sanya did not invite her in. Over Sanya's shoulder, Pamela saw another woman moving around, staring at her with interest.

'When am I seeing you again?' asked Pamela, finally.

'I don't know.'

Twice Sanya made as if to speak, then stopped, unsure of the right words. Finally she said, 'I don't want to be your friend.'

'But ... '

'Please go away.'

'But Sanya ... why ... ?'

'Please.'

'But what have I done?'

'I don't ... ' tried the Russian, then halted again. She was shaking, Pamela saw.

'Look, Sanya, let's talk ... '

'Go away,' erupted the other woman. 'Leave me alone. You smother me. You won't let me breathe.'

She slammed the door. Pamela heard her run back into the apartment. As calmly as possible, she turned and slowly walked out of the foul-smelling block, gulping air as she regained the street.

Chapter Nineteen

Fear would give him the chance to re-establish some control over the writer, thought Josef. Endelman sat apart from them, hunched in a dressing-gown. Despite the central heating, he appeared cold, shudders going through him in spasms.

'A man died,' Josef told the writer. 'Now there will be police inquiries. If you are implicated, the Nobel Foundation will withdraw the award. You'll probably be arrested, when you return to Russia.'

The arrogance and contempt of the previous days had vanished.

'Help me, Josef. I need you to help me.'

Josef sighed, wearily. 'No more scenes,' he stipulated.

'I promise, Josef. Honestly.'

Endelman sighed, contemptuous of the writer's collapse.

'And I want to know what drugs you're taking,' demanded the negotiator. 'Pills or marijuana didn't put either of you into the condition that you were in last night.'

Nikolai looked to Endelman. He seems to need help from everyone, thought Josef.

'What are you going to do if we don't tell you?' asked Endelman, turning to face him at last.

'It's still not too late for the facility of travelling with us to be withdrawn,' tried Josef, the hollowness echoing in the threat.

Endelman laughed at him, openly. 'It *is* too late,' he said. 'Isn't it, Nikolai?'

The writer shifted on the bed, but said nothing.

'You're a fool, Josef,' continued the American. 'You try to convey the impression of being so worldly, but you're a fool.'

The photographer jerked his head towards the briefcase that lay by Josef's leg.

'You walk around like a clerk, with a briefcase and a pocket full of pens and try to convince people you're something special. But that's all you are, Josef. A clerk.'

Their roles had changed, realized Josef. Endelman was showing the arrogance that Nikolai had attempted and now the writer had the subservient part.

'Show him your arms, Nikolai,' ordered Endelman.

Made aware of it, Josef realized that Nikolai was sitting with his shirtsleeves buttoned. The writer half folded his arms, running his hands over them. Endelman had been doing that, as he emerged from the bathroom at the party, remembered Josef.

'Please, Jimmy,' pleaded the writer. The man's skin was greased with perspiration. He looked desperately ill, thought Josef. He moved forward to the bed and Nikolai tried to crab away. Josef caught him easily, and jerked the cuff of the shirt. The button broke away and Nikolai's arm, up to the elbow, was exposed. The veins were blackened tributaries along the inside of his arm, which was marked, near the inside of the joint, with bruises, as if a strong man had grabbed and squeezed. Medev's arms had been like that, Josef recalled. And his legs, too, after he had defied the guards and given help to Josef and his father and then been taken away to be trussed in a metal frame, like a bed without springs, and beaten. Medev had been a brave man, thought Josef. And stayed one. Even at the worst moments, reduced to tears, he would have rejected narcotics, Josef knew.

'Oh God,' said Josef, slowly. Nikolai refused to meet his look. 'You fool,' said Josef. 'You stupid, bloody fool.'

'Please don't be angry, Josef.'

'For Christ's sake, stop it,' snapped Endelman. He stood up and walked over to Josef, staring down from his superior height.

'You knew he'd smoked heroin, because he told you. So don't perform the outraged protector now. You should have known bloody well that having smoked it, he was going to start mainlining it.'

Josef moved away from the bed, needing to get space between himself and the two men. He stared directly at the photographer.

'You did it deliberately, didn't you, Endelman?' he demanded.

The photographer laughed, a jeering sound. 'Josef Bultova, the psychoanalyst,' he mocked.

'You gave him heroin knowing that he would become dependent upon it. And if he needed heroin, he needed you. So now you're in command.'

Nikolai began whimpering, very quietly, and Josef stared at him, distastefully. What a fool, thought Josef.

'So?' challenged the photographer, knowing his strength.

Again, there was nothing he could do, accepted Josef. To seek help from Semyonov would provide the man with information that would be immediately channelled back to Devgeny.

'We're all the same, us fags,' said Endelman. 'We're all bent on destruction.'

He threw something he took from his dressing-gown pocket on to the bed and Nikolai snatched at it.

'I *do* look after him, Josef,' said the photographer. 'That'll set him up for the day.'

Josef turned to leave, but Endelman stopped him.

'Stay, Josef,' he ordered, challenging a refusal.

One difficulty disappears and another rises to take its place, thought Josef. He remained, looking on, his face expressionless. Nikolai dissolved the powder into the bowl of a spoon held over Endelman's cigarette lighter, sucked it into a hypodermic he took unsterilized from the bedside-table and injected into an artery he swelled in his left arm by binding his tie around the elbow joint. Josef felt nothing.

'See what a good pupil he has been?' mocked Endelman.

Nikolai sat, hands clasped between his knees, and looking down, waiting for the feeling to engulf him. The photographer prepared his own injection. He was very practised, saw Josef.

'You can go now,' commanded Endelman. 'You wanted to know and we showed you.'

Theatrically, Endelman stopped him as he was about to go through the linking doors.

'And Josef?'

'What?'

'Be a little more polite, in future.'

Back in his room, Josef stood staring out over the whiteness of Central Park, seeing nothing. It had been another vow that never would anyone treat him with the complete disregard he'd suffered during imprisonment. But now it was happening again, he thought. He was jumping at the snap of fingers, running at the whim of everyone, like a common black-marketeer negotiating a squalid deal on Gorky Street.

They were ready in an hour for the Algonquin meeting with the *New York Times*. The change in Nikolai was remarkable. Now he was almost as he had been during the early days in Stockholm, obeying Josef without question, turning to him in deference before answering any question. Publicly, Endelman behaved perfectly, always working unobtrusively.

Blyne joined them back at the Pierre before the publishing magazine lunch. He looked worried and tired.

'Have you seen the papers? The pictures in the *Daily News* are incredible. They got into the party before it broke up.'

'We'd have had some indication before now if anyone had linked Nikolai with it,' said Josef.

Blyne moved his never-still hands uncertainly.

'I think we should get out of New York,' said Blyne. 'Tonight's reception at the United Nations is the last thing here. Why don't we go down overnight to Washington? You're staying at the embassy there, so Nikolai will be under some sort of control.'

The only objection to going to Washington was that Endelman could not stay at the embassy, so it would mean he would have to shuttle between 16th Street and the hotel in which the publisher and his party were staying, ferrying the writer's drug supply. He could not, he knew, make Nikolai's addiction known immediately he arrived at the American capital. The Washington ambassador, Semyon Vladimirov, had been an attaché under Josef's father in Paris, an able, eager diplomat. The old man had nurtured him, guiding him so he avoided the pitfalls, recommending his promotion with personal letters to the Praesidium. During the trial, Vladimirov had denounced them both, seeing a short cut to even greater promotion, giving graphic evidence of totally fictitious meetings with members of the Sûreté and the C.I.A. Vladimirov had been in court when the sentence had been announced, Josef recalled. And had found the shock on the old man's face particularly amusing. To make Nikolai's addiction an embassy matter would be a tactical mistake, Josef decided. But there was common sense in Blyne's suggestion.

'Is there a shuttle down to Washington tonight?'

'I'll hire a plane,' said the publisher, anxious to cocoon the writer as much as possible.

Josef telephoned the Washington embassy, curtly instructing them to arrange overflow accommodation. Illinivitch would be staying at the embassy, thought Josef. He would need to speak to the deputy Minister immediately he arrived, he decided.

Endelman refused to attend the videotaping of the television show, excusing himself to develop the film he had taken during the tour. Josef felt a lurch of uncertainty at the thought that the photographer was tiring of the association with Nikolai. Thank God he had a commission that would keep him with them until the time came for Nikolai's return. The recorded shows, both for radio and television, went remarkably well, as had the lunch that preceded it. He wondered if the public success of the tour could be produced as a partial defence against any inquiry. It was inevitable that there would be an investigation, he accepted, once Nikolai's addiction became known.

Josef had forgotten his time stipulation upon the film company and was surprised to find Wasnet and Artman waiting for them when they returned to the Pierre from the TV studio.

The contracts were perfectly drawn and needed no amendments and Josef signed the Americans' copy after the first reading. The anxiety seeping away from Wasnet was almost visible, although Artman managed to control himself slightly better. Watts had withdrawn, Josef decided, because he feared a disaster, shifting responsibility entirely upon the production chief. If Moscow accepted the deal, Josef wondered if Watts would allow the man credit for the successful conclusion. Probably not, he thought.

'Thank you,' said Wasnet, nervously, as Josef signed. He was still unsure, Josef knew.

'How long before Moscow's approval?' asked Artman.

'Difficult to say,' avoided the negotiator. 'Within a month, perhaps. I would hope no longer.'

'So would we,' said Wasnet, with feeling.

'I was wondering whether I could come to Moscow, next month,' pressed Wasnet. 'Just to see everything is going smoothly.'

They *were* nervous, concluded Josef. But there was an element of personal protection in the idea.

'An excellent suggestion,' he agreed. 'I'll recommend it.'

Semyonov had taken great care with the reception, Josef realized. Only the Chinese had refused the invitation, and because every other delegation was represented, the majority by their ambassadors, the Peking rejection appeared petty and rebounded in Russia's favour. Diplomacy, reflected Josef as he moved into the room overlooking the East River, often resembled schoolgirl dormitory politics.

Officiously, Semyonov took the initial role of translator, moving from group to group, introducing Nikolai. He actually enjoyed the reflected glory, realized Josef. The vanity of important men frequently surprised him. Endelman had arrived an hour before the reception, spending most of the time alone with Nikolai, who towards the end of the afternoon had grown irritable and nervous, unable to remain still, as if he were suffering a skin irritation. Now he was relaxed again, a shy man accepting Semyonov's guidance. Another injection was the most logical explanation. It was always possible, Josef supposed, that they had gone to bed together. He waited for a personal reaction to the thought. There should be disgust, he thought, or a shudder of contempt. He felt nothing, only the emptiness of non-feeling that had existed when he had learned of Pamela's betrayal and watched Nikolai jab a filthy needle into his arm. How much of him, wondered Josef, had died in Potma? Was something else buried in the shallow ditch into which he had rolled the already stiffening body of his father?

'It goes well, doesn't it?' demanded Semyonov. An aide had taken the role of translator, saw Josef.

'Yes,' agreed the negotiator. The ambassador was tense and smiling, like a man with a secret.

'Did you read of the tragedy in the city last night?' said Semyonov.

'Which one did you have in mind?' rejoined Josef. Schoolgirl repartee, he thought again.

'A shocking example of Western decadence,' said Semyonov, reciting dogma. 'A man, dressed as a woman, leapt from an apartment where, according to police reports, nearly everyone was homosexual. There are amazing pictures in today's newspapers.'

'No,' said Josef. 'I didn't read about it.'

So they knew of the party. Sledgehammer finesse, he thought. If that were an example of the ambassador's ability, Semyonov must need Devgeny's constant support. Unless, of course, Semyonov knew through Devgeny of moves in Moscow which meant the man could be careless in his clumsy innuendo. It was obvious they would have been watched, he supposed, but he had not imagined the surveillance would have been so complete. Perhaps Moscow might dispense with an inquiry and move immediately for a trial.

'It is fortunate that Russia is free of such filth,' said Semyonov, disappointed that Josef had not risen to the bait.

He was very clumsy, thought Josef. He stared at the ambassador, refusing him any satisfaction.

'I'm sorry if this reception isn't up to the usual standard to which you're accustomed,' the man blundered on, determined to extract some reaction from Josef.

'Do you enjoy America?' threw back Josef, irritated.

'No,' said the ambassador, immediately. 'I judge my presence here necessary.'

'Perhaps you'd like me to recommend a transfer?' suggested Josef.

Concern etched Semyonov's face, then cleared into a sneer. 'You?' he queried, contemptuous of Josef's influence.

'I think it's time you had a change, ambassador. Your conversation is most strange for an event such as this,' said Josef, happy at planting the seed of uncertainty.

The reception became oppressive. Nikolai realized that Semyonov and the other Russians were studying him, like a laboratory experiment, and became nervous, and Josef's exasperation grew. He rejected the traditional invitation of a tour of the building, careless of offence, pleading that they had a plane to catch to Washington. Semyonov's reports would be devastating, Josef realized, as he hurried from the building.

Their luggage was already packed in the waiting limousines, so they drove straight to La Guardia, Nikolai and Endelman slumped in their seats, hostile to everyone. The photographer was making Nikolai suffer for his brief moment of independence, decided Josef.

'Jimmy and I will be able to meet, won't we?' asked Nikolai, urgently, as the Grumman Gulfstream taxied towards the Washington terminal.

'Of course,' assured Josef. Sex or drugs, he wondered.

'I mean ... ' stumbled the writer.

'There won't be any difficulty. I promise you,' said the negotiator. Drugs, he decided. Nikolai would have no other interest now.

The cars were drawn up with diplomatic dispensation on the apron. Blyne and Endelman went to the second car and Josef ushered Nikolai into the leading vehicle. Nikolai stopped as he was entering the car, so that Josef collided with him, pushing him forward. Vladimirov, grey-haired and thinner than Josef recalled, was in the far corner. The ambassador stared unsmiling across at the man he had last seen standing in a court dock in Moscow, alongside a weeping old man. He said nothing. At least, thought Josef, he wasn't a hypocrite. On the jump-seat, but smiling a welcome, sat Illinivitch.

'Hello Josef,' said the deputy Minister, extending his hand. Josef made difficulty of entering the car to avoid taking it.

'You know our ambassador, of course,' Illinivitch said, unperturbed by the rudeness.

'Yes,' agreed Josef. 'He has a reputation for court appearances.'

Illinivitch's smile faded at the antagonism.

Nikolai retracted tortoise-like into his shell, muttering one-word responses to the greetings of the two men, burrowing into the corner of the car. Josef sat opposite Vladimirov and stared at him, pointedly. Illinivitch kept the courtesy lights on in the car, the windows of which were curtained. The vehicle pulled out of the airport and began moving towards the city.

'We've a lot to talk about, Josef.'

'A great deal,' agreed the negotiator. 'Has Moscow been getting my reports?'

'We've been getting a great many reports,' returned the deputy Minister, enjoying himself. He turned to the writer. 'Quite an historic speech you made at the Nobel ceremony,' he said.

Nikolai did not reply. Josef had noticed that his briefcase supply of drugs was again diminishing and assumed Nikolai was the thief. He wondered if his current behaviour were the result of librium or methalaquone mixing with heroin. Endelman might have given him some amphetamine, he thought.

'How was it received?' asked Josef. He saw Illinivitch and the ambassador exchange looks at the writer's attitude.

'Liked by some. Not by others,' fenced the tall Russian, glibly.

'Not approved,' predicted Josef.

'I didn't say that,' protested the deputy Minister.

'There aren't many occasions, Comrade Illinivitch, when you actually do give an opinion,' accused Josef. Vladimirov was shifting uneasily at the brittleness of the conversation. Josef was glad to disconcert the man. He remembered his father, dazed and bewildered, looking around the court, seeking friends and finding none. How easy it would be now, to seize him by the throat, judged Josef. All he would have to do was stretch forward and then grab and squeeze. The ambassador shifted under Josef's unblinking attention.

Illinivitch laughed. 'There's great value in vagueness, Josef.'

'Do you prefer vagueness, Comrade Vladimirov?' demanded Josef, determined to create the maximum discomfort. 'Or do you find it easy to be dogmatic and accurate in everything you say?'

'The question is difficult to understand, Comrade Bultova,' replied the ambassador, seeking help from Illinivitch.

'The last time we encountered each other,' jabbed Josef, viciously. 'You found questions only too easy to follow.'

The ambassador was spared by the arrival at 16th Street.

'I would like to talk to you, tonight,' announced Josef, looking straight at the deputy Minister.

Illinivitch consulted his watch, which showed eleven forty-five.

'It's important,' stressed Josef, delaying his exit from the stationary car.

'Thirty minutes,' agreed Illinivitch.

Josef shepherded Nikolai into the embassy and took him immediately to his bedroom. The writer appeared whiter than usual, the negotiator thought, as he undressed. Nikolai had no embarrassment about nudity, decided Josef. He was remarkably small, like a young boy.

'Want a sleeping pill?'

The writer nodded.

'Anything else?'

'I've made a mess of it, haven't I?' blurted Nikolai, suddenly.

'No,' contradicted Josef. 'It only becomes a disaster when lots of people know. So far we've only harmed each other.'

'I'm sorry, Josef,' said Nikolai. 'About ... about everything. I've betrayed you in every way possible. But you

216

stayed my friend. There can't be any forgiveness for what I've done, but I'm truly sorry.'

Did he mean it, wondered Josef. Or was this another performance? Genuine, determined the negotiator. Nikolai's period of performances was over.

'You'll get something from Jimmy for me, won't you?' asked the writer.

'Yes,' undertook Josef.

'I'm desperate, Josef.'

'I know.'

Illinivitch and Vladimirov were waiting in an upstairs study, but the deputy Minister turned to the ambassador as Josef entered.

'Perhaps,' he said gently. 'You would excuse us ... '

'This is my embassy ... ' the ambassador began, but Illinivitch raised his hand, almost wearily. Illinivitch was practising sinister behaviour, thought Josef. He wasn't very impressed. Devgeny was really much better.

'Please,' coaxed Illinivitch, his voice still very soft. 'I'm sure you'll understand.'

Josef smiled as the man left the room, an exaggerated expression that Vladimirov saw.

'I guessed you'd speak more freely without witnesses,' said Illinivitch.

Josef nodded. So, he thought, might Illinivitch.

'Nikolai has become a drug addict. And he's also a committed homosexual,' proclaimed Josef, abruptly.

'Really,' said Illinivitch, smiling. So he already knew, decided Josef. The surveillance had been very good.

'You knew that Endelman was a heroin addict when I telephoned from Stockholm, seeking Ministry approval, didn't you?' demanded Josef. 'You knew from Semyonov and still approved his accompanying us, even though you guessed from Nikolai's unstable behaviour in Moscow that there was a likelihood of his experimenting.'

217

'That's clever of you,' praised Illinivitch.

'Did you know?' pressed Josef.

'Of course. I knew he was a homosexual, too. But even I didn't imagine he would seduce the man.'

Illinivitch wouldn't have cleared the permission to allow Endelman to accompany them on the trip, Josef decided. That meant that from Moscow's point of view, the decision was Josef's alone.

'Why did you come to America?' asked the negotiator. 'It wasn't necessary for the Presidential reception.'

'The scandal I had created between the photographer and Balshev, to use against Devgeny, had been too well hidden,' said Illinivitch, simply. 'You were being far too successful in disguising what was going on. So I used the reception as an excuse to get here, to create a situation that you have been avoiding.'

Josef ignored the last part of the sentence. 'I *have* remained successful, haven't I?' he boasted.

'New York was very close, wasn't it?' returned Illinivitch, swallowing the lure. He really was very stupid, thought Josef.

'Semyonov has been very thorough,' said the negotiator.

'He's a very able man,' said Illinivitch. 'Although we must be fair. In the beginning, Vladimirov helped with the investigation into Endelman. You've no idea how carefully we had the man investigated.'

'Semyonov is a protégé of Devgeny's,' mused Josef. 'How, I wonder, have you got his report of the drug party so quickly?'

Illinivitch laughed at Josef's suspicions. 'Because he thinks I'm supporting Devgeny, not opposing him,' explained the deputy Minister, convincingly.

'You've done a great deal of planning,' agreed Josef, returning to a familiar theme. 'You must have powerful support in the Praesidium.'

Illinivitch smiled again. 'You'll get the names when I get your unconditional support,' he rejected. 'Being the liaison man has enabled me to make many friends. So far you've shown no friendship, merely guarded interest.'

The deputy Minister sat back, staring up at the ceiling, an artificial pose.

'I can use that drug party,' he said, after a long silence. He was like that Swedish count whose name he couldn't remember, thought Josef, attempting something beyond his ability.

'Wouldn't it be embarrassing if there were newspaper leaks that Nikolai might have been a guest there?' he asked, smiling. 'Imagine that appearing in the Jack Anderson column on the very day of the Presidential reception. I wouldn't be surprised if the President wouldn't cancel the whole thing.'

Josef looked at Illinivitch for several minutes. It was the moment of decision. He had to commit himself now, categorically. The risk, he thought, was appalling.

'I will not sacrifice Nikolai,' he announced. 'Particularly to the detriment of my country, to settle an imagined score with anybody. If newspaper stories appear linking Nikolai with that party, I shall leave America immediately, fly back to Moscow before the Presidential reception and give to the Praesidium a full report of what you have been demanding that I should do throughout the tour.'

For a moment, Illinivitch sat completely still, robbed of any movement.

'And whom do you imagine would believe you?' he sneered, finally. 'You'd need evidence to convince anyone. And at the moment, the only person who stands to be utterly disgraced on the evidence available is yourself. You don't imagine Semyonov or Vladimirov would confirm what you say, do you?'

He was right, thought Josef. Here at least the man had

been clever. He wondered if Illinivitch were as frightened of an inquiry as he was.

'You really are very immature,' said Josef, sadly.

Illinivitch glared, his face colouring.

'Don't you see how you've been outmanœuvred?' demanded Josef. 'To be the danger that Devgeny suspects you of being, you would have to be in Moscow, where you can gain allies and alienate him away from his supporters. Here you're just where he wants you, far away so he can whittle down whatever support you ever had. You're dead, Illinivitch. You've been outwitted and you've lost. Utter one word of what happened in New York and I shall go back to Moscow and denounce you.'

Illinivitch began to shake, but it was anger, not fear, Josef thought. He wasn't prepared to call his bluff, Josef realized.

'So we've both failed,' conceded the deputy Minister, with difficulty. 'But I remain on the Praesidium, which is something you have forgotten. I'll make you a solemn promise, Bultova. If Devgeny fails to get you purged, and I don't think he will after the disaster of this tour, then I'll have you back inside a prison camp within a year.'

Josef laughed, an uncaring sound, and for a moment thought the other man was going to hit him. His face suffused into a puce colour and his hands bellowed open and shut. If he hits me, thought Josef, it'll hurt like hell and my eyes would probably water with the pain, which would be embarrassing, because Illinivitch would think I was crying. With great effort, the deputy Minister got himself under control.

'You'll regret this,' he said.

'Perhaps,' said Josef.

Later, as he undressed upstairs and took his customary sleeping pills, Josef found himself humming.

There seemed no need, so Pamela hadn't bothered to wash. Her hair was matted and unkempt and she ran her hands through it, grimacing at the tangles, pulling faces at her own reflection in the dressing-table mirror. Nikolai's eyes had been red-veined and rheumy, like hers were now, she remembered, that night they got drunk at the dacha. She shuddered. The recollection still embarrassed her. She looked for her glass and found it on the bedside table. Funny. She couldn't remember putting it there. She stared at its emptiness, like someone gazing stupidly into an empty wallet after encountering a pick-pocket. The bottle was on the lower table. She'd have to do something about the mess, she thought, before Josef returned. He had that fetish about tidiness. She shrugged. But he wasn't returning for several days yet. She wondered why he hadn't telephoned in the last few days. She stood at the window, watching the babushkas far below chip and hack at the snow. She hoped Josef would be home by Christmas. Perhaps they could go to church. She'd like that, she decided. Perhaps, if she made a promise which God knew she meant, He'd listen. She really would keep her promise.

'Honestly,' she said, aloud, in the empty, dirty apartment. She heard the delivery flap click and turned, staring at the box. From her mother, she predicted. So there was no hurry. Time for another drink. Like a child saving the best part of a birthday trifle until last, she waited fifteen minutes before seeing what had arrived. It wasn't from her mother, she realized, recognizing the Moscow franking and the officialdom of the envelope. Careful not to spill her drink, she opened it. It was a short letter. It had been impossible, it said, to guarantee a re-entry visa if she chose to leave Russia. She squeezed her eyes shut, then re-focused, reading the letter again to ensure she hadn't misunderstood. She dropped the rejection on the hall table and went back into the sitting-room, refilling her glass from the emptying bottle. She wondered why she didn't feel any disappointment.

Chapter Twenty

It would have been easy for Endelman to have given him sufficient heroin the previous night, Josef realized, as he drove to the Hay Adams. He had even suggested it on the aircraft coming to Washington, but the photographer had lied about having to make contact with a Washington supplier, waiting for Josef to begin an argument he would have to lose. Why was it necessary, wondered Josef, for everyone to see him run errands? He felt a coldness, but no anger. Endelman was lounging in his room overlooking the White House. He'd regained some of his former elegance, thought the Russian.

'How very prompt,' said Endelman. He was enjoying the role of bully, thought Josef.

The Russian put his briefcase by the chair and sat down. 'I've got to be,' replied the negotiator. 'Have you any idea the state Nikolai is in?'

Endelman made a careless gesture. 'He'll be better an hour from now. You know, Josef, you really are like a clerk. My memory of you will be of a fat little man with a briefcase welded to his arm.'

'And my recollection of you will be of a man who knowingly set out to destroy someone with more talent than you could imagine.'

'Nikolai knew what was happening,' rejected Endelman.

'How many times did you meet Semyonov before you came to Stockholm?' asked Josef, unexpectedly.

Endelman shrugged. 'Two or three times,' he confirmed.

'A letter came from some Ministry in Moscow after Blyne had requested permission for me to accompany you, suggesting I call upon the guy.'

'Did he know you were a heroin addict?'

Endelman laughed at him. 'I don't wear a lapel badge.'

'But you don't go to much trouble disguising it.'

'Why should I?' asked Endelman, aggressively. 'I'm not particularly ashamed. Or of being a fag. I can afford both.'

'So it wouldn't have been difficult for anyone to find out?'

Again Endelman laughed, mocking him. He was excited at the confrontation, Josef knew.

'Not employing the methods that you're used to, no,' agreed the photographer. 'Are you trying to frighten me that there's a dossier on me in Moscow, for seducing their favourite author?'

Josef smiled and Endelman looked surprised. The Russian stood up, holding out his hand. Endelman shook his head.

'What's the matter now?' asked Josef.

'So far,' said the photograper, 'the exchange between Nicky and me has been, shall we say, for love. But we both know there isn't any love left.'

'How much?' asked Josef, simply.

'It's not easy any more,' said Endelman, wanting to prolong the meeting. 'It's getting tighter on the Mexican border. So the stuff's scarce. It's inevitable that the price will go up.'

'How much?'

'And I do feel you should contribute to all the stuff I handed over free of charge, don't you?'

Josef stood, refusing to join in Endelman's game, waiting for the demand.

'I think,' continued the photographer, 'that a thousand dollars would be fair. After all, Josef made some of his most impressive public performances strung out on what I'd given him.'

'That's bullshit.'

Endelman raised both hands, palm upwards, in feigned horror.

'But we can't afford to fall out, can we?'

'I've only got five hundred now,' said Josef.

'We don't extend credit,' said the photographer.

'You know you'll get it,' said Josef. It would be another occasion when he would have to come running, the negotiator thought. Endelman would like that.

From the bedside drawer, Endelman took the glassine envelopes and handed them to the Russian.

'I want the money,' he insisted.

'You'll get it,' said Josef.

Nikolai was hunched, cross-legged, in the middle of his bed when Josef returned to the embassy. He had been crying, Josef saw. The sheet was pulled-up, rope-like, and was creased and filthy where the writer had sat clutching it, like a baby sometimes holds its bedding for comfort. He grabbed the envelope from the other man and prepared his injection. Some of the powder fell on to the bed and he carefully brushed it back into the spoon. It was sexual, thought Josef, the slow entry and withdrawal of the needle. A bubble of blood popped up on Nikolai's arm as he withdrew the hypodermic and Nikolai stared at it, hypnotically. It looked like a tiny cherry, thought Josef. Or a nipple. Sex again. Abruptly, the writer smeared the mark with his thumb, looking up at Josef.

The negotiator felt a sudden moment of pity for the other man. He looked so frail and small, as if he were collapsing inwardly. Countries had tossed him about like children playing with a ball until it became dirty and punctured. And, like children, there weren't any regrets.

Before leaving the embassy that morning, Josef sought out the doctor, a bullish, shock-haired Georgian named Ravil Shevardnadze. The doctor's genial greeting soured within minutes of their conversation, and he grew angry, but Josef argued patiently, frequently reminding the man of his rank. Fortunately, the hostility of Illinivitch and Vladimirov had not permeated through the embassy. Josef finally got his way, as he knew he would.

Before the reception, there was more publicity sightseeing to the John F. Kennedy Memorial Centre and the Lincoln Monument, and lunch at the National Press Club. They divided into ridiculous, hostile camps, the ambassador and Illinivitch isolating themselves, Nikolai and Endelman together but hardly talking and Josef thrown into constant contact with Blyne, to which he did not object.

'Not like a scene out of happy families,' mocked Blyne, as they drank before lunch.

Josef smiled, knowing there was no hostility in the American's remark.

'Ridiculous, isn't it?' he said.

'Yes,' agreed the publisher. 'I don't envy your position.'

'No,' said Josef, sincerely. 'Neither do I.'

Vladimirov had chosen to be the interpreter, as Semyonov had in New York. Illinivitch stood to one side looking more at Josef than at the writer.

'What are you going to do about Matheson?' asked Josef.

'I don't know,' said Blyne, as if the matter were not important. 'He fouled up.'

'Have you fired him?'

'Not yet.'

'I don't think you should,' said Josef. There were too many casualties already, he thought.

Blyne looked surprised.

'What happened to him would have happened to either of us if we'd been there,' said Josef.

'Probably,' agreed the publisher, doubtfully.

'There's no doubt,' stressed Josef. He stared across at Endelman, who was quietly taking pictures. Throughout everything, Josef realized, the man had remained the complete professional. They all had, he supposed, reflectively.

Blyne's swearing had diminished, thought Josef. It had obviously been a nervous gesture.

Once again, in public, Nikolai performed well. As he stood beside him, translating his answers to the questions that followed the press lunch, Josef thought how odd it was that a narcotic that was destroying the man could make it possible for him to behave with such confidence. The pendulum began swinging back at the end of the meal. Nikolai started shifting as if it were impossible to become comfortable and surreptitiously he scratched his arms and then, trying to disguise the movement, his legs. Josef saw Illinivitch and Vladimirov watching intently, then bunch in conversation.

There were three hours before the Presidential reception. As soon as they returned to the embassy, Josef took Nikolai to his room and gave him another envelope. The negotiator had insisted on holding each dose until it was necessary. The sight of the writer injecting himself had begun to disgust him, so he left the room to find Vladimirov's secretary waiting in the passageway to say Illinivitch wanted him in the upstairs study. The ambassador was there, too, when Josef entered.

'A disgusting scene,' began Illinivitch.

He's accepted that whatever move he planned against Devgeny has failed, decided Josef. So now it was time for the deputy Minister to start rebuilding bridges.

'What?' demanded Josef, truculently.

'The sight of Russia's foremost writer, groping and snatching at himself because of a filthy addiction.'

Vladimirov was smiling, delighted.

'No doubt', said Josef, 'you will have made a full report to Moscow?'

'Yes,' said Illinivitch. 'Of course. I'd be failing in my responsibility as deputy Minister if I had not done so.'

'And no doubt', coaxed Josef, speaking to Vladimirov, 'you have fully endorsed what Comrade Illinivitch said.'

'Nothing has been overlooked,' assured the ambassador. Already, thought Josef, he's imagining another trial. He would enjoy the second much more than the first.

'You fully support Comrade Illinivitch in what he is doing?'

'Of course. And always have done,' said the ambassador, smiling at the deputy Minister.

'We have considered trying to get tonight's reception cancelled,' said Illinivitch. 'Because of Balshev's condition, there is a risk.'

'I'm far better able to judge Balshev's condition than either of you,' said Josef, curtly, knowing his tone would unsettle them. They would expect him to be frightened. 'He has just had another injection,' continued the negotiator. 'He will be quite capable of attending the reception. To pull out now, after Nikolai's successful appearance at the press luncheon, would be a direct insult to the President ... '

He looked pointedly at the ambassador. Illinivitch would have told him very little, guessed Josef. They could both manipulate the man to give the answers they wanted.

'Do you think it advisable that such an insult should be allowed, particularly with the growing American rapprochement with the Chinese?' he asked.

Vladimirov hesitated, seeking the trap to the oddly formal question. Unable to find it, he said, 'No, I don't think it should.'

The deputy Minister stared curiously at Josef. He's worried, thought the negotiator. That was good. It might lead to mistakes. Illinivitch regretted the ambassador being present, decided Josef. He was unsure at the way Josef had taken over the conversation and could not see the point to some of the questions.

'This is degenerating into the sort of inquiry that will be

necessary elsewhere,' he said, heavily. 'Comrade Vladimirov will formally introduce Balshev to the President and to the necessary members of the diplomatic corps, but I will expect you to act as interpreter otherwise.'

Josef nodded. They were even frightened of association now, he realized. His earlier thought about Nikolai reoccurred. The punctured ball was being discarded.

The reception was in the East Room of the White House and was even more crowded than that in New York. The Chinese appeared to have realized their mistake, he thought, as he entered through the bottom door. The communists, whose presence in the American capital had been agreed upon after the Kissinger visit to Peking in 1973, were in an isolated group near the canapé table on the left. They all wore their dark grey, buttoned-to-the-neck tunics, emblazoned only with the crimson Mao badge. They looked immaculate, thought the negotiator.

The conversation hushed as the party entered, then picked up again. People stopped eating and most turned towards them. Vladimirov and Illinivitch were either side of the writer, for the introductions. Endelman walked slightly to one side, to get the pictures he wanted. Josef walked alone, almost ostracized. Blyne was strangely quiet, awed in the presence of the President. Nikolai seemed perfectly controlled, relaxed even, walking quite confidently through the crowd, returning the smiles of strangers. The President was at the top of the room. He was a small man with grizzled hair and ears that stuck out, which embarrassed him. It had become an habitual gesture to finger them, as if he were trying to disguise their size. He did it now, as they approached. He wore built-up shoes, Josef noticed. He was sixty, Josef knew, and the Russian had expected him to have more grey hair. Perhaps he dyed it. The man smiled, with the quickness that Josef usually associated with nervousness, then came forward to meet them. Over his shoulder, Josef saw Morrison Rodney, the foreign affairs advisor whom he had met in the earliest stages of the wheat negotiations between America and Russia, after the disastrous harvest in the Soviet Union in 1972. The American smiled and nodded to him.

Ahead of Vladimirov's introduction, the President reached out, took Nikolai's hand and then covered it with his left hand as well, holding it for the benefit of photographers. There were two, apart from Endelman. It was an electioneering pose, thought Josef. The President turned, indicating members of the cabinet, then the Senate and Congress leaders and Nikolai smiled and shook hands. Then the American leader began to move with the writer among the ambassadors who pressed forward.

Morrison Rodney approached through the crowd and the two men shook hands.

'Quite a triumph,' said the advisor.

'Do you think so?'

The American, as susceptible to nuance as Josef, looked curiously.

'That's how it appears to us,' he said. 'Although I personally was surprised at your involvement. Not your sort of thing.'

'No,' agreed Josef. 'I haven't enjoyed it.'

'It was my idea to throw a reception,' said Rodney. 'The President became very keen.'

'Thank you,' said Josef. So there was a point to their conversation. He waited.

'We've been a little alarmed that relations have been tightening up with Moscow lately,' continued the advisor. 'We wanted to make a gesture.'

There was more, Josef knew. He felt comfortable, like someone wearing his favourite slippers. This was what he was used to and enjoyed, shading words with colours.

'There's been increased communist activity in Indo-China.

Do you know, I wouldn't be at all surprised if Laos wasn't on the maps in ten years time. Our intelligence says all the support is from Peking.'

The American indicated the group of Chinese, who stood watching Nikolai's perambulation of the room.

'The idea of this reception caused quite a lot of annoyance,' continued Morrison Rodney. 'We got the feeling Peking had misunderstood just how far we were prepared to let Russian relations slip in our keenness to maintain our accord with them.'

'I'll convey the thought to Moscow,' said Josef, knowing he had been chosen as a message carrier. So Peking had become slightly too confident and an apparently innocuous reception had been staged to remind them of their biggest fear, a renewed and stronger link between Russia and America. Nikolai was making slow progress back towards them. The punctured ball had been picked up for one final game, thought Josef. He owed Morrison Rodney a debt, he realized.

Nikolai reached them, looking strained, thought Josef. Vladimirov introduced Josef to the President.

'I've heard a great deal about you, Mr Bultova,' said the American leader. He infused meaning into the cliché.

'I'm afraid a great deal of fiction is written into what I do,' he dismissed, easily.

'Have you enjoyed your visit this time?'

'Very much. But then, I always enjoy America,' replied Josef. He wondered why the man's parents hadn't had his ears corrected by surgery when he was a child.

'I found Moscow interesting when I was there,' said the President. 'I thought the jewellery in the Armoury was magnificent. I was very glad to strengthen the bridges between our two countries.'

Another hint, thought Josef. 'I think everyone appreciates the growing friendship between the countries of the world.

And the part you are personally playing to make it possible,' he said.

Diplomatic sleight-of-hand, thought the negotiator moving words around like a conjuror. The challenge was to find the shell beneath which was hidden the word that mattered.

The President's glance towards the Chinese was hardly discernible.

'I'd like to talk with Mr Balshev privately for a moment,' he said, looking around for the ambassador. Vladimirov had obeyed Illinivitch's instructions and withdrawn to the other side of the room. He appeared deep in conversation with the deputy Minister.

'Please,' said Josef, quickly. 'Allow me to interpret.'

The President hesitated, uncertainly, aware of the slight diplomatic discourtesy in not involving the ambassador. Vladimirov remained with his back to them. Shrugging, the President led the way to a side room, with Josef and Nikolai following. The negotiator saw Vladimirov and Illinivitch turn too late. They looked worried. Only by hurrying could Vladimirov cross the room before they entered the side chamber and that would have attracted attention. As they went through the door, Josef turned and smiled at them. An idea had begun forming in Josef's mind. Poor Morrison Rodney, he thought.

It was a small study, directly off the East Room complex. The American translation of Nikolai's book lay on the desk. The whole charade had been staged for the benefit of those outside, so once in the tiny room there was little to say. The President indicated the book.

'I enjoyed *Walk Softly on a Lonely Day*,' he said.

Nikolai looked surprised, as if he had expected something more profound from the man.

'Thank you,' he said.

'Perhaps you'd sign it.'

'I'd be pleased to,' replied Nikolai, still disappointed.

There was the arranged knock on the door and one of the official photographers entered. In years to come, thought Josef, the photograph would hang in some personal museum in the man's home town. The picture session took exactly five minutes, then, as if rehearsed, the photographer stopped and the President began moving towards the door. Stop-watch diplomacy, thought Josef. Now it was his turn.

As they approached the door, Josef said to the President. 'We were talking earlier of the growing friendship between the countries of the world ... '

They passed into the main room as the President looked inquiringly at the negotiator.

' ... I would not like any offence created, however un-intentional,' continued the negotiator, 'by Nikolai not having properly greeted the representatives of the People's Republic of China ... '

They were in the middle of the room now, being approached by members of the Cabinet. Several heard the remark. The Chinese stood about twenty yards away, still by the food table. The President frowned, looking suspiciously at Josef. It had been calculated to the second, Josef congratulated himself.

'I'm sure ... ' began the American, seeking an escape, but Josef gestured towards the Chinese, openly, so they would realize they were being talked about.

'They have waited,' stressed the negotiator.

The tiny knot of men went completely quiet. Several shuffled, embarrassed. They all knew it would be taking the rebuke too far. But not to approach the communists, now they knew they were being discussed, would be as bad as avoiding the meeting. Morrison Rodney stood on the edge of the group, his face burnt with anger. He had been seen talking to Josef and would be blamed. It was unfortunate, thought Josef, but in similar circumstances he knew Rodney would do the same. The Chinese were moving restlessly, talking among themselves. Across the room, Vladimirov and Illinivitch stared, aware of the discomfort but too far away to discern the reason. They had utterly misjudged the reception, decided Josef. His father had been wrong to champion Vladimirov all those years ago. The man was not a good diplomat.

Reluctantly, the President moved towards the Chinese, smiling at their interpreter. It was a frozen, hostile encounter, Nikolai moving forward like a robot to barely touch hands with the Chinese envoy, who actually tried to look away at the moment of contact. There was a glitter of flash-bulbs. Whatever harm had been done by the Stockholm press-conference would be erased by that one photograph, Josef knew. He wondered if his acquaintanceship with Morrison Rodney were irreparably harmed. Probably, he decided. The President was glaring at him, fixedly, not trying to disguise the hostility. The man knew he had been tricked, although he probably guessed for the wrong reasons. He had badly damaged his credibility for any future negotiations with America, Josef knew. It didn't matter. He was striving to survive.

Having touched hands like dancers in a medieval court, they parted. The President was furious, Josef saw. There was a muttered conversation with people around him and the indication that the reception was over rippled through the room. Vladimirov and Illinivitch moved forward with Nikolai and Josef, making the first farewells as chief guests. The President shook Nikolai's hand and smiled, knowing the writer was unaware of what had happened. He looked directly at Josef when their hands touched.

'Goodbye, Mr Bultova,' he said. There was great finality in the three words.

'You caused an incident,' accused Vladimirov, in the car returning to the embassy. 'There'll be a complaint.'

He panicked easily, thought Josef. His father had

definitely been wrong. He felt disloyal making the mental criticism.

'I demand to know what happened,' said Illinivitch.

Josef smiled at him, in open defiance, ignoring the statement.

'If there is a complaint,' he said. 'Any inquiry will clearly show that you both abandoned Nikolai.'

They were frightened, he knew. That was good.

Shyly, the girl entered the Kremlin office and stood, down-faced with embarrassment in front of the Minister.

'Don't be nervous, Sanya,' soothed Devgeny.

Still it was impossible for her to talk.

'You did very well,' congratulated Devgeny. 'I want you to know that. The authorization for your family to have a flat of their own has gone through today.'

Chapter Twenty-One

Josef slept even worse than usual, eventually abandoning the pretence before dawn and sitting looking out over the American capital, waiting impatiently for the day. It was snowing again, with a muffled, hissing sound, whitening everything. The snow had been an enemy in the camp, he remembered. Not because of the cold, which was bad enough, but because it halted movement. The authorities welcomed it and watched, hoping to find tracks that would show them the after-dark communication between the barrack blocks. But he'd beaten them, he reminisced, smiling. Until Medev had begged him not to because of the danger, and even after that, when the man was sick and needed the medicine Josef knew existed in the camp and could be purchased at extortionate prices with the money he made black marketeering, he had ventured out after curfew, a tree branch secured by wire around his waist and trailed, like a rake, so that the slight indentations made by his sack-wrapped feet were erased seconds after he had made them.

Outside it began to lighten into a grey day. Washington would have its white Christmas. He'd enjoyed Christmases in America. His father, who could remember the celebrations before the revolution, had allowed the occasion to be recognized. It had been mentioned at the trial, he recalled. On the first or maybe the second day, nearly the whole morning had been taken up by the prosecutor talking about the holiday and present-giving and at first Josef had smiled, unable to see how anything so innocent, even to a country with an atheist dogma, could be made into something so damning. It would be snowing in Moscow, too, he realized. Moscow looked attractive in the snow, he always thought, like a nostalgic old woman wearing her faded wedding-gown.

Without conscious thought, the idea of defecting suddenly came to him. It would not be difficult, he decided. This early he could slip from the embassy and no one would know. His role with Nikolai had finished. The writer could easily be returned to the Soviet Union without Josef's guidance. Money would be no problem. Despite the denials to Illini-vitch, there were subsidiary accounts in Switzerland and it would probably be possible to clear his American account before they moved against him. He could go south, to Mexico, then hedge-hop through South America. He had enough money available in America to stay there for several months, maybe a year even. La Paz would be pleasant. The height had never worried him. Or Lima. He could easily get lost in Peru. But that would mean abandoning Pamela, who had thought nothing of abandoning him. There had been a women's camp in the Potma complex, he remembered. Was it Camp 23 or 25? He wasn't sure. There had been a lot of talk about the women's camp because the first substitute for sex was to talk about it. They degenerated worse than the men, according to the stories. The long-termers, those who accepted they would never get out, became like animals, actually discarding speech. In the end, even the guards were frightened and wouldn't go into their enclosure. Food was pushed through hatches until that became too much trouble and the problem was solved by starving them to death. He couldn't allow Pamela to become an animal, he thought. And to defect would be to become a bad Russian.

He waited until seven-thirty before going to Nikolai's room. The writer was awake, the hint of desperation already evident. Wordlessly, Josef handed him the transparent container and looked away while the man attended to himself. He looked dissolute and ill, Josef thought, his skin chalk-white but dirty-looking, despite the custom of two daily showers. His eyes were black-ringed, so completely that it looked almost like some strange make-up, and although he was maintaining his personal cleanliness, he had started to neglect the clothes he had bought with Endelman and of which he had been so proud.

Nikolai would have to be cured, Josef determined. And it would have to be done as soon as possible. That would mean his being met immediately they arrived in the Russian capital by doctors who could take him to a sanatorium. It would have to be kept from Nikolai, of course. He couldn't know until the moment of arrival.

There had to be goodbyes, Josef realized. He had hardly spoken to Blyne at the reception and he still had to settle his outstanding debt to Endelman. He left Nikolai packing and instructed the ambassador's secretary that he wanted to see Vladimirov at eleven o'clock, then drove to the Hay Adams. The publisher was already packed, Josef saw. There was coffee on a side-table and Blyne poured.

'So,' said the publisher, 'it's goodbye.'

Josef nodded.

'I can't pretend I enjoyed it,' said Blyne. 'But it's been a success publicly. No one can remember a subscription like there's been for this book. The initial print for the book club is one million. Currently, the paperback bidding is four million dollars.'

Josef supposed he should be interested in the figure. He had forgotten the eventual financial reward. Perhaps, he thought, it wouldn't matter anyway.

'It'll go higher,' predicted Blyne. 'We're letting them create their own hysteria.'

'We've been extraordinarily lucky,' said Josef. A great fatigue seemed to be engulfing him.

'Matheson is staying, by the way,' added Blyne.

'I'm glad,' said Josef, sincerely.

There was silence between them. They were encountering that odd, embarrassed etiquette people always stumble over before parting.

'I'm putting Nikolai under treatment as soon as I get back to Russia,' said Josef.

'Good,' said Blyne, shortly. Then he added, 'How is this going to affect you personally?'

'I don't know,' said Josef.

Blyne detected the depth of Josef's doubt.

'If there's another occasion ... ' he began, awkwardly. He stopped, then tried again. 'I mean, if there's another chance of publishing something from the Soviet Union ... '

'I'll remember the promise I made in Vienna,' said Josef.

'I hope it works out. Personally, I mean.'

'Thanks. You had a letter', reminded Josef. 'From Moscow, after you sought permission for Endelman to accompany me.'

Blyne frowned, trying to remember.

'Yes,' said the publisher, vaguely.

'Have you still got it?'

The publisher went to his briefcase and leafed through the papers there. He finally extracted a single sheet.

'May I have it?'

'Of course,' agreed Blyne.

Again the conversation lapsed.

'Perhaps we could keep in touch,' offered the publisher, like a holiday acquaintance promising to exchange letters.

'Yes,' said Josef. Both recognized the emptiness of the gesture. Josef stood up, wanting to end the meeting, and offered his hand.

'Thank you,' he said, with feeling. 'Without you and Matheson, what happened in New York would have been a disaster.'

'I had as much to lose as you,' pointed out Blyne.

238

Endelman was waiting in his room overlooking the White House, on the floor above that which Blyne had occupied.

'Honouring your debt, Josef?' he asked. The early diffidence masked a very unpleasant man, decided Josef.

'Yes,' said the Russian.

'How's Nikolai?' smiled the photographer. At that moment Josef felt more dislike for the man than ever before.

'About the same as any heroin addict needing at least two fixes a day,' replied the Russian.

'Poor Nikolai. You know, he actually insisted the first time? Kept on about the need to experience everything. But he was frightened of the injection. They often are, in the beginning. I had to give it to him.'

The man spoke boastfully. He was very proud of what he had done, decided Josef. The Russian handed over five one-hundred-dollar bills.

'Thank you,' smirked Endelman.

'You might as well have this,' said Josef unexpectedly.

The photographer looked at the envelope.

'I'm not going through Canada carrying heroin,' explained Josef. 'I'm going to give Nikolai an injection just before we leave so that he can last the trip. As soon as we get to Moscow, I'm putting him under treatment.'

Endelman accepted the packet. He had only recently had an injection himself, Josef knew. His pupils were dilated and several times he had smiled for no reason.

'Well, it's goodbye then,' said Endelman. He stood up and extended his hand. Josef looked at it, turned and left the room without speaking. As he closed the door, he heard Endelman laughing.

Vladimirov was waiting for him alone in the study when he returned to the embassy. He was smiling and looked very confident.

'Comrade Illinivitch has decided not to return with you.'

Josef frowned, trying to assess the significance. The man obviously felt there was some advantage in remaining and that could only be to obtain something harmful to be used against him.

Josef's mind slipped sideways. He had made it quite clear to Illinivitch that any move against Devgeny had failed. It was obvious there would be an inquiry immediately he returned. Surely the deputy Minister, fearing that he would now be purged, hadn't decided to defect? He couldn't recall anyone of Illinivitch's rank going across. And he personally could benefit, he decided. He had consistently opposed the man and been seen to do so. And Devgeny would have been responsible for allowing Illinivitch to come to the West. The man's defection, Josef decided, would be very good. It was the second time the thought of defection had arisen that day, he realized.

'When *is* he returning?' he probed.

The ambassador gestured uncertainly.

'A day or two. Maybe longer.'

'Has Moscow approved?' asked Josef, knowing the question would offend.

'Of course,' said Vladimirov, sharply. 'And such a question is hardly correct, coming from you.'

'Vladimirov,' said Josef, carefully calculating the weariness of his voice. 'There is a great deal of this tour about which you know nothing. Please don't challenge me.'

Josef wondered who hated him more, Devgeny or Illinivitch or Vladimirov.

'I want something done in advance of my return,' resumed Josef. He was almost over-stressing the imperious attitude, he realized. 'I have decided that Nikolai should be placed under immediate hospital treatment. I want a message sent to Moscow.'

'Full reports have already been sent about the man's addiction,' said Vladimirov.

'I've no doubt of that,' said Josef. 'Just do as I say. I want an ambulance to meet me when I get to Sheremetyevo. '

He stood, preparing to leave the room.

'Wait, Bultova,' commanded the other man.

Josef turned.

'I feel we will be seeing each other again very shortly,' said Vladimirov.

'Yes,' said Josef, without the fear the ambassador had tried to engender. 'I'm sure we will.'

He walked from the room, leaving Vladimirov sitting at his desk, blank-faced with doubt.

Josef had timed their trip meticulously. Over the days, he had carefully calculated how long Nikolai's injections lasted, and assessed that the injection just before they left the embassy would be sufficient until they reached Moscow. As a precaution he still had one envelope left, despite what he had told Endelman. He was travelling on a diplomatic passport so there would be no difficulties with customs in Montreal, particularly as they would be in transit.

Nikolai spent the initial stages of the trip to Canada in the familiar withdrawn state that followed his injection. In Montreal Josef refused an airport press-conference and they spent forty minutes in a V.I.P. lounge. They were the first to go out to the Ilyushin. The captain walked with them, settling them into a specially curtained section of the aircraft. Nikolai's depression seemed to be increasing now they were finally going home.

'It's going to be very different, isn't it Josef?'

'Yes,' agreed the negotiator.

'I've done nothing about a sequel to *Walk Softly on a Lonely Day.*'

'I know.'

'I haven't even got an idea.'

'It'll come,' Josef encouraged.

241

'Not in Moscow, it won't,' disagreed the writer. 'The place presses down on me. I can't think properly there.'

After a while, Nikolai lapsed into a snuffling, uncertain sleep, occasionally whimpering, like someone in pain. The negotiator ordered vodka and sipped it, reflectively. How accurate would Nikolai's prediction be, he wondered, staring into the glass. Things would be different, he decided. Very different. He shivered, unconsciously, and the stewardess misunderstood and handed him a blanket. He accepted it, rather than attempt an explanation. December was the worst time in the camps. It was too cold for any outside work, even though a new commandant would occasionally try, abandoning it only when the number of men who died reached a level unacceptable even there. The cold became a physical pain, gouging into the body and creating a perpetual numbing ache. Everyone slept bent into the person next to them, trying to steal some warmth. A blanket could cost twenty roubles and the barrack trustee had to be bribed a rouble a day to ensure it wasn't immediately stolen. It always was, of course. Josef had knowingly re-purchased the same piece of coarse material three times during the second winter until, in the end, it had become so foul covering his father, who was incontinent by them, lying constantly in his own, embarrassed filth, that it became unstealable. He fingered the covering the stewardess had handed him, appreciating its thickness. A man could establish the financial basis for several years in black-market trading in Potma with one blanket like this, he thought. He checked his watch. Two roubles? Surely more than that now. Any camp guard would surely pay six. From the time he realized that they would be over Russia. Nikolai was next to the window and Josef strained, looking out over him. They had passed through the time zone and it was dark outside the aircraft. They would be down there, somewhere, he thought, dotted along the winding river like an infectious disease, collection places

242

for the dissenters and the political malcontents or just the plain unfortunates who had become of so little consequence that the camps they occupied were not thought important enough to justify names, just numbers. Part of a prisoner's number identified the camp to which he belonged. It took only a short time to realize that the number was more important than your name, because you were always summoned by your number and to mistake it or ignore it meant punishment. The name ceased to be important, which was part of the psychology. People who accepted themselves as ciphers behaved like ciphers, never creating trouble.

He felt the aircraft begin to lose height and Nikolai stirred. Another injection would not be necessary, Josef thought gratefully, certainly not while Nikolai was under his control. He quickly got up and locked himself inside the cramped lavatory, taking the remaining envelope from his pocket. He dropped it into the lavatory bowl, then watched it disappear in a swirl of disinfectant water. When he returned to his seat, Nikolai was shivering and staring around the aircraft. He made no greeting as Josef sat down.

'I feel awful,' he said.

'I'm sorry.'

'What am I going to do about it ... you know, now I'm back?'

Josef was surprised the question had been so long coming.

'It will be all right,' he said, vaguely. 'I'll arrange something.'

They were below the clouds now and even though there was no moon, Josef could detect the reflection of whiteness. So it had snowed. The wheels grabbed at that moment of landing when airline passengers hold their breath, snatched again and then the plane settled on the runway.

'We're home,' said Nikolai. He sounded very sad.

'Yes,' agreed Josef, with equal reluctance.

The steward beckoned Josef forward immediately the

plane came to a stop and he edged into the cramped flight-deck. The pilot gestured out through the port side.

'Control tower had just told me the ambulance is waiting,' he said. Was there censure in his voice? Probably not. There was no reason why there should be. He was becoming over-sensitive, which was stupid.

'Does he know?' asked the captain, jerking his head back towards where Nikolai was sitting.

'Not unless he sees it out of the window.'

'He's on the wrong side.'

He returned to the seat and Nikolai smiled up at him, a grateful expression.

'Thank you, Josef,' he said.

'What for?'

'For not abandoning me.'

Josef detected the sound of the disembarkation ramp locking into the aircraft.

'Come on,' he said. 'It's time to go.'

It had begun to snow, very lightly, but the wind was screeching across the tarmac, grabbing it in handfuls and throwing it into their faces. Nikolai hunched into his topcoat and it wasn't until he got to the bottom of the steps that he focused and saw there was no welcoming party. He turned, squinting, as the snow stung at his face, seeking an explanation. Three men emerged from the shelter of the ambulance, grey and nondescript, bent forward for protection. Nikolai stared at them, at first unaware they were anything to do with him. Then he saw they were coming directly towards him and came back to the negotiator.

'What is it Josef ... ?' he said. The words were picked up and jostled by the wind, so that it was difficult for Josef to hear them.

'You need treatment,' said Josef.

The men were alongside now, nodding to Josef, positioning themselves around the writer.

'No Josef. Please. You're my friend. You know what it will mean. Please Josef. No.'

They were waiting for his permission, Josef realized.

'Goodbye, Nikolai,' he said.

'But Josef. No. Please Josef. No. Help me.'

The negotiator nodded and the men either side grabbed Nikolai's arm, turning him towards the vehicle. He tried to snatch away, but they were experts and held him easily. Nikolai attempted to baulk, wedging his heels into the ground, but they were prepared for that too, half lifting him, so the protest ended with his slipping on the ground. Desperately, as they took him away, Nikolai turned, wild eyed now, screaming back at the negotiator, but the wind took the words and discarded them, so that Josef never heard what he said.

He stood, watching the vehicle grunt into life and then move slowly away, the wipers fashioning half-moon eyes in the snow. Track marks formed behind it, like two skeins of wool unwinding. Josef waited until the ambulance was completely out of sight and then looked around for the car to take him to the terminal building. The tarmac was deserted. They had expected him to accompany Nikolai to hospital, he decided. It would be another thirty minutes before the bus arrived for the other passengers, he thought. It would be quicker to walk. His clothes encrusted with snow, he crunched off towards the lights, head down against the wind, trying to draw back into his coat. He stopped inside the arrival building, stamping the snow from his shoes and billowing his coat, trying to shake off the cold and dampness. He wiped his hair and face with a handkerchief which became soaked, so he discarded it in a refuse bin. The arrival was a familiar scene, he thought, wearily. How many times had he entered this building, washed yellow with its unshaded lights, with the immigration desks like the traps from which racehorses emerged in America and Britain? Behind them the narrow, low benches of the customs officials were deserted. He walked forward, towards the nearest immigration channel, nodding as he passed through to the man in the tiny cubicle.

'Comrade.'

'What?'

'Passport.'

Josef stared at him, aware for the first time of a difference. There were hardly any passengers in the terminal building, yet there were more airport officials and people than usual.

'My name is Bultova,' he said expectantly, 'Josef Bultova.'

'Passport,' insisted the immigration official, doggedly.

'I see,' said Josef. He groped into the briefcase and produced the document. There was hardly any conversation in the hall, Josef realized. The man was steadfastly leafing through the pages, even making the pretence of checking against a hard-bound, loose-paged book at his side. It took a full ten minutes.

'Thank you,' he said.

Josef nodded, his face expressionless, passing through into the customs hall. His suitcases stood, isolated, on the very middle bench, in full view of the entire hall and in a spot where he would have to walk at least forty yards to claim them. He was aware of his own footsteps, as if the ground upon which he were walking was hollow. There was no official near his baggage. He waited, gazing straight ahead, ignoring the attention. It was nearly fifteen minutes before anyone approached him.

'Your baggage?'

'Yes.'

'Open them, please.'

'Which one?'

'All of them.'

There were three cases. Josef unlocked the smallest first, ending with the largest. They were painstakingly packed, the suits with tissue paper in the arms and legs to prevent creasing, the shirts laundered and neatly packed, in the American fashion. The customs official rummaged them all, taking everything out, snatching the paper from the suits, unfolding the shirts, reducing the cases to chaos.

'The briefcases,' he demanded.

Josef offered both to him. The man jumbled through them, sorting aimlessly through the tapes and miniature recorders, then shuffling the papers into a disorganized mess. He lifted Josef's pills from the second case and dropped one of the bottles. It smashed against the concrete and sleeping pills rolled everywhere. The man looked at him for reaction, but Josef said nothing.

'Follow me.'

Josef walked to the cubicle with the man and entered and stood, waiting.

'Personal search,' announced the official, shortly. The hut was created from pressed cardboard sheets and there was no heating. The temperature would be near freezing, thought Josef. Naked, he stood while the man explored his pockets, rifling through his wallet and credit-card holder. Thank God, thought Josef, he had got rid of the heroin on the plane. He clamped his teeth together, determined not to show his discomfort. The cold was drawing the feeling away from his legs. As he finished with each piece of clothing, the official was tossing it aside on to a bench, but Josef held back from reclaiming it. He had to await permission, he knew. How easily the old rules came back.

'Thank you,' the man said, flatly.

The cold had permeated Josef's body and so even dressed it was difficult for him to walk. He hobbled to the bench across which the contents of his cases were strewn and stood, looking at the man. He was still in charge, Josef accepted.

'That's all,' said the official.

Slowly, Josef picked up every pill from the floor, taking

an unused tape from its cardboard carton and using that as a container. He laid his suits out, replaced the tissue paper, then folded the shirts into their original, pressed creases. He worked unhurriedly, with no sign of stress. The official stood attentive, aware of the occasional snigger from people watching. The other passengers had been allowed off the plane, but prevented from entering the customs area. Josef could hear the babble behind him and knew they would be staring over the partition, curious at the scene.

'May I go?' asked Josef, finally. He was very polite.

'Yes.'

'Thank you, sir.'

The 'sir' came automatically.

He knew there would be no car waiting, so he looked around for a taxi. Several stood in the reserved bay, but there were no drivers. He opened the door of the first and sounded the horn, but no one came. Sighing, he carried his bags to the bus and humped them into the baggage section. The negotiator managed to get a taxi at the terminal and slumped back as it drove towards the apartment. He felt exhausted, almost unable to move, as if someone had tapped an artery and drained the blood from him. He was unaware of the car stopping and felt stupid when the driver turned, looking quizzically at him, and announced his arrival. He loaded the cases under his arms, backed in through the apartment door and found the lift had been turned off. He made two trips up and down from the fourth floor, to get his belongings into the apartment.

It stank. And was filthy, dusty with neglect, several unwashed glasses lying on pieces of furniture, all of which was disarranged. There were several cushions half on, half off the chairs and embers of a long-dead fire mottled the fireplace and the carpet in front of it. Ashtrays overflowed, some even spilling their contents on the floor. The cow. The filthy, spoiled cow.

He went from place to place, putting back cushions, emptying ashtrays. Anger flooded over him, a reaction to the dirtiness of the flat and to the carefully orchestrated humiliation since he had stepped off the plane.

Josef burst into the bedroom, flooding it with light. It was as filthy as the main room and a sour odour hung over everything.

Pamela snored, an ugly, phlegmy sound. Savagely, he snatched the clothing from her, staring down, waiting for her shocked awakening. She was completely naked, her hair matted over her face, which was swollen and red, almost as if she had been slapped. An overpowering smell of alcohol wafted up at him. She shifted and groaned, but did not wake up. His eyes swept over her nakedness, almost clinically. He stopped, concentrating on her navel, then reached out, touching her pubic turf with his finger, like someone apprehensive that contact might burn. She murmured and turned over. There was no feeling, he thought. No desire, not even lust. She moved again and there was an odd sound and he saw she had urinated in the bed and was lying in it, unconsciously. Gently, anxious not to awaken her now because there was nothing to say, he replaced the bed covering and walked softly from the bedroom. He made the couch acceptable, then sat down. She was disgusting, he thought, utterly disgusting. How prescient Nikolai had been on the homecoming plane.

Everything was different. Completely different.

Chapter Twenty-Two

She looked at him curiously, as if he were a stranger. Neither spoke. Her eyes carried on, moving over the apartment that had taken him three hours to clean. He had worked carelessly, disregarding the noise, purposely creating it in the beginning hoping to awaken her, but there had been no movement within the bedroom. Now it was almost noon. The front of her towelling robe was stained and the hem had become unstitched, he saw. The belt had gone, too. She held it across the front of her body, defensively.

'Hello,' she said. Instinctively she ran her fingers through her hair, fussing it into shape.

'Hello,' he said.

'Didn't know you were coming back. Should have told me. Telephoned or something.'

Properly constructed sentences seemed too much for her. She was still half drunk, he realized. Pamela came unsteadily into the room and sat down opposite him. Her feet were dirty where she had walked around the flat for several days without stockings or shoes. They stared at each other, seeking a bridge to cross.

'Nice you're back,' she tried.

He said nothing.

'Trip.'

'What?'

'Good trip?'

He shrugged.

'Place was a mess,' she confessed.

'Yes.'

'Should have told me. Didn't know.'

'Why?'

She squinted to understand the question.

'Why?' repeated Josef. 'The filth? And the drink?'

Pamela began to move, then realized she was holding her robe and risked exposing herself. She stared down at her hand, reluctant to release it, then back up at her husband. She squinted again.

'What?' she mumbled.

'What's happened to you?'

'Lonely.'

'That isn't sufficient reason.'

'Unhappy. Don't like it.'

He went to the kitchen, made coffee and then served her, refilling the cup as she emptied it, watching without sympathy as sobriety came to her. She grew more and more uncomfortable under his stare.

'Better?'

'Suppose so.'

'I know,' he announced. He had decided it had to be done abruptly.

'Know?'

'About Nikolai. At the dacha.'

'Oh.'

'He took great delight in telling me.'

'I thought he would.'

'Why?' he demanded, again.

'He got me drunk.' She jumped immediately into the practised defence.

'No,' he refused.

'We *did* drink.'

'You knew what you were doing.'

'I was frightened.'

'Frightened!' It was a sneer.

'Yes, Josef. Frightened because I knew I was inadequate … that I couldn't make a proper wife. Can't you imagine what it was like for me, married to someone like you, terrified to say or do anything, knowing it would be wrong, frightened of the look that would show you were disappointed or ashamed … '

'Was Nikolai better than I was, when my turn finally came?' he asked, bitterly.

'Oh God,' she said.

'Was he?' he pressed, savagely.

'Don't,' she said. 'Please don't.'

'Don't be stupid,' he said.

'Isn't the aggrieved husband act a little false?' she accused. 'You knew I wasn't a virgin.'

'I didn't know it was him.'

'Ah,' she said, given a sudden explanation. 'So it's pride more than love.'

'I never questioned what you did before we married,' he said, refusing her the excuse.

She looked into her lap, rehearsing the words. 'I *am* ashamed, Josef,' she offered. 'There wasn't a time when you were away when I wasn't terrified of the moment you'd find out, knowing that b..stard would eventually boast that he'd screwed your wife … '

Josef winced and her words clogged as she stumbled to a halt.

'I'm begging forgiveness, Josef,' she said. 'Please. I know I've hurt you, terribly. But I want help.'

'I saw your mother in London,' he said and she stared at him, unable to understand the change of direction.

'We talked about visas.'

Pamela's face cleared. She looked very sad. 'Oh,' she said, understanding.

She would cry now, thought Josef. Then her eyes would look worse than they already did. He hoped she would avoid it. She really did look quite ugly.

'Did you try?' he asked.

'Yes,' she said, resigned.

'And?'

'They wouldn't give me re-entry. But I can go out, of course. Any time.'

'Yes.'

'I saw my parents' marriage collapse. Don't let it happen to me. I know I've no right, after what I've done. I can't even offer an explanation or a proper excuse. But let me stay, Josef.'

'Your mother wants to see you again.'

The tears finally came, marking parallel paths down her face. Her nose was running, too. Disgusted, he threw a handkerchief across the gap separating them.

'Can't you forgive anyone, Josef?' she sobbed.

He continued looking at her, saying nothing.

'I hope to God', she said, 'that you never know the need for pity.'

'Why don't you take a bath?' he said, rising. 'You smell.'

Chapter Twenty-Three

He had to wait three days to appear before the inquiry committee of the Praesidium. By coincidence, it was the day Pamela was flying to London. She had made a desperate effort since the homecoming, accepting the separate sleeping arrangements, keeping the flat clinically clean and not, as far as he was aware, touching any alcohol.

Twice, when she realized his determination, she had pleaded again, staying completely controlled, not giving way to tears, which Josef admired. He had matched her control and rejected her. Everything was still very civilized, he thought.

He saw her struggling to get her cases from what had been their bedroom and moved to help her.

'Thank you,' she said.

There had been another time, between the Stockholm visits, when they had been over-polite and courteous to each other, Josef recalled.

'There's an important meeting. I'm afraid I shan't be able to take you to the airport.'

'It doesn't matter.'

'I'm sorry.'

'It really doesn't matter.'

'I'll make arrangements through my London bank for an allowance. And some drawing facilities on the main account.'

'Please don't bother. I gather my father left me a lot of money.'

'I'd like to.'

'I shan't use it.'

'I'd still like to.'

'As you wish.'

She looked very lovely. She would have opened out like a flower in the sunshine of Sochi, he thought. It was all very unfortunate.

'Perhaps I'll write,' she offered.

'All right.'

'I suppose we should be sensible. About a divorce, I mean. You might meet somebody else. Or I might.'

'Yes,' he agreed. 'I suppose we should.'

'Will it be difficult, because of different nationalities?'

'I don't know.'

'You'll find out, though?' she asked.

'Yes.'

They stood looking at each other. Sometimes, Pamela thought, he looks just like a bear. But a friendly, cuddly bear, like they have in children's fairy stories.

'I must go,' she said. 'Or I'll miss my plane.'

'Yes.'

'You won't look me up in London, will you?' she guessed.

'Probably not,' he agreed.

'I *will* write.'

He wondered if he should kiss her. She seemed to expect something. Hesitantly, he offered his hand. She faltered, then took it.

'I'm sorry, Josef,' she said, for the last time.

'Yes,' he said. 'It's a pity.'

They stayed joined for several moments. Then, withdrawing his hand, he said, 'I'll help you down with your luggage.'

Josef was conscious of the awareness of people as he approached the main committee room in the Kremlin. Perhaps Devgeny's secretary had been voicing his opinion. He was kept waiting for forty-five minutes, but sat relaxed,

255

recognizing the psychology and untroubled by it. Devgeny's secretary summoned him, not quite able to keep the smirk off his face. Josef picked up his two briefcases and followed into the room, pausing just inside the door. Its size was imposing. Chandeliers hung from the high, vaulted ceiling and were augmented by strip lights, which gave everything a harsh, unreal glare. Windows stretched from ceiling to floor almost the complete length of one side, and facing walls were bare of any decoration. An enormous table occupied the centre of the room, slightly curved at either end, so that the men before whom he was to appear sat in a half moon, facing out towards the windows. In front of them, there was a small table, also half-mooned, for officials and secretaries, and then, isolated, a table at which only one man could sit, positioned so that the occupant had his back to the light. He walked in front of the expressionless men, towards the smallest table he knew was his. He paused, then put his briefcases beside the chair and turned, awaiting permission to sit. Devgeny was half-way down on the left-hand side, he noticed. Illinivitch was sitting next to him. Korshunov was several seats further along. Ballenin was far away, among the lesser important. In the centre sat the Party Chairman, Mikhail Beilkin, with the Secretary, Ostrap Svetlova, on his right. Josef was always surprised when he saw them. Such men should be over six feet, he felt, and large, their stature befitting their positions. Both, in fact, were quite small men. But then, so were Krushchev and Beria. Both men sitting before him were assessed to be tougher and more ruthless than either of them had been. The sixteen men of the Politbureau were all on the inquiry committee. That gave it the highest rank possible, he realized.

The Party Secretary nodded his head and Josef sat down. Devgeny stared at him, his face blank. He looked better, thought Josef, than when they had last confronted each other. Even his suit was freshly pressed and there was no sign in his face of the excessive drinking that Josef had suspected before he went on tour with Nikolai. He moved on to Illinivitch. The man was looking at him as if he were a stranger.

'This preliminary inquiry into the recent tour of the West with Comrade Balshev is to establish whether a criminal investigation should be undertaken into your conduct,' began Svetlova, officiously.

He nodded towards Devgeny.

' ... The Minister of Culture lays the complaint against you. It is serious ... '

Devgeny shifted in his seat, his excitement needing movement.

'There is, in fact, a demand that you be placed on trial,' the Secretary went on. 'This Committee will decide whether such a trial is justified ... '

The man shuffled through the papers lying before him, found the document he wanted and looked up.

' ... There is provision for a charge against you under Section 190 of our Criminal Statute,' he said. 'The allegation is of anti-Soviet activity ... '

Why had the man to go through the charade of finding the document? It was always Section 190. That was the panacea indictment thrown like a fishing net over the Russian judicial system. It as always possible to mount a prosecution under Section 190, no matter what offence, real or otherwise. How bewildered his father had been when the allegation had been made against him, a man to whom such action would have been anathema. He had shaken his head, refusing to accept it, actually challenging the court clerk in the belief that the charge was wrongly made and there had been some terrible mistake.

'Do you have anything to say?' asked the Secretary.

Josef cleared his throat, rising to his feet. Whenever challenging a fact or addressing the committee, he had to stand, he knew.

'I categorically deny the accusation laid against me,' he said, formally, and sat down. Movement shuffled along the table and several of the committee looked sideways to their partners, as if they had expected Josef to say more.

The Secretary nodded to Devgeny, who rose and walked around the table, so that he could command the full attention of everyone. The Minister stood, one hand lightly resting on the huge table, savouring the moment. This, thought Josef, was the occasion for which the man had waited for nearly fifteen years, the moment of Devgeny's vindication. Now he would extract the apologies far more demeaning than those which Josef had been insisting upon for a decade and a half.

Perspiration was causing the inside of Josef's legs to irritate. He scratched himself surreptitiously. As he withdrew his hand he saw that it was four-thirty. Pamela's plane would be taking off now. She would be happier in London, he knew. And safer. Certainly safer. He wondered if she would ever realize that.

'There have been occasions in the past', began Devgeny, 'when this committee has had to make preliminary inquiries of this nature. Because of the fairness of the Russian legal system, many of those accusations have been dismissed as unfounded … '

He paused, for effect, but it was an unhappy hesitation, seeming as if the Minister were awaiting challenge upon the assertion of fairness. Several other people had the same impression, Josef knew.

' … Others, however, have not,' took up Devgeny. Even he regretted the pause, speaking quickly to make up for it. 'The accusation I make today will come into the second category. Rarely will this committee have encountered a worse case of anti-Sovietism … '

How many hours had gone into Devgeny's rehearsal, wondered Josef. He felt the briefcases at his side, a needless reassurance. He should have returned with more sleeping pills and tranquillizers, he thought. Devgeny seemed very confident. Hardly, decided Josef, with growing conviction, a man with little support in the Praesidium.

'The facts', went on Devgeny, 'are as simple as they are horrifying. At the beginning of this year, the Ministry of Culture heard that the Nobel Foundation was considering one of Russia's most brilliant writers, Nikolai Balshev, for their literary award.'

Was it really only a year ago, questioned Josef. It seemed a lifetime.

'Balshev's talent is undenied. There is probably no one in the world today with greater lyricism. He has been publicly acclaimed in every country in the world. More, he is a good Russian. It was decided that Balshev should be encouraged to accept the award if he were the eventual recipient, and that he would be allowed to make a literary tour of the West, in which the sales of his books were to be negotiated.'

He stopped, sipping from a glass of water. Dramatically he extended his hand, pointed at Josef.

'That man was entrusted with the task of negotiating those sales and arranging the tour. It was also his task to let the Foundation know, in a diplomatic way, that every facility would be made available for Balshev to accept.'

How easy it sounded, thought Josef. It was the job of a junior counsellor at a minor embassy, a mission in which nothing could go wrong.

'Bultova was selected because of his unrivalled knowledge of the West, to which he travels frequently ... '

Another pause, for effect.

' ... Some may think too frequently. He was to do more than just organize the tour. His principal job was to safe-guard Nikolai Balshev. The writer is a shy, unworldly man. His very lack of sophistication is one of the major delights of his writing. The Soviet Union had to be spared any embarrassment that such innocence might have unthinkingly created.'

Devgeny stopped for more water. It was a brilliant denunciation, conceded Josef.

'Because of the immense importance to the Soviet Union, I had our overseas security service constantly in attendance,' admitted the Minister.

They were very good, thought Josef. Not once had he recognized them. Devgeny would know of everything, of course. Like a croupier dealing cards, the Minister handed the security reports along the table.

Devgeny cleared his throat.

'Today Nikolai Balshev is a patient in a sanatorium. He is a hopeless, committed heroin addict. His creativity is utterly destroyed. In a few moments, I shall call a doctor to tell you that apart from his craving for drugs, Balshev has only one interest. He returned from the West a sexual deviant, a savage pederast. For the protection of the other patients, some of whom are young boys, Balshev has to be kept locked in a private ward.'

It was hardly surprising the secretary with thick spectacles had made up his mind, thought Josef. No doubt he'd witnessed the organization of the evidence, perhaps even typed the draft of Devgeny's opening address. Devgeny took a document from a folder.

'Many of you will be familiar with the press-conference in Stockholm. I refer to it again. Rarely can there have been an occasion so mismanaged as to create greater public criticism of the Soviet Union than this. Within twenty-four hours of that disastrous beginning, Bultova abandoned the man to become hopelessly drunk at an official reception while he telephoned his wife in Moscow ... '

He paused. ' ... to tell her he loved her.'

Sukalov had done more than just report the incident,

decided Josef. The ambassador had obviously decided there would be a purge and backed what he thought was the winning side. It didn't come as a shock to realize his telephone had been tapped. Josef shrugged, discomforted by the heat, wishing he could remove his jacket. In the camp, he remembered, there were many times when he wished he had just such a covering, instead of the thin cotton uniform that the wind and cold penetrated so easily.

'It was in Stockholm that the destruction of Nikolai Balshev began. Many of you will remember his demeanour when he left Moscow. He was apprehensive of his responsibilities, knowing he was going to the Nobel ceremony not only as an author, but as a representative of his country. He was a man needing help. He was a man needing assistance and guidance ... '

Another sip of water. Never again, Josef knew, would Devgeny experience a moment like this.

'Did he get it?' resumed Devgeny, rhetorically. 'He did not. Instead he was provided with drugs, to give him false confidence. The doctor will tell you the sort of man Nikolai Balshev is. He is brilliant, but unpredictable. His uncertainty in himself is deeply rooted. He is, in fact, just the sort of person to whom drugs should not be made available, because he will become psychologically dependent upon them. But by Josef Bultova they were given freely. He always travels with a briefcase stocked with stimulants and sedatives.'

He stopped, allowing every implication of the smear to settle in the minds of the committee. 'Josef Bultova apparently finds the work he does for his country a great strain,' he added.

He would never know another enemy as implacable as Devgeny, Josef knew. Illinivitch would never match him.

'But even that was not enough,' continued the Minister. 'Balshev was immediately thrown into contact with an American photographer, a famous man. His name is James

Endelman. He is a homosexual. And a heroin user and trafficker. It was with this man that Balshev, already introduced to drugs, terrified of being in a strange country and desperate for friendship, was placed. So he started using heroin. And was perverted into homosexuality ... '

Illinivitch was smiling, Josef saw, a triumphant expression.

'Unquestionably,' Devgeny went on, 'Balshev was under the influence of drugs when he delivered his speech at the Nobel ceremony. I have no doubt Bultova will point to the world-wide reaction to that address and argue it as a credit to Russia. There are many who feel otherwise.'

His voice was becoming hoarse from so much speaking. He was coughing occasionally and the water glass was almost empty. Josef wondered if it were just water, or whether he was taking confidence from vodka. He had little need for artificial confidence, accepted the negotiator.

'Publicly, the visits to England and America were successful,' conceded Devgeny. That was clever, thought Josef. It conveyed the impression of balanced criticism.

'Privately,' continued his accuser, 'the tour was a disaster. I have in my possession for introduction into any court proceedings reports from London, New York and Washington that fully show the depth of degradation to which Balshev was reduced by a man in whom he placed his full trust.'

Devgeny was supporting himself against the table now, physically strained.

'By far the most horrifying was a party which Balshev was allowed to attend in New York.'

Semyonov had done well, thought Josef.

'There were no women at the party, although half were dressed as such. Available was every sort of drug and narcotic. Balshev was allowed to go because at the time, Bultova was negotiating at considerable financial reward to himself the sale to an American film company of the rights to the novel.'

There isn't one member of the committee who hasn't decided already on a trial, thought Josef.

'Men freely copulated with men,' went on Devgeny. 'It was a scene of sexual degradation almost beyond comprehension.'

The Minister drained his water glass.

'Bultova got the man from the party, largely by the help of the American publisher and an assistant. As they left, a man later found to be under the effect of lysergic acid diethylamide leapt to his death. Balshev's departure was just fifteen minutes before the arrival of the police ... '

He paused, allowing the point to register.

'Ambassador Semyonov has returned from New York and is at hand to give evidence should you require it,' he said.

Devgeny's determination was incredible, thought Josef.

'You will be aware,' continued the Minister, 'that the President of the United States gave a reception in Washington, honouring Balshev. I have also recalled Ambassador Vladimirov to tell you of indications he has received from the State Department that as a result of Bultova's behaviour at that function, our relations with America have visibly cooled.'

Devgeny stopped, his voice weak.

'There appears only one result of Josef Bultova's involvement in this matter,' resumed Devgeny. 'With publishing houses in England and America, he has entered into contracts under which fifteen per cent of all royalties earned by this book goes, on commission, to himself into Swiss banking accounts. Further, there are massive commissions upon film sales. Not only, I submit, is Josef Bultova guilty of anti-Soviet activity, he is guilty of currency speculation on a criminal scale that should be added to his indictment.'

He stopped, triumphantly, happy with the opening.

'I call the doctor,' he said.

The doctor was clearly very nervous. He was tall and

extremely thin and in his apprehension kept removing and then replacing his spectacles, as if they were permanently uncomfortable. His voice carried a Siberian blur to it and he stammered, coughing frequently. He identified himself as Ravil Maturin, listed his qualifications and said he was head of the sanatorium at which Nikolai was being treated. The Minister took the man quickly through his evidence. Maturin asserted that Balshev was deeply addicted to heroin and that treatment would be long and painful. He had been subjected to several psychological and psychiatric tests, all of which showed deep mental disturbances, some of which could be permanent. He showed no inclination towards writing, actually rejecting the suggestion from therapists. Balshev was fully and painfully aware of his condition and blamed his success as a writer for creating it. He was also a committed homosexual.

Devgeny sat down and Maturin removed his spectacles yet again. Because of the arrangement of the furniture, Josef was obviously the man accused. He knew Maturin, in awe of the Praesidium committee, would judge him guilty of whatever he had been charged and would react in Devgeny's favour to any questions. Josef awaited the invitation from the Party Secretary, then rose, nodding to Maturin. The doctor stared back.

'You have had many sessions of analysis with Balshev?'

'Of course.' The hostility was obvious.

'He recognizes his addiction and regrets it?'

'I have already said that.'

'Quite so,' agreed Josef. 'He blames his exposure as a writer for putting him into a position of needing drugs?'

'Yes,' sighed Maturin.

'He blames being a writer — not people?'

'What?' demanded the doctor, realizing the questioning wasn't aimless.

'During your several examinations, has Balshev ever blamed any person for introducing him to drugs?'

Maturin hesitated, looking to Devgeny for guidance.

'I'd like an answer, doctor.'

'Not directly,' said Maturin.

'Whom does he hold responsible?'

Again Maturin went to Devgeny. The Minister remained unmoved, as he had to.

'Tell the Committee, doctor, whom does Nikolai Balshev blame for his addiction?'

'He talks of the need to experiment, discover new experiences,' said Maturin, clumsily.

'So he does not blame any person,' drew out Josef. 'Rather, he accepts the responsibility himself?'

'I suppose so,' said the doctor, reluctantly.

'Have you talked about me, personally?'

'Yes.'

'What is his attitude towards me?'

'One of dislike, hatred almost.'

Devgeny, who had been ignoring the questioning, fumbling through papers and box files before him, looked up and smiled.

'Why?' demanded Josef.

'He considers you betrayed his friendship.'

'Why?'

'Because you arranged for his immediate admission to hospital upon his return to this country.'

'Would you explain that further to the committee?'

'He is undergoing acute discomfort because of the necessary treatment. He has accepted that his talent, if not gone, has been severely impaired for some years.'

'So his feeling towards me is one of resentment, for putting him into a position of suffering discomfort and facing reality about his writing?'

'Yes.'

'What would have happened to Nikolai Balshev if I had not insisted upon his immediate treatment?'

'He would have remained a heroin addict, of course.' Maturin looked at Josef, as if he were stupid.

'Let us suppose he could have obtained heroin, here in Russia, what would have happened?'

'He would have needed bigger and bigger doses.'

'And?' pressed Josef.

'Eventually he would have died.'

'Now he is undergoing great discomfort and it could be several years before he will be able to write again at the level of his earlier ability. But the discomfort will go, eventually. And he *will* be able to work again?'

'Probably,' concurred Maturin, still reluctant.

So well had the case been prepared against him that Josef knew he could leave nothing unsaid.

'By arranging his admission to hospital, I have saved his life?'

'Yes.'

'And made it possible for him to write again, some time in the future?'

'I cannot make a prediction like that.'

'But it *is* possible, surely doctor?'

'Yes,' agreed Maturin. 'It is possible.'

'It is a fact, isn't it doctor, that some people are more susceptible to drugs than others?'

Maturin frowned, trying to see which way the questioning was going. He was alert now, realizing he had frayed the points Devgeny had been trying to establish.

'Yes,' he agreed, slowly.

'Some men are psychologically able to disdain drugs, others recognize their medical benefits but can avoid addiction, as with sleeping pills and tranquillizers, for instance ... but others imagine a need for them?'

'I have already indicated that,' replied Maturin, his confidence returning.

'Into what category would you place Balshev?'

'I thought I had already made that clear, too,' he said. 'He is basically an unstable man ... I would diagnose him the sort of person who would find it easy to rely on drugs.'

'An easy way which might have been indicated by a predilection towards excessive drinking?'

'Yes.'

'Is it possible to recognize, psychiatrically, someone with homosexual tendencies?'

Maturin frowned, shaking his head. 'Not merely by psychiatric examination, no. By a combination with physical and medical tests, one can reach certain conclusions.'

'What sort of physical examination?'

'Chromosome imbalance, genital size, which might indicate hermaphroditism ... '

'Have such tests been carried out upon Balshev?'

'Yes.'

'Having subjected Nikolai Balshev to a number of psychiatric examinations and with the advantage of being able to consider these examinations in conjunction with the medical tests, are you surprised at the man's sexual tendencies?'

'It is difficult to say ... '

'What conclusions have you drawn, doctor?' demanded Josef.

'No one can be categoric ... '

'Are you surprised at Nikolai Balshev's homosexuality?' he pressed.

'No,' conceded Maturin, finally.

'Given that a man has homosexual tendencies, it is possible for him to resist them?'

'Yes.'

'Putting Balshev in proximity with another homosexual however, particularly at a time when he was under great stress, was undoubtedly wrong and dangerous?'

Maturin looked surprised at the question which supported Devgeny's accusation.

'Yes,' he agreed quickly, 'undoubtedly.'

'Thank you doctor,' said Josef, sitting down. It was eight o'clock, he noticed. The inquiry had gone on for over three hours. Pamela would be in London by now. She was safe.

Devgeny was standing again, still confident despite the admission Josef had extracted from the doctor.

'I believe', he concluded, 'that there is unquestionably a case for Josef Bultova to answer before a criminal court. As I have indicated, I have a great deal more evidence available. I consider it unnecessary at this stage. I move that a charge be formulated and that until his trial, Josef Bultova be held in custody.'

Josef looked at Illinivitch. The deputy Minister leant sideways as Devgeny whispered something and both men smiled, finally resolving the doubt in Josef's mind. He had made the right decision, Josef decided, all those months ago when Illinivitch had come to his apartment within hours of the false challenge to Devgeny. Illinivitch had never worked against the Minister, but always with him, trying to prompt the indiscretions and demanding commitments to incriminate Josef in case the tour was successful. The man had travelled to Washington to co-ordinate every scrap of evidence that Semyonov and Vladimirov could gather, to ensure his destruction.

Why, he wondered, had Illinivitch exposed himself so completely? The threat — or promise — must have been enormous. He stared at the man, thinking again of that apartment visit and his anxiety to show his prowess with languages, and found another answer. His comments about the apartment hadn't been contempt, corrected Josef, but envy, the stupid lapses into French and English like a boast, to prove he was as clever as Josef. If Devgeny's purge were successful, Russia would need another negotiator and Illinivitch saw the role as his. How bad he would be, decided Josef.

'It is now your opportunity to speak,' said Svetlova. His voice clearly showed he had already made up his mind, like the rest of the examining committee.

Josef rose, pushing his chair to one side.

'At the beginning of these proceedings,' he said, 'I denied the accusation levelled against me. I repeat that denial. Throughout I behaved with the best interests of Russia foremost in my mind ... '

Illinivitch and Devgeny whispered and smiled. They wanted him to know, in the end, of the conspiracy against him, Josef realized.

'I am not', reiterated Josef, 'guilty of anti-Soviet activity. It is, I submit, an astonishing charge to be levelled against someone who has been to almost every country in the world, representing the Soviet Union.'

He had their attention, he knew. An overwhelming indictment had been prepared against him and he wasn't frightened. They wanted to know why. Neither Illinivitch nor Devgeny was smiling.

'I stand before you this evening,' continued Josef, 'as a victim of personal animosity. One man, a member of this committee, has attempted to destroy me, quite disregarding that to do so would be to disgrace the Soviet Union.'

He paused, using the silences to much greater effect than Devgeny. I *am* better than he is, thought Josef.

'And so, before continuing,' he said, 'I invite the Minister of Culture to withdraw these unfounded accusations.'

And then he sat down.

The effect was remarkable. The committee stared at him, each man with complete incomprehension. So surprised was Illinivitch that when Devgeny gestured, he missed the command for a whispered conversation.

'Do you wish to offer no defence?' demanded the Party Secretary.

Briefly, Josef rose. 'I have a complete defence,' he said.

'And one which I wish to produce before this committee if the accusations against me are not retracted immediately.'

'Minister?' invited Svetlova, looking sideways along the table to Devgeny. The Minister stood. He was controlling well his bewilderment, thought Josef. Perhaps he would be experiencing the first flicker of apprehension, Josef hoped.

'I can only believe that Comrade Bultova is suffering from the strain of this appearance. Or that he isn't capable of formulating any defence.'

The Party Secretary looked back to Josef. He stood, matching Devgeny's stare.

'I demand,' he said, 'for the last time, that this accusation be withdrawn.'

Devgeny looked in both directions along the table, humping his shoulders to indicate his astonishment. The Party Secretary caught his gesture and came back irritably to Josef.

'Do you wish to address this committee or not?' he demanded, curtly.

Josef looked to the smaller table, where the officials sat. 'I wish to be fully recorded the number of times I made the request for a withdrawal.'

He bent, placing both briefcases upon the chair, so he would not have to stoop when addressing the committee. From the larger briefcase he began unpacking cassettes, building them into a tiny wall between himself and the committee. One side of each cassette was completely occupied with dates and annotations. Josef arranged them in careful order, then looked up at the committee.

'Each of you know', he began, 'that fifteen years ago I was released from imprisonment, because the Soviet Union decided there was a need for someone to commence negotiations with other countries of the world which might be embarrassing for more formal, diplomatic contacts ... '

'We are aware of your impressive history,' interrupted the Party Secretary irascibly.

'These contacts', continued Josef, unperturbed, 'were with few exceptions largely those of trade or for tentatively establishing relations. I was never before involved in any literary negotiations. It was a point I made most forcibly when I was first told what the assignment was to be ... '

He stopped, turning to a folder he had taken from the briefcase at the same time as the cassettes.

'I would like formally to submit to the committee the letter I wrote when I was first assigned to arranging Balshev's tour to the West, making the point abundantly clear.'

He handed the letter to one of the officials at the smaller table, who passed it to the Party Secretary. Josef waited while the man read it, then moved it along the table.

'I am aware', went on Josef, 'that the life-style I have followed since my release from imprisonment has been the subject of some criticism ... '

He paused, staring first at Devgeny, then at Illinivitch. Was there the slightest indication of fear yet?

'One particular criticism', he picked up, 'has been the fact that I have extensively employed the use of scientific aids largely manufactured outside the Soviet Union.'

From the larger of the two briefcases he took one of the tape recorders he had purchased in Japan. He held it before him.

'Tape recorders, for instance,' he said. He was looking directly at Illinivitch. The man huddled sideways, to Devgeny. Squirm, you bastards, thought Josef.

'It has always been my practice from whatever part of the world in which I am working, to send nightly taped reports of the negotiations upon which I am involved. I am tonight going to ask you to listen to a number of tape recordings. I feel sure the allegation will be made that these recordings are fraudulently produced. To those accusations I say two things. Firstly, our own scientists can subject them to electronic tests, voiceprints, which will establish that the voices upon them are those of the people I claim them to be. Secondly, that as I did not know what specific accusations were to be made it would have been impossible for me to prepare them in advance. From the length of the tapes, it can also be determined that I have in no way edited them for my own benefit.'

'I protest,' erupted Devgeny, but Josef was expecting the interruption.

'To what?' he demanded.

It was a brilliant rebuttal. Devgeny stood there, stranded.

'There's no proof of authenticity,' he floundered.

'Comrade Bultova has already answered that objection,' pointed out the Party Secretary. He turned to Josef. 'You are prepared to subject every one of the tapes you wish us to consider to scientific examination?'

'I am,' undertook Josef. 'They will become the property of this examining committee.'

The Secretary looked back to Devgeny, who sat down. It was important, Josef knew, to block any escape. If he failed in what was to follow, he could never again expect release. What he was to say could, he supposed, be construed as treason and bring a death sentence.

'With your permission,' he said, to the Party Secretary, 'I wish to directly address a member of this examination committee.'

The Secretary frowned, then nodded.

'Is there anything you wish to say to the committee?' said Josef to Illinivitch.

Illinivitch flushed. He sat quite still, his hands resting on the table before him. Devgeny was the first to turn and stare at him, saw Josef, followed by the rest. Even the officials sitting in front of the large table screwed round, looking at the man.

'I would like the committee to note the offer I have just extended to Comrade Illinivitch,' said Josef.

He picked up the first of the cassettes, holding it up to the committee.

'This', he said, 'was made by me at the second meeting at the Ministry of Culture, when Comrade Balshev's tour to the West was discussed. Many of you might regard the habit of tape recording committee sessions as reprehensible. I do it so there can never be a mistake in any instructions I am given. Upon it, you will hear me voice the objections to the assignment that I have already conveyed in writing, both to the committee and to the full Praesidium.'

He fitted the cassette into the machine.

'You will hear something else,' he warned. 'A somewhat surprising exchange between Comrade Devgeny and Comrade Illinivitch.'

He pressed the 'on' button, adjusting the volume. The quality was excellent.

'An argument in committee,' defined Josef, when the tape had finished. 'One member, Comrade Illinivitch, apparently expressing opposition to a Minister, Comrade Devgeny. Nothing, perhaps, particularly remarkable about that. You actually heard Comrade Korshunov stress such disagreements were to be expected. I would now ask you to listen to a second recording.'

Josef fitted it into the machine, but delayed starting it.

'It was made', he said, 'the evening of that committee disagreement. It is a conversation I had, in the study of my apartment in Moscow, with Comrade Illinivitch. The visit was to involve me in political moves to replace Comrade Devgeny as Minister of Culture. Had I agreed, I would have been guilty of exactly the charges that have been made against me here this evening. You will hear my rejection of that approach.'

As the recording progressed, Devgeny turned and stared at Illinivitch. It was a clever move, appreciated Josef, the sort a man would make on hearing a plot outlined against him. It would be hard for Illinivitch later to try to argue that he acted on instruction from Devgeny. Illinivitch had been abandoned and he knew it.

He let the tape run on, through the assertion of Praesidium backing, then stopped it again. 'I would like the committee to listen most carefully to what follows,' said Josef. 'It was my reaction to this approach. It was made many months ago, as I have made clear. But it stands tonight as my reply to the accusation of anti-Soviet activity.'

He started the machine and again his voice filled the room, telling Illinivitch of his arrest, trial, the burial of his father in Potma and defection approaches from countries in the West and concluding, ' ... despite what has happened, I remain a good Russian. I won't do anything to damage my country.'

Josef ended the recording and gestured a clerk to take another document.

'This is a sworn statement from the concierge of my apartment block, whom I ensured that night witnessed Comrade Illinivitch's departure. Her evidence is independent corroboration of his visit.'

Illinivitch was looking fixedly at the table.

'There was another committee meeting,' Josef continued. 'After the announcement that the Nobel Foundation had awarded the prize to Balshev. Afterwards, Comrade Illinivitch walked with me from the room, again insisting I attempt something during the tour which would disgrace Comrade Devgeny.'

Josef slotted into place the recording he had made as he and the deputy chairman had walked towards his car, the briefcase containing the tape between them. The committee listened in complete silence. He stopped, staring across at them. An hour ago, he thought, and they had already convicted. He wondered if Devgeny, confident of success, had already demanded the papers of accusation from the Ministry of Justice.

'A great deal has been made of my having supplied pills,' said Josef. 'I would like the committee to consider this.' He played the tape of his argument with the author in the hotel bedroom, when he discovered that the man had stolen drugs from the briefcase.

'You will discern from that,' said Josef, when he stopped the tape, 'the state of mind in which Balshev was prior to the Nobel ceremony. You may feel, as I did, that the need for pills was justified. But I submit that this tape recording makes it quite clear that I did not introduce the man to dangerous amphetamine or barbiturate drugs. On only one occasion, judging it necessary, I gave him tranquillizers. From then on he took them, unknown initially to me, from my briefcase. You have not an hour ago heard Dr Maturin identify Balshev as the sort of man who, knowing such drugs were available, would rush to take them.'

Josef coughed. His throat was becoming sore, as Devgeny's had.

'Stress has also been put upon my allowing Endelman to make the tour with us. That was not my decision. It was that of Comrade Illinivitch.'

Another tape went on to the machine, the recording beginning with static and the international operator securing the number, which was clearly identified on the call. It was that which Illinivitch had given him on departure from Moscow.

'Has there been any decision on my overnight query regarding Endelman?' Josef's voice could be heard to ask, after the customary greetings.

'Let him accompany you,' Illinivitch's voice said.

'Are you sure?'

'Quite sure.'

'Have you had the man checked out?'

'Thoroughly, to my satisfaction.'

'What about the satisfaction of the Ministry?'

'It's the same thing.'

Josef stopped the recording. 'That investigation,' he said, 'was carried out by a man who has been brought back to this country to give evidence against me, Comrade Semyonov.'

He produced the letter he had taken from Blyne on the day he left Washington.

'This letter was sent to Endelman in response to the American publisher's request to have the photographer accompany us. The signature is difficult to decipher, but it purports to be from the Ministry of Culture. I have no doubt that the same scientific examination to which these tapes will be submitted will show the typewriter to be that to which Comrade Illinivitch has access. I feel the handwriting will be shown to be his, as well.'

Josef fitted a further tape into the machine.

'This', he explained, 'is a conversation with Endelman. In it you will hear him say he had two or three meetings with Semyonov and that both his homosexuality and drug addiction were not difficult to discover. I contend that it was known, but kept secret by men well aware of the risk of disgrace that would hopefully arise by putting Endelman in close contact with the author. I am not suggesting, of course, that they were aware then of Balshev's homosexual tendencies. It was, I consider, a calculated decision that someone they knew to be a heroin addict and a sexual deviant could create trouble. Merely for the man to be arrested in our company would have been sufficient.'

Illinivitch was glancing around as if seeking escape.

'I would like here to mention the drug party in New York. I was negotiating the film sale of the book, as instructed by the Ministry of Culture. I got Balshev from that party admittedly only minutes before a scandal. I was accompanied by the American publisher and his assistant. Everyone else was a homosexual or a transvestite. Yet a complete description of that party has been given to this committee.

How? I submit because Ambassador Semyonov, whom I have proved connived at the introduction of Endelman on to the tour, had someone at that party, an *agent provocateur*, trying to enmesh Balshev in just the sort of situation from which I removed him.'

Josef selected another cassette.

'This', he said, 'was recorded at the Washington embassy. In it, you will hear Comrade Illinivitch threaten to leak details of the party to American newspapers, specifically to wreck the President's reception. You will hear my reaction to that threat.'

Devgeny was staring at him with a look of complete hatred. Illinivitch was hunched in his chair, gazing back at the table. Josef was coming to the end of the recordings. Without introduction, he played those of his conversations in Washington on every other occasion when he had confronted Illinivitch.

'It is clear from the last recording', said Josef, 'that Comrade Illinivitch was still urging me to allow the tour to collapse. He was a senior, responsible man in the Ministry for which I was currently working. To ignore that order amounted to insubordination. I decided upon insubordination to avoid exactly the situation of which I am being accused today.'

His back ached. He would be glad to sit down.

'When I discovered that Balshev was a heroin user, I obtained it from Endelman and supplied it to him,' confessed Josef.

He inserted the tape in which Endelman boasted in the hotel room of making Nikolai dependent on drugs. 'That is the man responsible for Balshev's addiction,' said Josef. 'A man whose association with the writer was arranged by Comrade Illinivitch and his willing helpers in America.'

He paused, feeling confident.

'Once I became aware of it, I knowingly allowed the use

to continue,' he conceded. 'I knew that if the man did not have drugs, he would collapse and need admission to hospital. By supplying him, I prevented his addiction becoming public knowledge in the West, with the consequent scandal that would have been created. Every public moment of the tour was a complete and outstanding success, culminating in that amazing picture of representatives of the People's Republic of China being forced to acknowledge publicly the superiority of a Russian author.'

He paused, nearly finished.

'That, Comrades, is the cause of the American anger. You have heard that the Washington ambassador is here. I suggest you ask him the real reason for the reception. It was given to illustrate to Peking they were striving too hard to capitalize upon the friendship negotiated by Nixon and Kissinger. We were, if you like, duped into the reception for this purpose. By manœuvring the introduction to the Chinese representatives, I reversed the whole thing into a sole triumph for the U.S.S.R. Perhaps you might also question Comrade Vladimirov about this ... ' he said.

He played the tape in which the Washington ambassador was linked with Semyonov's investigation of the photographer by Illinivitch's boast the night they had arrived in Washington.

'By arranging an ambulance to be at the airport, I have saved Comrade Balshev's life. You have heard from the doctor it is possible he will write again. I will concede that the press-conference was bad. You have been able to establish from the early recordings that the writer was in an incredibly nervous state. I was trying to do what was expected of me, present Balshev to the world's press, but at the same time protect him from any interrogative reporting. Because of a certain notoriety, I became the object of the press-conference. You will see it did not happen again. I reiterate what I said at the beginning of this inquiry. I am innocent of the charges laid against me. Further, my actions throughout the tour were always pro-Russian. I remain what I always have been, a man proud of my country, determined to do nothing to disgrace it.'

It had gone well, decided Josef, reaching the climax. Very well.

'I believe I have established', he concluded, 'that Comrade Illinivitch, eagerly assisted by Comrades Semyonov and Vladimirov, embarked on a plot to disgrace myself and Nikolai Balshev, in an attempt to displace, eventually, the Minister of Culture.'

He sat down, gratefully. An official walked over and carefully collected the tape recordings. The Party Secretary muttered with the men sitting either side of him, then looked at Josef.

'Thank you, Comrade Bultova,' he said. 'The Committee wishes you to retire. Perhaps you would wait in the anteroom.'

Josef bowed, formally, picked up his empty briefcases and left the room. Illinivitch was still staring fixedly at the table as he passed.

Chapter Twenty-Four

It took exactly an hour and fourteen minutes before there was movement from the committee room. Josef timed it exactly, sitting opposite one of those large, numeralled clocks that always seem to hang in official places, and watching its slow, minute-by-minute progress.

Finally, when the door opened, only Devgeny came out. For several moments they stared at each other. Then Devgeny said, curtly, 'The committee has completely exonerated you.'

Oh no, corrected Josef, immediately. They had done more than that. There were at least a dozen minor officials and secretaries who could have been deputed to tell him the verdict. But the committee had ordered Devgeny to do it, so that everyone would know the disfavour into which he was now held for accusing the wrong person. Josef had expected to win, but not so completely. Devgeny's credibility before the Praesidium was badly damaged, even before the accusations that would come from Illinivitch.

The other man's humiliation would be made greater by reserve, knew Josef. He remained expressionless, gathering his briefcases yet again.

'I haven't finished,' said the Minister. Josef faced him, curiously. He seemed more controlled than the negotiator would have expected.

'What?' He allowed a smear of insolence.

'My office,' demanded Devgeny and moved off, quickly, before Josef could protest. The ministerial suite was quite near the committee chamber, at the side of the Kremlin. Josef followed, surprised. After what had happened that evening, Devgeny would do nothing to expose himself further, he felt, so the summons didn't make sense. Did the man want a truce, Josef wondered. Did Devgeny realize the closeness of official censure or maybe even arrest after Illinivitch was questioned and intend abandoning any pride in the sheer effort to survive? Perhaps. How wonderful, thought Josef, to reject him. It would be the final victory.

Devgeny motioned him to a chair and settled comfortably behind his large desk. He appeared quite relaxed. Suddenly he smiled, that ugly expression Josef found so unpleasant. Devgeny nodded to the briefcases.

'You want to record everything, of course,' he mocked.

This wasn't right, thought Josef.

'Of course,' he agreed, lifting the briefcase on to the desk and starting the machine. If it weren't so serious, the behaviour would be childish, decided Josef.

'No doubt you will be making a recording,' he said.

Devgeny indicated a drawer on the left-hand side of his desk.

'Illinivitch has been arrested,' reported the Minister. 'Semyonov and Vladimirov have been detained for questioning, too. There's little doubt they'll face trial.'

Josef remained expressionless, waiting.

'You've been very clever, Josef,' conceded Devgeny. 'It was brilliant, restricting your defence only to Illinivitch, leaving me out completely. To try to link us, without evidence, would have weakened your case.'

Josef stared at him, watchfully.

'Illinivitch wanted to be Russia's negotiator, didn't he?' guessed Josef, anxious for confirmation. 'That's why he involved himself.'

Devgeny smiled slowly, in admiration.

'You *are* very good,' admitted the Minister. Answering the

question, he said, 'I've never known anyone covet anything as much as he envied what you did.'

Josef nodded, satisfied. He'd make the tape available, he decided, as additional evidence.

'I was so sure that there was no way you could possibly extricate yourself,' continued the Minister.

Josef remained mystified. Devgeny wouldn't admit involvement in the precarious position in which he knew himself to be, aware it was being recorded, he decided. Not unless he was sure Josef could never use the tape.

'But it doesn't matter,' said Devgeny, abruptly. 'It doesn't matter at all.'

Conscious of both recordings, Josef sneered, 'If there is a point, can we get to it? I don't imagine Illinivitch will face trial without listing precisely your role in the affair. Both Semyonov and Vladimirov will support him. Shouldn't you be preparing a defence?'

Devgeny nodded, still admiring. 'I can see why you are so good at what you do, Josef. You've always got control. I like that.'

Josef sighed, too obviously.

'I was too confident,' admitted Devgeny. 'A little like you are now. I was so sure that I had sealed every escape route that I was careless before the committee. I imagined the court was the place at which all the evidence should be produced and you would be absolutely crushed. But I was wrong.'

He paused, briefly, then added, 'But I've won, Josef.'

'Devgeny,' said Josef, purposely using only the surname to increase the disrespect. 'I am beginning to doubt your mental condition ... unless you're trying to apologize ... '

Devgeny cut him off, with a laugh. 'Stop performing for the recording, Josef,' he said. 'You won't put this tape before anyone else.'

Josef felt the first prick of uncertainty.

'I decided to destroy you, utterly,' confessed Devgeny. 'Nothing was overlooked. I covered everything.'

He leaned back in his chair, looking over Josef's head. 'I got every report and piece of information and in the end I missed the entire point of it. I didn't realize it until you were defending yourself and by then it was too late.'

He patted the mound of documents before him, then lit a cigarette, one of the cheap ones of which nearly half is an empty cardboard tube.

'The recording of your row with Nikolai, because he stole your pills, was the first indication I had. There was a point to the other conversations, but not that. No one would have recorded that unless he anticipated a subsequent inquiry. Why?'

He looked down at the negotiator, as if he expected an answer and moved two of the files, as if it would be there instead.

'And Endelman troubled me, from the very beginning. It was Illinivitch's idea, to keep the letters from you, so that you'd have no opportunity to argue it before the Ministry Committee. It was to be the clearest indication of a plot against you, to try to prompt you to over-compensate and make a mistake. But it still didn't make sense for you to accept it as easily as you did. You had the power to refuse and you knew it. But you placed the request on official record and then trapped Illinivitch. Why? Why record the conversation with Nikolai and then accept Endelman so easily?'

Josef sat completely motionless, leaning slightly forward as if anxious not to miss anything the other man said.

'There has to be a point, I knew. But even as you were talking in there, I couldn't see it. Then you asked a question and I remembered something I had seen in one of the earliest reports I'd ever read. So I looked it up while you were destroying everything I had carefully built up and realized the mistake it was too late for me to rectify.'

'What the hell are you talking about?' demanded Josef.

'It was the camp, wasn't it Josef? It all started way back there in the camp and I was too stupid to appreciate it.'

He paused, trying to increase Josef's discomfort.

'You were fond of Medev, weren't you Josef? He was kind to you, after your father died. I have a report from the commandant showing how upset you were by the old man's death and how Medev looked after you. He really wanted to care for you in every way, didn't he?'

He patted the folders again. 'Your whole life is here, Josef.'

'You're mad,' said the negotiator.

'It didn't work, Josef, that rope you gave him. Oh, we knew about your suicide attempt. An informer saw you. I knew even before your release, the following morning, but I couldn't overrule a decision that had been made by the Praesidium. I was in disgrace again and had to bend with the wind.'

The question churned in Josef's mind, but he refused Devgeny the satisfaction of asking it. The Minister anticipated it.

'Medev tried to hang himself the day after you were released. But your attempt had strained the rope. It snapped.'

Poor Medev, thought Josef. Poor, sensitive, kind Medev.

'Were those questions very important to you?'

Josef shook his head. 'You're not making sense.'

'The question you put to Maturin, back there in committee. "Is it possible to recognize a homosexual?" you asked. It is for you, isn't it Josef? It's the easiest thing in the world. And it isn't just your American training as a psychologist. You're ashamed of the attraction you feel, aren't you? But as you got the doctor to admit, some men who feel the attraction can resist it, providing it's not too sustained, can't they? That's why you gave Medev the suicide rope, after pretending to make an attempt to satisfy your own conscience, wasn't it Josef? You didn't intend to kill yourself. I know that. That attempt was a charade, performed entirely for your own benefit. Refusing to accept the fact, even to yourself, is how you resist it, isn't it Josef?'

Josef shook his head, unable to find words.

'But you knew Medev would try, didn't you? Just as you knew you'd give in, if you stayed together much longer. And you thought you were there for life, after all. The risk had to be removed, hadn't it Josef?'

Josef just stared.

'You always intended Medev to have the rope, to remove the threat. And you knew Balshev would take your tablets. That's why you let him know they were there. He had to be destroyed, just like the temptation in the camp. That was why you had to record the argument, to establish your innocence before you'd even been accused. It was easy for a trained psychologist to recognize Balshev's homosexuality, long before the tour began, wasn't it? That was what you objected to, not involving yourself in literary negotiations. You were frightened, weren't you Josef, just like you were at the camp, that it would become as big a temptation as it had been with Medev.'

The Minister paused, expecting Josef to speak, but the negotiator said nothing.

'And then Endelman arrived and there was more than one homosexual,' resumed the Minister. 'So you changed your attack upon Balshev. By throwing them together, you achieved two things. You hastened Balshev's destruction, certainly sexually, and you lessened the risk of either making an approach to you that you would have found difficulty in resisting. There was no surprise, finding them in bed, was there? That was inevitable. He's dead, incidentally.'

'Who?'

'Endelman. He took the one hundred per cent pure heroin you got from the doctor in Washington. Vladimirov made a full report about that, too. I thought, initially, you'd got it for Nikolai. Endelman took it, as you knew he would, not realizing its purity. I suppose you waited until you knew he had taken an injection, so he wouldn't question how you were able to return one envelope. Vladimirov's report contained the conversation you had with the embassy doctor. You were insistent, weren't you Josef, on knowing the effect of such a pure dose upon an addict? The doctor recalls telling you quite clearly it would kill. I didn't quite understand why you had to kill Endelman. Perhaps it was because he made you suffer and had to be punished. We mustn't forget your vindictiveness, must we?'

Josef was shaking his head, bemused. 'Incredible,' he said, contemptuously. 'Absolutely incredible.'

'We bugged your apartment,' admitted Devgeny. 'So I know what happened between you and your wife when you came back. It was easy to send her back, wasn't it Josef? Nikolai has told the doctor all about his seduction and how difficult it seemed for the marriage to be consummated. It was cruel, Josef, convincing the poor girl it was her fault, when all the time it was you. She'll always wear the guilt, Josef. And really the marriage was your experiment, just like those that Nikolai made. An attempt to be normal that went very wrong for you.'

'You're insane,' judged Josef, finding the proper rejection difficult.

'Was it hard, Josef, to walk away from that party in New York? You went too far that time, letting Nikolai get out with that young American, didn't you? If you made one mistake and let control get away, that was the moment. But once you got to that party, you wanted to stay, didn't you? You wanted to join in, like everyone else. You'll give in one day, you know, Josef.'

The negotiator felt the onset of that hollow feeling.

'All the facts fit, don't they Josef? First Medev, then

286

Nikolai, then Endelman. Every time you encounter someone with unnatural sexual tendencies, you have to react. It's a danger, so it has to be eradicated. I know it's your weakness, Josef. So I've won. Whenever I want to, I can use it. I can create the situations and expose you to the temptations and then wait until you finally give in and destroy yourself. And you'd have to kill yourself, if you ever gave in, wouldn't you Josef?'

'You're deranged, Devgeny,' said Josef, easily. 'I *shall* produce this recording. I'll make it available to the committee, both as an example of your involvement with Illinivitch and of your insanity.'

He stood up, shutting off the machine and snapping the briefcase shut. He paused, once more, gazing down at the Minister and shaking his head, a pitying movement. Then he turned and moved to the door.

'He's dead, Josef,' called Devgeny.

The negotiator hesitated, then stopped. 'What?' he asked.

'Medev, the man you loved. And who loved you. He died in the punishment block, where he was sentenced after the suicide attempt you set up. He went quite mad in the end. The only lucid thing was his hatred for you. They treated him very badly in the punishment section. You know the sort of things they do there. And he blamed you for it. It was the only thing he said before he died ... '

Devgeny paused, then said, 'Listen Josef.'

From the drawer he had indicated earlier, Devgeny produced a tape just like that which Josef had used before the inquiry. It was an old, scratchy recording. Devgeny turned the volume up, filling the room with noise. It wasn't human, decided Josef. No man could sound like that. It was an animal, a terrified, frightened animal, snared in a trap and screaming its agony. Then he caught it, indistinct at first and then clearer, over and over again.

' ... I hate him ... I hate Josef ... '

287

Josef walked unhurriedly from the Kremlin. It had snowed and it took him several minutes to clear it from his car. He drove slowly because of the weather conditions and got to within a mile of the apartment before he had to stop.

Carefully he parked the car and switched off the engine. It wasn't true, he knew. The recording was a fake. It had to be. Asher Medev would never have hated him, no matter what had happened. Josef began crying, great racking sobs pulling at his body. Not Asher. It just wasn't possible. Even though Josef had refused, he knew Asher had loved him.